FROM RUSSIA
WITHOUT LOVE

FROM RUSSIA WITHOUT LOVE

A Special Operations Group Thriller

Stephen Templin

All Rights Reserved © 2015 by Stephen Templin

Published by Stephen Templin
www.stephentemplin.com

ISBN-13: 9781516800162
ISBN-10: 1516800168

Cover design by Nuno Moreira

Sometimes the heart sees what is invisible to the eye.
—H. Jackson Brown, Jr.

PROLOGUE

SUMMER 2015

SEAL Team Six veteran Chris Paladin shot up in his sleeping bag, torn from a nightmare he couldn't remember. A cool sweat covered his body, and he was cold. Rain rapped on the windowpanes of the rented office in the financial district of London, like fingers ominously beckoning someone to open the windows. Sitting in front of the surveillance monitors, CIA officer Hannah Andrade had the early-morning watch. She turned her head from the live feed to the frozen image of a man who they'd nicknamed "Business Tourist" on the second monitor. The man dressed like a businessman yet hung around the area and peeked about like a tourist. They weren't entirely sure what he was up to.

Chris shook off the dream and rose to his feet. He nodded a quick hello to Hannah before getting dressed and preparing breakfast—microwave meals courtesy of Tesco, the Walmart of Great Britain. The aroma of bacon, sausage, omelets, hash browns, and baked beans in tomato sauce filled the office, making Chris's mouth water. And he clearly wasn't the only one.

Solomon "Sonny" Cohen, their teammate, hopped out of his sleeping bag dressed *au naturel* with a loud sniff. When Chris first met Sonny, the short, bald man was riding nude on a donkey crossing a Syrian road in the dead of night. By now, Chris should've been used to seeing Sonny's naked backside, but his system still experienced a shock. Hannah didn't seem to care. She was *one of the guys*.

"Morning," Sunny mumbled, changing into his suit pants, shirt, and tie.

Hannah was wearing business slacks, but she too got ready for the new day. With one eye on surveillance, she changed blouses. Chris had seen her change before, and he should've been accustomed to seeing her wearing only a brassiere, but in that moment, his usually-cool blood ran hot and wild. Not only was she a super spook with whom he'd worked during the Iraq War, running covert operations across the border into Syria to root out terrorists, but she was stunning when she allowed herself to be. In the Middle East, she appeared Arab, but here in Europe it wasn't clear what her ethnicity was, and the story of her background changed depending on whom she was talking to.

Sonny stared at her without inhibition, and Chris shot him the evil eye. The man continued to stare.

Now it was Hannah's turn to glare. "Sonny, have you ever been kicked in the eye by a former MMA middleweight?"

Chris snorted. Few people knew she had competed in Mixed Martial Arts, winning her region, before she joined the Agency, and Sonny was about to find out the hard way.

He seemed to give the question some thought.

"It's not a trick question," she said.

"Then, no," Sonny answered.

She smiled sweetly and batted her eyelashes. "Would you like to be?"

Chris, Hannah, and Sonny served together under the Special Operations Group (SOG) and were on yet another mission. As an arm of the Agency's Special Activities Division (SAD) focused on high threat intelligence and paramilitary operations of which the US could deny any knowledge, it was dangerous, high-stakes, and something Chris could no longer imagine doing full time the way Hannah did. He and Sonny were under special contract, and this was a far cry from Chris's regular job as an assistant pastor. Sonny worked for the Army's Delta Force, aka the Unit, which loaned him out to SOG when needed.

"What I'd like to do is eat," Sonny said, then walked to the TV and turned it on.

"Fair enough," Chris said just as the microwave beeped. "Breakfast is served."

The three sat down in a small circle, Hannah taking a spot where she could watch surveillance as they ate. Their surveillance focused on Business Tourist, who seemed connected to the focus of their hunt. "If Business Tourist takes the same route, today," she said, "Chris, you can handle the first leg of surveillance and follow him along Charles II Street until he reaches the arcade. When he exits the other end of the arcade, I'll follow. Then, when he arrives at Green Park, I'll disengage and Sonny will take over, hopefully discovering his final destination."

"What if he doesn't take the same route as before?" Chris asked.

"We can take turns following him in the same order—you, me, Sonny—and we'll just have to improvise."

Hannah's Agency training, experiences, and instincts made her better at mobile surveillance and countersurveillance than Chris or Sonny, so he nodded, happy to let her call the shots on this part of the mission. Sonny chewed on a mouthful of baked beans and grunted.

And so it began.

By 0745 the rain had stopped and the trio was already done eating breakfast, so they prepared to move into their surveillance positions. Business Tourist appeared, wearing the same conservative business suit and taking the same route along Duke of York Street as he had before.

Chris grabbed a light tactical vest, custom-made by the Agency, loaded with eight rifle magazines. One magazine sat vertical along each breast, and below that were three horizontal magazines on each side. The middle of the vest was free of gear, handy when wearing a suit jacket. When worn under a suit jacket, it was indistinguishable from a normal vest.

Sonny and Hannah donned similar vests, and they all watched their mark carefully.

Business Tourist continued along St. James Square, passing his target—the headquarters of United Kingdom Petroleum. No sooner had Business Tourist turned on Charles II Street than he slowed down his already leisurely pace and pulled out a phone. He stopped walking and started talking.

"He's making a call," Hannah said.

Chris expected Sonny to make some kind of snarky "Captain Obvious" comment, but he only chuckled. "Looks like an invitation to me."

"It's time to put our dancing shoes on." Chris pointed to St. James Square. "I can take my position behind the tree line there."

Sonny nodded. "You'll be able to see if Lullaby approaches from Duke of York Street and cover UKP, too. And the trees will give you some cover."

Lullaby was wanted dead or alive by the US government for executing the White House Chief of Staff's son-in-law. They had reason to believe Business Tourist here was working with

Lullaby to pull off a deadly attack in the heart of London, and the pressure to wrap him up quickly was building minute by minute.

"From the ground it'll be hard to see what's coming down Duke of York until they're right on top of us, though," Chris said, a little worried. They had to be extra careful.

"I'll watch the surveillance monitors," Hannah assured him, "and report any odd movement."

"And I'll drive," Sonny said. "When Hannah reports a suspicious vehicle coming down Duke of York Street, I'll pull in front of them and block them from entering the Square. I'll pretend I'm having car trouble, get out, and talk to the driver. I should be able to get a look inside the vehicle that way, to see if anything's up. If it looks okay, I'll move and let 'em go. Then I'll drive back into my spot and wait until Hannah calls me up again—then block and inspect some more."

The three of them riffed off each other like jazz musicians as they outlined the plan they'd come up with the night before.

"They'll probably use vans or SUVs," Hannah said, "So keep an eye out for those in particular."

"Most likely," Chris agreed, putting on his wireless throat mic. Each throat mic was mounted on a band, which they concealed under their closed shirt collars. The clandestine microphones would transmit via vibrations in their throats rather than open-air sound. He leaned his head to the side as he inserted his small earpiece next, letting it drop into his ear canal. It was magnetic, so he could retrieve it with a small piece of metal, such as a key.

After a commo check to confirm the three of them could communicate on secure primary and secondary frequencies via their smartphones, he said to Sonny, "What if they recognize you when you stop their vehicle?"

Sonny grinned. "Then I'll recognize them, too."

"True," Chris said as he popped open his suitcase. Hannah was already assembling an HK416 assault rifle, and Sonny had attached the upper receiver of a customized M4 to its lower receiver. Chris pulled out a customized M4, too. The bittersweet fragrance of oil on metal smelled like the good ole times. His match-grade barrel was 10.5 inches long, topped off with an Advanced Armament sound suppressor. His US Optics 1-4x red dot sight enabled a shooter to touch someone up to four hundred meters out. And in Chris's hands, the weapon could reach out even farther. Hannah's HK416 was easier to maintain and could take more abuse, but the M4s were lighter and more accurate. Especially since Chris hadn't been training as much as he used to, he'd take whatever advantage he could get.

He slung his rifle over his shoulder, barrel down, and closed his suit jacket to conceal it. But in spite of the short barrel, it still poked out from under his jacket. He grabbed a copy of *The Times* and held it down at his side. He pressed his thumb into the paper, causing it to curve lengthwise and bend around the barrel to provide more concealment.

Sonny held a white plastic bag stuffed with something, possibly more plastic bags he could dispose of at a moment's notice, to cover the barrel extending below his suit jacket.

"See you in a bit," Chris said to Hannah.

"Don't wait up for me, honey," Sonny called over his shoulder as they headed for the door.

Hannah snickered. "See you guys."

They hustled to the staircase. Better not to experience close encounters with nosey business office renters in the confines of an elevator, or walk into a close-quarters ambush. They exited the building and strolled toward the road surrounding a lush, emerald-green park called St. James Square. The buildings around the square were mostly of Georgian architecture—named after the four Kings George—minimalist and symmetrical with paneled doors topped with rectangular windows centered in front and adorned with ornate crowns, pilasters, and moldings.

Cars, motorbikes, and people were already pouring into the square as Sonny went to fetch the car. Chris crossed the street and entered the park, quickly spotting Business Tourist, who didn't seem to notice Chris or his movement. As he ventured north in the park, the UKP building blocked Business Tourist from sight. Chris stopped at a spot where he had a good view of Duke of York Street and the St. James Square entrance to UKP, and waited.

Although passersby seemed uninterested in their surroundings and the trees partially obscured their view of him, he felt conspicuous at this early hour of the morning, standing alone on the wet grass in the park. He needed a cover story. Maybe he was waiting to meet a friend. It wasn't an ideal cover, but it would have to do. It was believable enough, anyway. Rather than ponder the details of what he might say if someone asked him what he was doing, though, he needed to focus on the impending attack. The rest he could do on the fly.

He watched in silence for a few minutes, and then Sonny pulled the car around and parked next to the curb, just before reaching Duke of York Street.

Within minutes, Hannah's voice sounded through Chris's earpiece. "Two dark Range Rovers on Duke of York heading your way."

Chris patted his suit jacket to make sure it was unbuttoned. He'd likely need to quickly swing out his rifle and make bang-bang. He'd already spotted the Range Rovers, too.

"They're behind a MINI Cooper, Sunshine," she said, using Sonny's call sign. "Let the MINI Cooper pass before blocking the road."

"Roger," Sonny said.

The MINI Cooper rolled into St. James Square and turned left. Sonny moved in behind it and stopped, blocking the Range Rovers before they reached the square. The lead Range Rover honked, and Chris's heart pounded so loud it seemed the whole of London could hear. He wiped his perspiring hands on his pant leg.

Sonny stepped out of his vehicle and approached the driver's side of the first Range Rover. "My engine stalled," he said. "Can you give me a push?"

The throat mic didn't pick up the voice of the driver, but Chris could tell by the man's angry gestures that he wasn't going to get out and push.

"Then I'll ask the guy behind you," Sonny went on. He left the first vehicle and walked to the driver's side of the second Range Rover.

The first Range Rover was blocking Chris's view, so he couldn't see the occupants in the second vehicle, but he heard Sonny go through the same spiel. This time, though, Chris couldn't see or hear the driver's reaction. A horn blasted from behind the second Range Rover.

"You don't even know my mother," Sonny said. He turned and headed back to his vehicle. "Range Rovers clear," he whispered. He got in his car and started the engine.

"Okay, let them pass," Hannah said.

Sonny backed up and parked by the curb again, standing by as the Range Rovers disappeared, and vehicles and pedestrians flowed steadily from Duke of York to St. James.

Chris was both afraid and unafraid standing there in the damp morning. *The people who say they aren't afraid are liars or idiots.* But sometimes, when civilians asked him about it, he'd say the opposite, claim not to be afraid at all. Contradicting answers to the same question seemed perfectly logical to Chris until Reverend Luther finally asked him about it. *How can you be afraid and unafraid at the same time?*

After thinking on it, Chris realized that fear was a double-edged sword. One side of the sword was debilitative fear, causing the wielder to flee when he should stay, freeze when he should act, or panic when he should be keeping his head. The other side of the sword was facilitative fear, steadying his nerves, empowering his body and mind, and tightening his focus to a ruthless efficiency. While the debilitative side of the sword wounded the wielder, the facilitative side wounded the enemy. The key was to employ the sword of fear against the enemy rather than oneself. From that first day of Basic Underwater Demolition/SEAL training, Chris had learned how to wield fear to parry, cut, and thrust, facilitating his enemy's slaughter. In his combat experience, when men became complacent and put the weapon of fear away, they risked certain death.

The possibility of letting Hannah and Sonny down, of a mistake on his part resulting in great harm to them, caused Chris the most fear. He pressed his arm against the hard metal of his rifle under his jacket to reassure himself. Then he touched the chest of his suit jacket until he felt the hardness of the ammo magazines attached to his vest. As a SEAL veteran, he understood the value of training, experience, preparation, equipment, and skill. But as a pastor, he knew these could only take a person so far. He said a quick, silent prayer to God asking Him if He might watch over them all—Hannah, Sonny, the civilians in the financial district, and Chris himself. Prayer gave him no crystal ball as to what the outcome would be, but it was an opportunity to align himself with a greater good. After he said *Amen*, an inner peace swept over him. Whatever was about to happen was going to happen.

"Business Tourist is moving your direction," Hannah said in Chris's earpiece.

Trying not to make any sudden movements that would alert someone, he scanned the area first moving only his eyes, and when he needed to see farther to the side, he slowly turned his head until Business Tourist appeared in his peripheral vision. Business Tourist crossed the road to the park side of the street, coming closer to Chris. It seemed he might be moving into some kind of support position.

Chris spoke quietly, like a ventriloquist, barely moving his lips. "I see him." He continued to watch, trying not to think about him, trying not to alert any sixth sense the man might have.

"Three-van motorcade just turned down Duke of York Street," Hannah said. "Vans are dark colored."

A sudden dump of adrenaline tweaked Chris's senses, causing the volume of his hearing to amplify and fade.

"Sunshine, they're right behind a sedan," Hannah said. "As soon as the sedan pulls out, block the road. The vans are right behind."

"Roger."

A white sedan pulled out of Duke of York Street and turned onto St. James Square. Sonny was so close behind that it looked like he was about to scratch the sedan's rear bumper. Sonny came to an abrupt stop, blocking Duke of York Street and the lead van. The van didn't honk as the Range Rover had. Was the driver showing the discipline of a courteous citizen or the discipline of an experienced terrorist?

Sonny stepped out, appearing frustrated at his vehicle, and began his act. Then he approached the driver's side of the first van.

Chris quickly scanned the civilians nearby. He didn't recognize any of them, which was a good thing. He didn't want anyone hanging around who'd seen Sonny's act with the Range Rovers to become suspicious and call the cops.

"Business Tourist is moving toward Sonny's position," Hannah said.

Chris's gaze shot back to the man, who carried something down by his side. Chris couldn't see it clearly, but in his bones he felt it was a handgun or other such weapon. Sonny's attention was on the vans, so it was Chris's responsibility to protect his teammate's flank.

"Business Tourist has something in his hand," Hannah said, her voice slightly shaky. "Could be a gun."

"Possible gun, aye," Chris said.

Sonny's verbal exchange with the driver seemed to go on for a long time. Getting no help from the first driver to push Sonny's vehicle, Sonny proceeded to the second van. Stepping to the side for a better view of the second driver, Chris maintained an eye on Business Tourist, who was still moving in Sonny's direction.

Chris still had no foolproof confirmation that a gunfight was about to take place, but he knew action was faster than reaction. He planted his feet like a boxer about to deliver a knockout punch, dropped his newspaper, and swung one side of his jacket out of the way, freeing his M4, which he brought up and aimed at Business Tourist. At about the same time, Sonny jumped away from the driver's side of the second van. He must've seen something from up close that Chris couldn't.

Then he saw it. The driver pointed a pistol at where Sonny had been standing. *Pop!* The driver's side window blew out, and a pedestrian screamed.

In one fluid motion, Chris shifted his red dot to the driver who'd taken the shot. He held his breath so his lungs wouldn't sway his body and squeezed the trigger once. Twice. Two puffs of air sounded, and the mixture of gas from the muzzle and the burning of oil in his weapon mixed into a sweet smell. The windshield imploded on the driver, causing his body to jerk. Two direct hits. Where the window broke, there was a white splash surrounded by spiderweb-like rings and lines, making it difficult to see if the driver was moving.

"Business Tourist definitely has a gun," Hannah finally said.

He swiftly transitioned his red dot back to Business Tourist, who was now raising what was clearly a pistol, bringing it to aim at Sonny, who now had his M4 out, too.

Chris popped Business Tourist once in the middle of his back. And then a second time. Business Tourist fell, biting the asphalt. Another civilian cried out, followed by more. Nearby people ducked and scattered.

"Sunshine! Third van, Sunshine," Hannah said. "Passenger in the third van aiming for you."

Chris moved to the side so he could see more of the rear van. Sonny had already opened fire on the passenger there, so Chris would immobilize the vehicle by taking out the driver. Two puffs and the body drooped like a glove without a hand, head resting on the steering wheel.

The lead van sped forward and hit Sonny's "stalled" vehicle with a smack and pushed it out of the way before turning onto St. James Square and proceeding towards UKP. The van behind it, riddled with bullets from Chris and Sonny, rolled forward into the intersection but didn't make the turn. A black taxi sped around the square and plowed into the van with a horrific metal *crack*, smashing the front of the taxi and knocking the van over on its side. The taxi driver appeared pinned between the steering wheel and his seat. He wasn't moving.

Behind the first two vans, the third van didn't go anywhere, but Lullaby and nine of his men—armed with AK-47 assault rifles—poured out of the tail of the vehicle. Chris tried to take a shot, but Lullaby ducked back behind the van before he could squeeze the trigger.

Sonny was vulnerable standing in the open without any cover or concealment, and he must've seen how outnumbered he was because he sprinted toward Chris, who covered him by laying suppressive fire into Lullaby's group.

"This is gonna get uglier before it gets prettier," Sonny said, huffing and puffing as he sprinted.

The first van had stopped in front of UKP. Its back doors flew open, and a tall blond man jumped to the pavement—Lullaby's protégé. He was a handsome man who could do ugly things. Then an armed gang of close to a dozen appeared.

Hannah reported the appearance of Lullaby's protégé and his men.

If we weren't outnumbered before, we're clearly outnumbered now.

She must've continued to report, but Chris's visual senses overrode his hearing. Lullaby and his men faced Chris and fired at him from near the third van. Sonny jumped over a fence surrounding the park area, and just after he weaved into the trees, an explosion lifted the tipped-over van completely off the street. The earth quaked, and Sonny stumbled.

The van must have been packed with explosives intended for UKP. The bomb was probably shaped, so if the van had been positioned on the street next to the curb, most of the damaging force would have been directed at the UKP building. But with the van on its side like it was, most of that blast went into the ground, causing the van to lift into the air. Its flight was short-lived, though, as it fell like a discarded toy next to the gaping hole in the earth it had created. A geyser sprouted up out of the ground like Old Faithful, spewing chunks of asphalt with it.

"What the hell?" Sonny shouted.

"Must've ruptured a water main instead of the intended target," Chris guessed.

"You see Lullaby?"

"He's behind the third van, but I can hardly see the van or the enemy through Old Faithful."

Hannah didn't chime in so she must not have been able to see him, either.

The number of civilian screams increased, and the volume of the steady noise became louder. They were in panic mode. The blare of nearing police sirens added to the racket. Droplets big as tadpoles streamed down Chris's face. At first he thought it was from the broken water main, but it was raining again.

"Chris!" a voice screamed from the chaos. *Lullaby.* "I know you are here. I will find you, and I will kill you!"

1

A week earlier...

C hris wore his clerical collar and minister suit, standing with a young couple at the wedding altar, trying to calm his anxious nerves. There were times he'd been shot at and was calmer than he was now. But there were different kinds of being shot at, ranging from direct hits to blind misses, and this was still closer to the blind-misses end of the spectrum. For Bobby and JoAnne this was the most important moment of their life together, and Chris didn't want to disappoint them.

Bobby tugged nervously at the cuff of his black jacket, and the lower half of JoAnne's white wedding dress trembled. Seeing that they were more nervous than he was calmed Chris's nerves. He tried to help them relax by allowing his inward calm to rise to the surface, forming a smile. The groom smiled back, and he stopped tugging on his sleeve, but the bride's dress continued to quiver. During the previous night's rehearsal, Chris had advised the bride and groom not to lock their knees, but he wondered if now in all the jitteriness, the bride had forgotten.

"Are you bending a little at the knees?" Chris whispered to her.

The whole congregation seemed anxious for him to begin the wedding vows, but Chris's mind blocked them out—just as he'd blocked out distractions while focusing on his rifle scope. There could be no ceremony without the bride and groom. He met her eyes.

"I am now," she said.

The groom reached out and held her hand, and she stopped shaking.

"Ready?" Chris asked them.

They both smiled and nodded.

Chris had read the wedding vows over and over again, even late last night when he was unable to sleep. But even so, this was his first wedding ceremony. *What if I mess up?* He swallowed, pushing down the anxiety, and banished the thought.

"Dearly beloved..."

Chris made it smoothly through the ceremony, and he let out a sigh of relief as Bobby and Joanne faced each other, ringed fingers intertwined. "By the authority vested in me by the state of Texas," he said, "I now pronounce you husband and wife."

They kissed, sealing their vow, and Chris couldn't help but smile. They stepped down from the altar and strolled out of the chapel to loud applause. The bridal party, family, and guests followed, Chris waiting until everyone was gone to go join in the outdoor reception himself.

Pastor Luther, whom Chris worked for, reached out to shake his hand when he entered the reception area. "I would've never guessed this was your first wedding," he said. "You handled it like a pro. And more importantly, you put Bobby and Joanne at ease."

Chris smiled. "Thank you. Coming from you, that means a lot."

Pastor Luther stepped away to mingle with the others, and a line of guests formed at a nearby table for hors d'oeuvres. Chris grabbed a bottle of water from a large bowl of ice and quenched his dry throat.

"Hey, stranger," a sultry voice said from behind.

Chris turned around to see who it was, and his breath caught. *Hannah...*

The sight of her lit him up like a white phosphorous bullet, but he tried not to let it show. She was a chameleon who could look like a geek one moment or the girl next door, but when she turned it on, like she did now, heads turned. Roses blossomed and faded, but Hannah's beauty was amaranthine.

He wanted to kiss her but remembered he was still wearing his clerical suit and was within sight of his congregation. He hugged her tightly.

"I thought we'd agreed to just be friends," she said with a raised eyebrow.

He was unable to control his smile. "And that was a friendly hug."

Then she kissed him on the lips, searing into him like a habanero. Her skin smelled of vanilla and oranges, and he breathed her in.

"I thought we'd agreed to just be friends," he said playfully.

"That was a friendly kiss," she said.

He chuckled. Though he hoped no one in his congregation had noticed, he couldn't fathom regretting a kiss from her. "Very."

But no such luck. Bobby and Joanne were supposed to be the center of attention, yet all eyes had shifted to Chris and Hannah.

"You sure do know how to crash a party," he said to her.

She flashed him a sly grin. "You speak with the voice of experience."

Although she lived in Virginia and he in Texas, they had dated when they could over the past year. He wished she could be the marrying kind, and she wished they could live together, but both were too stubborn to change. That left them here.

"You know, this setting suits you," he said.

"Not really," she said. "Not at all, actually. Isn't that part of the reason we decided to just be friends?"

"Well, I think it suits you."

"Because you believe in fairy tales."

"I believe in believing," he clarified. He offered her a drink of his water.

She held up her hand. "No, thanks."

He took a sip before going on. "I'm hoping you're here because you have some time off, but my instincts tell me you're here for business."

"You've got better instincts than any shooter I know."

"Flattery gets you everywhere."

"Flattery hasn't brought me all the way out to Dallas to see you," she said, keeping the playful tone in her voice.

"I'm happy to help you any way I can," he said.

"I left a message on your answering service and texted you."

"I was so busy with the wedding and all. I'm sorry I missed your messages."

Her tone became businesslike. "We don't have much time, so I'll get to it. The White House Chief of Staff's son-in-law was kidnapped."

"Kidnapped?" His mind switched into SEAL mode, and he forgot about his current job as pastor.

"A jet loaded with our gear is standing by at Addison Airport to fly us out."

Chris nodded, then remembered he was still in his clerical garb. "Do I have time to go home and change?"

"Everything you need is on the plane."

"Okay, give me a minute." He walked over to Pastor Luther and quietly pulled him aside. "Do you remember last fall, after I returned from my most recent assignment, I mentioned that sometime in the near future I might be needed again?"

Pastor Luther glanced at Hannah, then back at Chris as if he already understood.

"Thank you. I'm sorry this is such short notice."

Pastor Luther hugged him. "I'll cover for you, son."

The man was like a second father to Chris, and he couldn't be more grateful. "Please tell Bobby and Joanne I'm sorry I couldn't stay."

Pastor Luther nodded. "I will."

Chris rejoined Hannah amid numerous stares, and she led him to the parking lot where, instead of her yellow Mustang, she walked up to another vehicle, probably a rental. They hopped inside, and she fired up the engine and pulled out onto the street.

She had brought Chris back into the terrorist-hunting business less than a year ago, when they'd been racing down this same road. Back then, he had struggled with keeping the light of a preacher while immersing himself in the darkness of black ops, but he'd somehow found validation in both, saving souls and lives. Now, he couldn't help but wonder if he'd struggle again.

Pushing his concern aside, he focused on the mission. "Where was the Chief of Staff's son-in-law last seen?"

"At a US embassy party in Athens, Greece," she replied.

"Has anyone claimed responsibility?"

She turned the steering wheel and accelerated around a corner. "A Greek terror organization calling itself 21D."

He didn't recognize the name. "21D?"

"They're a pro-Marxist group with a history of attacks in Greece, opposing Greek ties with NATO and the EU."

"Any demands?" he asked.

"21D wants Greece to reject plans to create the Trans-Adriatic Pipeline."

He furrowed his brow. "Why?"

"European plans are for TAP to carry natural gas from Turkey to Greece and then to Albania, ending in southern Italy," she explained. "21D denounces TAP as another capitalist invasion into Greece."

"So why'd 21D choose the White House Chief of Staff's son-in-law? What does he have to do with the pipeline?"

She reached between her seat and the center console, pulling out a file and handing it to Chris. "His name is Michael Winthrop. He's an onshore civil engineer working for United Kingdom Petroleum. UKP is the central player in creating the pipeline, but it's not clear whether the terrorists know he's related to the White House Chief of Staff. It would've been easier for the terrorists to capture him at his home, so we think taking him near the embassy was an attempt to grab more headlines."

"Well, they certainly grabbed our attention. What's our mission?"

"Find Michael Winthrop and report his location so the US can launch a rescue," she said.

"Before 21D kills him," he added.

"Exactly."

Chris and Hannah boarded a nondescript Gulfstream jet at a private airport near Dallas. In the aft section of the plane, there were three sets of gear, marked for Chris, Hannah, and Sonny, but Sonny was nowhere in sight.

"Where's Mr. Sunshine?" Chris asked.

"Going to pick him up at Pope Air Force Base. We can make sure our weapons are zeroed when we get there, too," she replied.

The Agency already had Chris's measurements, photos for ID, weapons, and other equipment, so the plane was stocked as Hannah had promised. He located his garment bag hanging in a closet. After unzipping it, he found a fine dark gray wool suit he'd never seen before. The wool would breathe well in the heat and insulate against the cold—highly durable. When he changed out of his clerical clothes and put on the suit, it fit perfectly.

"You really wear that suit," Hannah said.

He smiled. "Not nearly as well as you wear that dress."

He smoothed his hands along his jacket, feeling something stiff inside the left breast pocket. He checked and found a US diplomatic passport. He opened it to find his alias printed inside. They'd kept his preferred real first name—it was easiest to remember, especially under stress—but the last name, *Johnson*, was an alias. The agency had even signed the document in Chris's handwriting. "I guess this means we're diplomats?"

"Legal attachés investigating the kidnapping of Michael Winthrop. The US embassy in Athens has agreed to cooperate, but they don't know we're really working for the Agency. Our code name for the embassy is *Olympus*."

Being the son of diplomats, Chris was accustomed to life in and around embassies, which would come in handy. "Will we be the only search team from the US?"

"I asked but didn't get a straight answer," Hannah said, "so my guess is there will be at least one more team working the kidnapping."

Chris checked his bags for the small container that held his spare prosthetics. In 2009, during a covert mission to capture a Syrian terrorist, the bastard had bitten off a large chunk of Chris's ear, and he'd ended up losing the whole thing. He wore a prosthetic, and the Agency kept a regular spare and a camouflage spare to pack with his mission gear whenever they called him to action.

He located his Glock 19 Gen 4 pistol, magazines filled with ammo, and his Raven concealed holster. Checking over the weapon, he was relieved to see that the Agency had customized it to his specifications, replacing the plastic sights with metal, plugging the gap in the magazine well, and swapping out the factory barrel with a KKM match grade barrel. He wore it on his hip, and his mind shifted from his weapon to finding Michael. He might be using his Glock sooner rather than later.

"You've got that look in your eyes," Hannah said.

"What look is that?"

"That bleeding-edge stare. Like you're about to kill someone."

"I'm just thinking," he said.

"About what?"

"I hope we find him while he's still alive."

2

They touched down at Pope Air Force Base in North Carolina, where they rendezvoused with Sonny. They greeted one another on the plane, and Chris immediately noticed how well Sonny was moving after their mission last year when he took a bullet, which lodged near his spine. "You finished with your physical therapy, then?"

"I don't know," Sonny said. "The nurses have been giving me extracurricular exercises, but I'm running out of excuses to keep visiting them. My back never felt better."

"You look great," Chris said.

"I wish I could say the same for you." Sonny was wearing a camera on a strap around his neck. He adjusted its telescopic lens.

"Were you out on recce?" Chris asked, assuming it was part of some surveillance training.

Sonny glanced at Chris. "Kind of."

"Kind of?"

"I know this may seem funny to some people, but I'm a bird watcher."

Chris and Hannah stared at him as if he were spouting science fiction.

"Yeah, I take photos of birds. What of it?" Sonny said. "Been doing it since elementary school. I was smaller than the other boys and the only birdwatcher, so they beat the shit out of me for it. Now... say hello to the Rat." With a twinkle in his eye, Sonny pulled out a knife that Chris recognized right away, named after a Team guy named Tom Ratzlaff. "Well, I guess the Rat would be overkill, but you know what I mean."

Sonny handed it to Chris, who examined it with admiration. With a blade length of three and a half inches, it was small enough to conceal but long enough to stab internal organs and arteries. It had a narrow blade width for fitting into tight spaces between bones, and its narrow spear point could penetrate military clothing. It wasn't designed to open envelopes or survive in the woods. It was designed for one thing and one thing only: killing.

He returned the knife to Sonny, who put it back in its sheath. "Anyway, bird-watching is about the hunt, challenging yourself to find what's out there. Improving your skills. I once tracked a golden eagle for five days to get a clear pic of it. If I have a couple hours to get outdoors, I throw my pack in the truck and I'm in the woods. I'm addicted to it. Maybe I need a psychiatrist, but what do I care? Life is short and pleasure is shorter, so you have to seize the moment." With that, he walked aft and checked the bags waiting for him.

After flying over the Atlantic Ocean, southern Europe, and most of the Mediterranean Sea, they touched down in Athens, where they unloaded. The air outside was hot and dry, and Chris was tempted to loosen his tie, but he waited, expecting that their car would have air-conditioning. He was right. The engine and air-conditioning were already running in the BMW supplied by the Agency. The trio stuffed their gear in the trunk, and Sonny crawled into the backseat and lay down.

Chris took the driver's seat and adjusted the mirrors. "After we find Michael, who'll be tasked with the rescue mission?" he asked Hannah, who sat in the passenger seat beside him.

"Your former Teammates," she said. She mounted a pre-programmed GPS on the dash and turned it on. "Six will be stationed at Minotaur, but we won't have direct communication with them, and they'll need permission from Washington before they can launch the rescue." Minotaur was their code name for the US Naval Support Activity, Souda Bay in Crete.

Sonny groaned. "The Hollywood Whores," he said in his pained, nasally Queens accent.

"I don't get it," Chris said.

"Because you're slow," Sonny said, cutting him off.

Chris shook his head and eased out onto the highway, following it southwest.

"Sonny," Hannah said, "last year, you seemed so excited about the three of us working together again. What gives?"

Sonny wrinkled his face like a dried prune. "*Excited* is such a strong word. Besides, that was last year and I was in the hospital under heavy sedation at the time. Truth be told, I wouldn't follow you two into a hot tub full of naked strippers."

Hannah rolled her eyes, and Chris smiled. He followed the violet trail on the monitor, turning right onto another highway that took them northwest through farmland before rounding the northern base of Mount Hymettus. The mountain reached a kilometer in height, topped with a transmitter park for TV and radio stations. It stretched sixteen klicks to the south, running from Athens to the Saronic Gulf.

It didn't take long before they entered the urban sprawl of Athens, though, passing the Olympic Aquatic Center and a mall before reaching Sofias Avenue, where the embassy stood. Hellenic Police were posted on each street corner and at the gate of a three-meter-high steel fence surrounding the embassy. Inside the fence, an armed US Marine stood watch. This was one of the more heavily guarded embassies Chris had seen.

"Why can't I get Ankara out of my mind?" he wondered aloud. The embassy in Turkey was where Chris and Hannah had been falsely imprisoned by US authorities before Sonny helped them escape. He prayed they never had a repeat of that event.

"This time will be better," she said.

"Don't know how it could be worse." Chris stopped at the gate and handed his passport to the police officer.

The officer motioned for Hannah and Sonny to hand him their passports, too, which they promptly did. He examined each of the passports and studied the trio's faces before stepping away from the vehicle. Soon, he returned the passports.

"Welcome," he said, "Ambassador Garcia is expecting you."

"Thank you." The vehicle barricade lowered, and Chris drove into the compound. "So far, so good."

He parked the BMW and then stepped out with Hannah and Sonny. The embassy was closed for normal business, but before they reached the nearest building, a heavyset man greeted them.

"I'm Bob Garcia."

They each returned the ambassador's greeting and shook his hand.

The man's gaze lingered on Chris. "You must be the legal attachés from the States, yes?"

The three nodded, but he continued to stare at Chris. "Do I know you from somewhere?"

While they might have met at a diplomatic function he'd attended with his parents, Chris didn't remember him. Maybe the ambassador knew his father—there was a strong family resemblance—but admitting his true identity now would blow his cover and that of his teammates.

"No, sir," he said.

Ambassador Garcia shook his head. "Hmm. I must be mistaken." He led them around the main embassy building to an annex in the back. "This is our Tactical Operating Center," he explained as he escorted them inside the TOC where a middle-aged man sat behind monitors looking at multiple views of the embassy. "Jason, here, is part of our diplomatic security, and he'll help you with whatever you need. My understanding is that you want to see the video of the event on the evening Mr. Winthrop was kidnapped?"

"Yes, sir," Hannah confirmed. "That would help us gain a better feel for what happened."

"Jason, can you run that video?" the ambassador asked.

Jason nodded and manipulated the video controls until a blank screen came to life, showing a party at the embassy.

"The Hellenic Police have already been here," Ambassador Garcia said. "And the British sent over an investigative team, too. You're the second group from the US, but nobody is sharing information with me about their investigations."

"I hope you can excuse us if we ask some of the same questions," Hannah said with a smile. "And we'll try to keep you informed about new information we find."

"Thank you," Ambassador Garcia said with a slight tilt of his head.

"What was the occasion for the party?" she began.

"We held an energy forum earlier that day, and the after-party was a time for everyone to discuss the forum and socialize."

Chris listened but also kept a close eye on the video monitor. Michael Winthrop's posture was relaxed on the screen, indicating he was comfortable meeting others. He wasn't a teetotaler, but he wasn't a drunkard, either. He drank sociably, and he seemed cheerful. It was ironic to watch him mix and mingle so freely, unaware that he was about to lose that freedom. Chris knew too well what being a prisoner felt like, and he had deep empathy for Michael.

Jason handed them a small stack of files with photos attached. "These are the bios and pictures of known Greek terrorists and suspects who aren't imprisoned."

Chris and his teammates compared the photos with people in the video.

"We already did that," Jason said. When Sonny gave Jason the stink eye, he shifted uncomfortably in his chair. "But you're welcome to check again."

The trio continued their comparison but discovered nothing new. Chris looked to Jason. "Do you have background files on everyone who attended the party?"

He sighed before stepping away from the table, then returned with a stack of files. He dropped them on the table with a *thud. That attitude won't get him very far,* Chris thought, and he didn't bother to thank the man. Instead, he, Hannah, and Sonny pored through the folders.

Minutes later, Sonny pointed to one of the files. "That guy has a thin file."

"That's Xander Metaxas, a friend of mine and a close ally of the US," Ambassador Garcia said. "He owns Athens Sustainable Energy. Xander has both Greek and American citizenship and is popular with many of the locals."

"Why is his file so thin?" Chris asked.

"I know Xander personally," Ambassador Garcia said. "I did not think there was a need to investigate him. But if you think thickening his file will be of use, I will help you get the information you need."

"Let's look at who came into contact with Xander," Sonny suggested.

Chris and Hannah nodded.

They rewound the video and played it again, noting the people who came into contact with Michael.

In the video on the monitor, Michael had stepped out of the camera view. Chris rewound and pointed to the tall man. "Xander?"

"Yes," the Ambassador said.

"When Michael heads for the exit, Xander puts his hand in his pocket," Chris said.

"What does that mean?" Ambassador Garcia asked.

"It could simply mean he put his hand in his pocket, or it could mean he's activating a remote signaling device," Sonny said.

"Not Xander." Ambassador Garcia shook his head. "Maybe someone else, but not him. He's not even looking in Michael's direction."

"Can you play the video again, from right before Michael leaves the embassy, please, Jason?" Hannah asked.

The diplomatic security officer tapped the keyboard.

As the video played, Hannah said, "There, pause the video."

Jason did as she'd commanded.

"That woman," Hannah said, "looks to be in her early twenties, she leaves just before Michael does. Wasn't she having a drink with him earlier? Rewind the video."

Jason did.

"Pause," Hannah said. "Right there."

The video froze.

Hannah pointed to the monitor. "There she is having a drink with Michael. Who is she?"

"That's Xander's daughter," the ambassador said. "Her name is Evelina."

"That babe's got a booty like a Bugatti," Sonny said.

The ambassador looked at Sonny like he'd just wiped his ass with a linen tablecloth.

"She seems to be flirting with Michael," Chris said.

"Ambassador Garcia, can you set up a meeting for us with this Xander?" Hannah asked.

"When?"

"As soon as possible."

Ambassador Garcia took out his phone. "I'll call him now."

While Chris and the others watched the video again and reexamined the photos and files, Ambassador Garcia called Xander Metaxas. The ambassador put the call on speakerphone.

"Bob, what can I do for you?" a man's voice asked.

"I have three legal attachés from the States who were wondering if they might meet you and talk about Michael Winthrop and his kidnapping," the ambassador said.

"I saw that story on the news and was shocked. Is Mr. Winthrop okay?" Xander asked.

"I haven't heard anything more."

"Yes, I will give them all the information I can," Xander said.

"When would be a good time for them to visit you?"

"Well, right now I am preparing for a cocktail party at my house tonight, so now would be difficult..."

"Could they attend the party?" Ambassador Garcia suggested.

"Wonderful. That is a splendid idea. It is semi-formal. There will be lots of hors d'oeuvres, so tell them to come with empty stomachs. It starts at seven o'clock."

The ambassador turned to face Hannah. She nodded. "Okay, I'll tell them. Thanks, Xander."

"If there is anything else I can do to help, just let me know," the voice on the line said. "Anything."

3

After finding no more clues at the embassy, they parted ways with the ambassador and drove several more minutes to their hotel. Once they checked in and got their rooms, the three met in Hannah's room to discuss their next steps.

"What's our plan to find out about Michael Winthrop's disappearance when we visit Xander Metaxas's estate?" Hannah asked.

"I can talk to Xander," Chris offered. "And you and Sonny can try to gain information from others at the party." His teammates nodded in agreement.

"And if we find ourselves on the wrong side of an unfriendly welcoming committee, what will our E & E be?" Sonny asked, moving on to their escape-and-evasion plans. "I'm not expecting such a committee, but just in case."

"If the threat is nonlethal," Chris said, "Hannah can use some of her MMA to drop some bodies, and you and I can use our bags of dirty tricks." For Chris and Sonny, *dirty tricks* meant exploiting any weakness on the enemy's body to subdue him. And that weakness dictated using the weapon that was most readily available, whether it be a fist, a drinking glass, or whatever. In turn, the weapon influenced how Chris and Sonny would move. For those lacking experience in violent confrontations, such a process might seem complex, but for Chris and Sonny, dirty tricks had become a natural extension of their being.

Hannah raised an eyebrow. "And if the threat is lethal?"

"We're all armed with pistols," Sonny said, patting his firearm. "So unless I'm in close and my knife is quicker…"

"That's a last resort," she reminded him. "If it gets too hairy, we can E & E to Olympus. Or if that isn't practical, we can make the journey to Minotaur."

Chris nodded. "If we get split up, I'll head for the water and try to lose them that way. Then I'll catch up with you two at Olympus. Or Minotaur. Whichever comes first."

"Why doesn't it surprise me that you'll head to the water first?" Sonny said.

Chris smiled.

"Okay, then," Hannah said. "Sounds like we've got ourselves something of a plan. I'm going to get ready." She waved the backs of her hands at them, shooing them back to their room to do the same.

Shortly before 1900 hours, they exited the hotel, got in the BMW, and headed toward Xander's. They passed the Parthenon as they drove, and Chris wanted to take a longer look at the classical Greek building perched high on the rocks, but there was no time. On the opposite side of the road stood the Temple of Olympian Zeus. No time for that, either.

Hannah sat in the front passenger seat, navigating as they cruised through the streets of Athens. "Did you enjoy being a diplomat's son?" she asked when there was a lull in the directions.

Chris flicked a glance in her direction. "I enjoyed the different people and their languages and food—the countries. The dressing up and the parties were just something that went with it all."

"Do you miss the dressing up and the parties?" she asked. He noticed her taking in his Agency-issued suit as she waited for his answer.

He smiled. "It's nice to wear a good suit once in a while. But at parties, too often I find myself against the wall not knowing what to do. How about you?"

"Why are you two talking about such boring shit?" Sonny piped up from the backseat.

"And what would you like to talk about?" Hannah shot back. She clearly didn't appreciate Sonny interrupting their conversation, either.

"I don't want to talk about anything right now," Sonny said, "but listening to you two talk about boring shit is denting my skull."

"Maybe you should stick your head out the window, Sonny," Chris said sharply. "You might see some birds."

"That'd be a hell of an improvement," Sonny mumbled.

Minutes later, they reached a white stone mansion perched on a bluff with a spectacular view of the setting sun. Below, the the dark-blue waters of the Aegean Sea contrasted the light-blue sky. Chris parked on the street behind several luxury cars, allowing enough space for their SOG team to make a quick getaway if necessary.

Walking onto Xander's property, they traversed a cobblestone pathway, past olive trees and grapevines, until they reached a thick oak door. Chris pulled out his cell phone and tapped it until his audio recording app came on, and he pressed *Record* before returning his phone to his pocket.

Sonny knocked.

Chris did a quick scan of their surroundings. If shit hit the fan and they were split up, the ocean was within walking distance, and he'd take to the sea and kick-stroke-and-glide while Hannah and Sonny escaped through the city.

There was no answer at the door, so Sonny knocked harder.

Finally, a tall man opened the door. Chris sized him up as being fit and about his same height, but the gray in the man's beard marked him as older. Chris introduced Hannah, Sonny, and himself.

"Ah, yes, the legal attachés. I'm Xander Metaxas," he said, his voice like honey. "Ambassador Garcia told me you were coming. I am so sorry to hear about Mr. Winthrop. Please, come in."

Inside the entrance hall, the high wooden ceiling was finely carved, and a grand piano stood to the side. The black marble floor looked somewhat dated, but it was shiny and clearly expensive.

"Nice floor," Chris said.

"Thank you." Xander led them across the hall. "This house has seen a fair amount of remodeling since the eighteenth century, but the floor is original. It is called Ashford Black Marble, imported from England, but it is actually limestone."

"It's beautiful," Hannah said as Xander gestured them into a spacious main room where a cluster of guests stood next to a grand fireplace and a butler served drinks to the guests standing under a crystal chandelier.

"A house as fancy as this," Sonny said with a snort, "and I'd think you'd at least be able to afford a new floor."

Chris clenched his teeth, and Xander gave Sonny a quizzical look. The New Yorker was going to get them into trouble before they could find anything out. Chris needed to find some way to build a rapport with Xander. And fast.

Xander was wearing what appeared to be a Yale ring. "I see you're a Yale grad." He pointed to the man's hand.

Xander nodded. "Did you graduate from Yale, too?"

"Harvard, actually," Chris said.

Hannah smiled at Xander, then at Chris. "Sonny and I will let you two exchange Ivy League stories." She looped her arm through Sonny's and pulled him along.

"Yes, please, help yourselves," Xander said.

She bowed her head graciously, and they strolled deeper into the house, where most of the guests were congregated.

Xander turned to Chris, a calm, carefree smile on his face. "Would you like a drink?"

"No, thank you." His purpose here was to find out about the hostage's kidnapping, and having a purpose helped him to relax. He didn't need a drink to do that for him.

"I had a friend in Harvard," Xander said. "Which dorm were you in?"

"Wigglesworth Hall."

"Ah. I do not know it. Sadly, I only visited the campus once."

Chris directed the conversation back to Xander's own experience. "Yale is an excellent university. And now you own Athens Sustainable Energy. That's quite the accomplishment."

Xander nodded. "The earth's resources are finite, so we must manage them effectively. Our descendants' survival depends on it. The twin pillars of my company are energy efficiency and renewable energy."

"Do you see yourself in competition with fossil fuels?" Chris asked.

Xander shook his head. "Not at all. The human race can only survive off dead organisms for so long. We're living on borrowed time. Whether Athens realizes it or not, she needs me. If not today, tomorrow."

"Michael Winthrop is living on borrowed time... if he's still alive," Chris said, carefully watching the man's reaction.

But Xander kept his face tranquil and his words even. "Yes, we attended the same embassy party. I first heard about the kidnapping on the news. It is terrible. And today your ambassador called me. Words desert me."

"I was hoping maybe you could help us."

"Of course, whatever I can do," Xander said. "Though I am not sure I will be of much use."

"What do you know about 21D? The kidnappers?"

"Only what I hear in the news. They are a pro-Marxist terrorist group with a history of attacks here in Greece. And they oppose the EU and NATO. That is about all I know." A knock sounded at the door, but Xander ignored it. "I did not know Mr. Winthrop personally, but I hope he will be okay."

"Do you have any idea what 21D stands for?"

Xander shook his head. The knock came again, but no one answered and Xander continued to ignore it.

"Have you ever talked to Michael before?" Chris asked.

"Not that I recall. There were a number of people at the party. It is possible we exchanged words." The knock turned into a pounding now. "I am sorry. I am short one staff member. If you will excuse me."

"Yes, of course."

Xander left and answered the door. More guests poured in, and he chatted leisurely with them. Chris waited a few minutes, but when Xander didn't return, he mingled with the other guests, keeping an eye on the host at all times.

The first two guests he approached spoke English as a lingua franca, and despite their European accents, their English was excellent.

"...NATO wants to recruit Ukraine as one of its members, so NATO can box Russia in," said a bespectacled man.

The woman nodded in agreement, her gaze piercing Chris's as she made eye contact. "Russia has a right to use its military to help Russophones in Ukraine."

The man took a sip of his drink. "The Russian government just wants to bring legitimacy and stability to the region."

"Exactly," the woman said. "They merely want law and order."

"And peace," the man added.

"Yes!" she agreed.

Chris listened quietly. Both of them sounded too socialist for his blood, and although he agreed Russia had a right to defend its land and its people, he firmly opposed Russia's military intervention in Ukraine. He politely excused himself and roamed the room looking for someone who might actually be willing to help him find Michael.

He suddenly remembered his recording cell phone, took it out, and pressed *Stop*. Then he used his phone to upload the recording to a colleague's website. The colleague, who was also a dear friend, was Young Park, a brilliant Agency tech who'd left the CIA but still did contract work. Then Chris sent an encrypted message requesting a voice-match analysis.

Young ran a twenty-four-hour service, so he or one of his assistants would respond soon.

Hannah emerged from behind a group of people.

"Where's Sonny?" Chris asked.

"Eating," Hannah said with an eye roll. "Did you learn anything from Xander?"

"He claims he doesn't know much."

"With all his connections?" She quirked a brow. "That seems unlikely. Greece is attempting to recover from massive debt, and Xander is living like a king. Look around you. He spends his money freely, but he's stingy with information."

"He did invite us here," Chris said.

Hannah frowned. "So we wouldn't suspect him of any wrongdoing."

"And he was kind enough to talk to me," Chris countered.

"A small sacrifice on his part," Hannah said. "The cost of retaining information."

"This might be easier if you try to enjoy it," Chris said.

Her voice was cold. "For some of us, life has never been easy."

He frowned. Somehow the topic had changed very quickly. "You mean growing up in East LA?"

"The haves eat the have-nots," she said. "My mother and I were the have-nots."

Sonny appeared then, chewing a mouthful of food and tugging on his tie. "I'm tired of this monkey suit, and I've lived in better zoos."

Hannah put her hand on Sonny's shoulder. "I need you to come help me with something."

Sonny grinned at Chris, as if to emphasize that Hannah had invited him to go with her rather than Chris.

"We'll be right back," Hannah said.

Before Chris could ask where they were going, she and Sonny were gone. Chris was grateful to her for keeping Sonny occupied, though. Operators like him were game changers to have in combat, but when the bullets weren't flying, they could be difficult to keep out of trouble.

Chris surveyed the room, his gaze landing on a woman in her twenties who was smiling at him. She had an easy-going expression and blond highlights in her light-brown, shoulder-length hair. He returned the smile before he realized who she was. The woman in the video of the embassy party... Xander's daughter, Evelina.

She disappeared in the crowd; his heartbeat quickened as he searched for her, and it continued to hammer steadily. She could have information about Michael's disappearance. He spotted her again, and she smiled at him again before exiting the house through a pair of French doors.

As Chris followed her outside, a brief panic grew in his chest. These same people were at the party where Michael was taken. If they were involved...

Will someone try to kidnap me, too?

No. That was silly. And even if they tried, he was well armed and had his team here for support. He took a deep breath and approached Evelina, who now sat in a lounge chair near an infinity pool. The sun had dropped behind the mansion, casting a shadow on the backyard.

"Mind if I join you?" he asked.

She gestured for him to have a seat. "Please." Her miniskirt exposed most of her legs, and she held a handkerchief in her lap. "I noticed you the moment you walked in."

He sat down across from her. "Have we met before?" he asked, worried for a second that maybe she knew him from somewhere and his cover as a legal attaché was in danger.

"No, this is the first time." She pulled her handkerchief farther up her lap, exposing the gap between her miniskirt and her thighs, showing the white triangle of her panties.

Is she showing me this on purpose, or is this an accident? Pastor Luther had told him, *Look once, you're human; look twice, you're not a pastor.*

Chris lifted his gaze and focused on her eyes. "Are you a friend of Xander's?" he asked, pretending not to know the answer. By asking a question she could answer truthfully, he could establish a baseline for her posture and speech when she was telling the truth. Then he could use deviations from the baseline to help him detect her lies.

"He's my father," she said, leaning forward with a smile.

Chris returned the smile. "Really?"

Abruptly, her eyes shifted to the French doors. She pushed her handkerchief forward and inched her chair away from Chris. He turned and saw a handsome man in his mid-twenties, with long blond hair and blue eyes. He stood there with a surprised look on his face as if he'd just been mugged.

The man made a slight motion with his hand that seemed as if he was about to apologize for interrupting what he hadn't heard. Suddenly, the backyard felt crowded. Quiet filled the air, awkward as an elephant, but the man appeared even more awkward, as if suspended in time and not knowing if he were coming or going. His eyes lowered first, then his head. And he walked back into the house.

"Do you know him?" Chris asked.

"That's Animus… my fiancé," she said. "He's also Daddy's protégé."

"Oh?"

She leaned forward. "Why'd you come here? To Greece?"

"My name is Chris. I'm a legal attaché for the US State Department," he said. "I'm searching for information about the kidnapped American, Michael Winthrop."

Her eyes widened.

"Is something wrong?"

She fidgeted with her handkerchief. "Nothing."

"You seem troubled."

"You better go," she said in response.

Chris paused for a moment. "A moment ago you were smiling…"

"You should really go."

"Do you know something about Michael's kidnapping?" he pressed.

"You have to go. *Now.*"

"I can protect you," Chris said. "Michael's life is in danger."

Abruptly, she stood up. "I'm sorry." She walked briskly across the patio, opened a French door, and disappeared inside the mansion.

Having stumbled upon something important, he felt dazed. Somehow, Xander or his family was involved. Concern for Hannah and Sonny filled him at the thought, and he hurried into the mansion. Once inside, he slowed down and tried to present an appearance of calm. There seemed to be nearly a hundred people inside the mansion now, and although Xander continued to mingle with his guests, Hannah and Sonny were nowhere in sight. He checked one of the restrooms, but it was empty. After more searching, he found

Sonny in a hall, but he shooed Chris away. Maybe Hannah was searching for intel inside one of the rooms while Sonny stood watch.

Chris returned to the main room and waited. Feeling conspicuously alone, he spotted some guests serving themselves from a wide silver platter of hors d'oeuvres and realized he still hadn't eaten anything. He made his way toward the table. Xander and a gaggle of guests flowed through the crowd in his direction, heading for the hors d'oeuvres, too, until Chris and Xander stood almost face-to-face.

"I met your daughter," Chris told him.

"Oh?" Xander raised an eyebrow. "I was not aware she was here."

"She seems like a nice girl." Chris ate a cube of feta cheese from a toothpick that also skewered an olive and some meat.

Xander glanced around the room. "She must have come through another door." His gaze returned to Chris, and his normally smooth demeanor ruffled around the edges. "What did you two talk about?"

"Nothing much. My understanding is that she was at the embassy party with you the same night Michael disappeared."

Xander picked up a drink without hesitating or trembling and took a sip. "Yes, she was," he said, his voice equally smooth once more.

"I'd like to ask you another question, if I may." Chris ate the olive from his toothpick.

"Yes, of course."

"How strongly do you support the creation of TAP in Greece?"

The mention of TAP seemed to cause the ears of nearby guests to perk up, and heads turned in their direction. Xander didn't answer.

"The Trans-Adriatic Pipeline?" Chris clarified, popping the piece of meat into his mouth.

"Yes, I know what TAP is," Xander said impatiently.

"Would you say you support it strongly?"

Xander's eyes were calm. "It is not for me to support or oppose."

"I like how you put that," Chris said with a nod.

"How is that?" Xander asked.

Chris forced a grin. "Carefully."

Xander stared.

"Maybe you can help me understand how you feel about Michael Winthrop's kidnapping," Chris whispered, glancing around. Now others were not only looking but *listening* to their conversation.

Xander frowned. "As I said, it is a terrible thing. I hope he is rescued soon."

Chris's gut told him Xander was lying, but he kept the tone of his voice polite. "Thank you. I'm sorry to have bothered you."

"No bother. I hope he is rescued soon." He picked up his drink. "Now if you do not mind, I would like to talk to some more of my guests."

"Certainly."

Xander walked away, and Chris couldn't get over how calm and cool he was—too cool.

He felt a gentle hand on his back and glanced over his shoulder.

"What were you two talking about?" Hannah asked, Sonny standing beside her.

Chris looked for a trash receptacle to dispose of his toothpick but saw none, so he handed it to one of the wait staff. "I'll explain in the car. Are we ready to go?"

Hannah and Sonny nodded and followed him as he weaved through the crowd toward the front door. Outside, they loaded into the BMW, and Chris flicked on the lights and drove away from Xander's estate.

Hannah checked the side-view mirror. "Sonny guarded the hall while I gained physical access to the laptop in Xander's study," she reported. "You remember after our last mission how Young showed us how to bypass the login?"

Chris nodded, focused on both Hannah and the road.

"I got into Xander's laptop and logged into Young's website." One merely needed to use the target's device to log into Young's website and then he could access the device remotely and begin hacking. Then he could install hidden monitoring software that wouldn't show up in the start menu, control panel, or index. Using the hidden software, he could keep a keystroke log of e-mails, chats, and other internet usage. In addition, the monitoring software took routine screen captures. "Young is hacking Xander's computer as we speak."

Chris grinned.

"What?" Hannah asked.

"I actually sent Young a digital recording of my conversation with Xander and asked for a voice match. The more time I spend around that man, the more my spider senses tingle."

"Me, too."

"Me, three," Sonny said.

4

In the villa north of the pool, Animus stood in the living room while Evelina sat slouching on the sofa. "What was that all about?" he asked.

"What was what all about?"

"Who was he?"

"Who was who?" Evelina said innocently.

He was determined to get an answer. "You know who I'm talking about," he said.

She sighed. "If you *must* know, his name is Chris. He's a legal attaché from the US Embassy."

A hard knock came at the door, and they stopped talking. Animus reached for his pistol, keeping it concealed under his suit jacket as he approached the door and looked through the window. "It's your father."

She stood up from the sofa. "You know how he doesn't like to be kept waiting."

Xander was more than a mentor to Animus, he was the father Animus never had. While Animus's contemporaries earned their bachelor's degrees in subjects like business and biology, he earned his in the art of killing. And Xander was his sole professor.

Animus answered the door and invited him in.

"I was looking for you," Xander said as he stopped in front of Evelina. "I could not find you in the main residence, so I came here."

"Is something wrong?" she asked, worry creasing her brow.

"Before the party, I tried to reach you, but your phone was off. I sent a text asking you to stay away from the party. And I left the same message with your answering service."

"I'm sorry. I was having trouble with my phone," she explained.

Xander took a deep breath. "It is okay. I understand, sweetheart." He paused for a moment. "There was an American here tonight from the State Department, a legal attaché."

Evelina hesitated for a moment. "Yes."

"Did he ask you about Michael Winthrop?"

"He did, but I didn't tell him anything," she said.

"Are you sure? I will not be angry. It is simply important that I know what you told him."

"I didn't tell him anything. When he brought up the subject, I walked away and came here."

"He was not like any diplomat I have ever met," Xander said. "Too calm for a bureaucrat. Did either of you see what his colleagues were up to this evening?"

Animus and Evelina shook their heads.

Xander hugged Evelina and kissed her on the head. "Could you bring us some drinks, please?"

She smiled and left the room.

"Our Albanian friends might need some help," Xander said to Animus quietly. "Make sure the rest of our people are standing by to back them up at a moment's notice."

He nodded. "Yes, sir."

"Kidnapping Michael Winthrop has already caused concern among the other UKP employees participating in the pipeline project. I tried to milk this for all it is worth, but with these attachés snooping around, we may have to kill the kid sooner than I expected. We may need to move on to Phase Two."

"UKP headquarters in London, sir?"

Xander nodded. "Go ahead and make reservations for our crew. Get us as close to the target as you can. I want to be ready to move in an instant. We can always cancel the reservations if we decide to begin Phase Two later."

"Yes, sir."

"We may not be able convince UKP's leadership to stop constructing TAP, but if we hit their employees hard enough, we should be able to slow construction down." Xander patted Animus on the shoulder and smiled. "Striking fear in their hearts is key."

5

C hris, Hannah, and Sonny were back in Hannah's hotel room when Chris's cell phone rang.

"Young," he answered, "I didn't expect to hear from you so soon."

"The computer hack Hannah initiated was terminated from the target's end," Young said, getting right to business.

"What does that mean?" Chris asked.

"Someone cut the power source and internet connection."

"Do you think he suspects we tried to hack him?"

"It's possible," Young said. "I haven't had time to analyze the data we were able to download, but a visual check is showing a lot of searches about Michael Winthrop and United Kingdom Petroleum."

"Hannah accessed the bathroom in the master bedroom, too," Chris said, "and she took a hair sample from a comb, I assume it's Xander's, but she'll send the samples to you by courier, so you can check the DNA and see if it matches anyone in our database."

"Will do," Young said.

"Can you get a cell number for Xander?" he asked. "And have NSA feed us the GPS coordinates in real time?" Xander's phone wouldn't even have to be switched on for NSA to track it.

"I'm on it," Young said.

"Thanks," Chris said. "Out."

He updated the others once he hung up, and Hannah requested an Agency courier to pick up the DNA sample. Within an hour, it had been picked up and was on its way. Soon after, Chris's phone rang again, and he answered it.

"NSA found a match for the digital recording of the first person in the conversation with you," Young said.

"The first person in the recording was Xander Metaxas," Chris said.

"NSA matched it with a Russian spy."

"Russian spy?" Chris asked, immediately sparking Hannah and Sonny's interest in the conversation. He met Hannah's eyes, then Sonny's. "Are you sure Xander is a Russian spy?"

"His code name is *Bayushki Bayu*." Chris recognized the phrase as something Russian mothers said to their babies to put them to sleep, but there was no direct English translation for it. "NSA and the Agency's code name for him is Lullaby. He's an FSB officer, a Non-Official Cover." After the USSR was dissolved, the KGB's foreign operations were restructured into the FSB, Russia's version of the CIA. "Rather than work as an official spy with diplomatic cover in an embassy, Lullaby operated away from embassies and trade missions. Although Lullaby didn't have diplomatic immunity, he had more independence and could mingle more easily in Greece, go into deep cover."

"I suspected Xander of being a Greek terrorist, but I'm stunned to hear he's a Russian spy. How sure are you about this?" Chris asked.

"Given the quality of the comparison recording and the quality of your recording," Young said, "it's almost a seventy-five percent match. It isn't one hundred percent, but these matches never are. Lullaby works under Directorate S, which handles illegal intelligence, including resident spies. It is believed that Lullaby assumed the identity of a dead Greek in Albania and lived there for a short time customizing the identity before moving to Greece. To help with his legend, he probably married a Greek woman, and it is believed that he lives in Greece."

Chris shook his head. "I guess it is what it is—until it isn't."

"One more thing," Young said. "I tapped the phone Hannah requested. Xander made a phone call to a man he called Talos. They spoke using code words about a 'package.' We're still trying to decode their conversation, but Talos's phone was tracked to the Kypseli neighborhood." Young gave the address.

Chris checked the GPS on his phone and found the location. "That could be where they're holding Michael. Kypseli is only five klicks north of our location."

Chris thanked Young, ended the call, and briefed Hannah and Sonny.

"Let's check it out," Sonny said.

"Better than just sitting here," Hannah said.

They left their room and took the elevator down to the garage where they loaded into the BMW. Hannah took her turn behind the wheel, started the engine, and mounted her GPS on the dash.

She drove to Kypseli, in the center of Athens, where the city became denser with apartment buildings and people— more foreigners than Greeks. The GPS coordinates corresponded with a brown, 1950s apartment building that stood four stories tall. As Hannah drove by, they searched for nearby surveillance, but all they found was a stocky man standing outside the apartment building.

Hannah drove two blocks away and found an open spot in a line of cars parked next to the sidewalk. Graffiti marked the wall beside them.

"My gut is telling me Michael is here," Chris said.

"Could be indigestion." Sonny chuckled.

Hannah and Chris both ignored him. "Tomorrow morning, we can pose as movie location scouts and rent out one of the apartments across the street from the target building," Hannah suggested as she turned the car away from the building. "Find out what's really going on here."

Early the next morning, they dressed casual, returned to Kypseli, and slipped through a back entrance into an apartment facing the target building. They went from apartment to apartment to request a room to rent, but the language barrier proved to be more of an obstacle than the movie production pitch.

They hit the jackpot on the second floor, though, when an elderly Pakistani man let them inside and showed them a room. One area of the wall was a patchwork of three colors: an unfinished yellow paint, the beige color beneath, and a worn patch of brown wood below it all. Scribbled on part of the beige color were childlike drawings, and a makeshift curtain hung from a rope by clothespins. Sonny opened the curtain partway, finding an excellent view of the target building across the street.

The Pakistani wrinkled his nose. "Albanian mafia, rude they are," he said.

"The men across the street are Albanian mafia?" Hannah asked.

The Pakistani nodded. "Communism fell. Albanians illegally immigrated. Crime organizations they make."

"What else do you know about the men across the street?" she asked.

"Albanian mafia, police hate."

"Anything else?" She showed him a photo of Michael.

The Pakistani shrugged as if he didn't recognize Michael. "Albanian mafia rude. Women buy and sell. Money take. You room want?"

"Human trafficking and extortion doesn't equal Michael being in there," Sonny said.

Maybe I'm wrong this time. But there's only one way to find out. "It's the best lead we've had," Chris said.

After some haggling with the Pakistani, they settled on a price.

Peering through the window, they could see there was a new guard across the street, taking the place of the one the night before. This guard was taller but not as stocky and had a permanent scowl.

"The right window on the fourth floor is protected with metal bars," Sonny noted.

Chris nodded. "Maybe these Albanians are more interested in keeping someone inside than keeping people out."

Smoke rolled out of an apartment window next to the Albanian building.

The Pakistani became agitated and pointed to the smoke. "Everyone say, 'she oil too much! She food burn!'" He walked out of the room, closing the door behind him.

Hannah sat down, opened her laptop, and typed. "I'm sending an update to the station chief, telling him we need Technical Intelligence to confirm what's inside that building."

After spending the night in the small room, a message returned from the station chief, telling the trio to keep an eye on the Albanian building until the agency's technical wizards arrived. In the afternoon, before TECHINT arrived, smoke poured out of the same apartment window next to the Albanian building.

"Looks like someone burned the toast again," Sonny said.

Soon, flames crept out of the side of the window. Shouting came from inside the burning building. Strangely, the smell reminded Chris of a backyard Texas barbeque. "If the toast wasn't burned before, it's burned now," he said. "I'm going to ask the Pakistani to call the fire department. It's getting out of control and the people in there are going to need some help."

Hannah nodded in approval.

Chris left the room and talked to the Pakistani, who made the call. When Chris returned to their room, an ethnic mix of people were noisily evacuating the burning building, carrying armfuls of papers, pictures, electronics, clothes, and other belongings. One woman dumped her things in the street and ran back into the burning building, presumably for more. Another tried to follow, but others stopped them.

In front of the Albanian building, the guard moved away from his position in front of the door and peered around the corner. Now the fire next door was licking the side of his building. He shed his composed demeanor and ran inside. Chris could hear the shouting from across the street. Two Albanians came out with the guard, and he showed them the situation, pointing up at the fire and gesturing wildly. His comrade shook his head and spoke loudly in Albanian. The guard became quiet, but the third man spoke up in a booming voice. The guard paced as the other men argued.

One of the Albanians pulled out a cell phone. Behind him, a man staggered out of the front door of the Albanian building. Plasticuffs were bound around his ankles, but the plastic band between his ankles was severed, and he had full use of his legs. His hands were bound by plasticuffs in front of him, still intact. Although the man was disheveled, he was clearly Michael Winthrop. The guard must have spotted him out of the corner of his eye because he turned and looked straight at Michael.

"Shit!" Without thinking, Chris burst out of the room, ran through the Pakistani's house, and dashed down the stairs. As he rushed out of the apartment building, he realized he had his pistol in hand, even though he didn't remember drawing it.

The guard tackled Michael, and Chris ran at him, instinctively pointing his pistol. "Get off him, now!" Chris commanded.

The guard turned his head toward Chris's voice. When he saw who it was, he let go of Michael, who crawled away. The guard got to his feet and reached into his waistband. Chris adjusted his angle so he could shoot the guard in the upper body without hitting Michael or the others in the street. It would be a tight shot, but he could do it.

His rapid breathing and stampeding heart caused his pistol sights to wobble uncontrollably. *Just pull the trigger when the sights wobble over the target,* Instructor Hickok had told him. Although he was aiming for the guard's chest, his first shot put a hole in the man's gut. The second shot caught the guard in the chest, knocking him backward. The guard pulled his pistol free and fired in Chris's direction but hit a woman in the crowd, who screamed as she fell. Chris's respiration and pulse calmed down a notch, and he aimed at the guard's head and squeezed the trigger. *Pop!* Gray brain matter spilled, and the guard fell to the asphalt as if he'd been pasted there. Screams came from all directions.

Pop! Another gunshot sounded. Then more gunshots. It sounded like Hannah and Sonny were shooting it out with the Albanians, but Chris couldn't be sure. His adrenaline was pumping so wildly out of control he couldn't tell whether he'd even been shot.

"Michael Winthrop, I'm from the United States government!" Chris blurted. "I'm here to save you!"

Michael turned and stared at him, his expression a mix of fear and confusion.

While helping Michael to his feet, Chris glanced behind him. One of the guard's comrades lay in the street, moving slowly, and the other seemed to have taken cover around the corner. The slow-moving Albanian aimed up at the Pakistani's window. Another gangster appeared in the doorway and aimed there, too. He could see Hannah now on the street level while Sonny remained upstairs providing overwatch, both firing at the Albanians.

With the fire in the building next door and the shootout in the street, a handful of the civilians waved their hands wildly and cried out. Chris had seen such pandemonium before. Some helped those in need, some ran away, some froze, and others collapsed.

In the pair of hostage rescues Chris had performed, he hadn't lost a hostage. Each rescue was intensely personal, and he wasn't about to lose Michael now. There was no time to waste; he had to trust Hannah and Sonny to cover his six, and he didn't have time to worry about their safety. He had to get Michael to the car... two blocks away.

Chris pushed at the small of Michael's back, propelling him forward, and Michael tripped. "Pick up your feet," Chris told him.

Michael did so with a whimper, picking up his feet and putting them down, but he wasn't going fast enough. The longer it took Michael to move, the more chance there was that none of them would make it out alive.

Chris grabbed a handful of Michael's trousers near the small of his back and lifted him up while pushing him forward, giving him a boost. In spite of his efforts, it still felt like they were moving in slow motion.

The Albanians are going to overtake us any minute now.

They turned the corner to head south, but Michael stumbled again, slowing them down. Chris pulled him to his feet and put his arm around Michael's shoulder, shifting much of the young man's weight onto himself, helping them move faster. They hurried south one block and then another, the gunshots behind them continuing.

Chris spotted the BMW. He pressed onward and assisted Michael into the backseat before he took the driver's seat. "I'm taking you to safety. You're going to be okay." Now Chris was too busy scanning for threats to see if Michael was even responding. Chris spotted no threats in the immediate vicinity, and when he put his key in and turned it, the vehicle started without any problems.

Hannah appeared around the corner then, sprinting faster than he'd ever seen her run. When she reached the vehicle, she gasped, "Sonny is right behind me." After taking her position beside him in the passenger seat and closing the door, she tapped the GPS screen and set the US embassy as their destination. "I called the station chief and told him we have the PC and we're gunning it out with Albanians, so now the chief is on the phone requesting approval from Washington for Six's assistance."

Come on, Sonny, where are you?

Gunshots sounded again, and Sonny charged around the corner like a bull with its ass on fire. "Enemy right behind me!" he shouted. He jumped into the car. Michael grunted as Sonny landed on him in the backseat. "Get us out of here!"

Without waiting for Sonny's door to close, Chris stomped on the accelerator. The BMW leaped forward just as an Albanian, armed with a handgun and speaking into a cell phone, came around the corner. Chris didn't slow down, hitting the man and knocking the pistol and phone from his hands. The Albanian landed on the hood, rolled up the windshield, and thumped the roof before Chris caught a glimpse of him in his rearview mirror as he landed in the street. It wasn't very reverend-like of him, but he didn't have the luxury of gazing into his belly button and soul searching right now.

Sonny closed the door, and Chris turned the corner with tires squealing, onto a street that cut southwest. "I'm heading for Olympus," Chris told Sonny, using their code word for the embassy. "We're only five klicks away."

Downtown Athens was such a confusing maze of one-way streets, particularly in the Kypseli neighborhood. He'd never been more thankful for Hannah's GPS. He was less worried about getting a traffic ticket or ending up in a head-on collision, and more worried about the Albanians.

Michael was still breathing heavily. "We made it, we made it," he said.

Chris didn't hear Hannah's phone ring, but she took it out and put it on speakerphone. It was Young. "Xander received a call from the Kypseli neighborhood, and now he's mass texting a shitload of people to converge on that area. And Xander himself is en route, too. If you're near Kypseli, you might want to consider getting the hell out."

"Already on it. We've got the package," Hannah said before she ended the call.

"What do these Albanians want with you, Michael?" Chris tossed to the backseat.

"I… I think they're working for the Russians," Michael answered. He seemed to be getting his bearings.

"Why would the Russians want you?"

"Russia's energy exports are the backbone of its economy," Michael said. "They supply a quarter of Europe's natural gas, allowing Russia to exert its influence on European politics."

"Lithuania, Estonia, Finland, and Latvia import a hundred percent of their gas from Russia," Hannah added.

"Right," Michael said. "Greece imports at least half, and countries like Germany and Italy import more than a quarter from Russia."

In the rearview mirror, a speeding car closed in on them fast. "We might have company," Chris said.

Sonny prepared his pistol to fire out the back window. "I'm on it," he said. The tailing car moved in closer. "They're armed. These guys aren't out collecting for the Red Cross."

The car neared them again, and Sonny pressed his pistol against the back window and fired through the glass. Michael yelped at the sound vibrating through the confines of the vehicle. The pursuing car swerved.

"One of them is an Albanian I shot at earlier," Sonny said.

Hannah checked her phone. "I've got a text message from Young. It says Xander is receiving more text messages, and he's sending another mass of texts. Young is still trying to decode the messages."

"I can decode the messages," Sonny said. "He's telling them to kill us."

"What is Xander's location now?" Chris asked, throwing a quick look to Hannah.

"Doesn't say."

"We need to reach Olympus before Xander reaches us."

"No shit," Sonny shouted. "A little help here?"

Hannah turned and aimed her gun through the back window at their pursuers, as well. Unfortunately, they were now shooting back.

Can this get any worse?

A bullet penetrated the back window and struck the windshield between Chris and Hannah. Chris's heart jumped, and he stopped wondering if their situation could get any worse.

He turned west on *Agiou Meletiou*, a large two-way street, but just as he reached the intersection of *Leoforos Konstantinoupolem*, cars were stopped at a railroad crossing, waiting for the southbound metro to cross. Sitting at a train crossing was not an option. When Chris hit the intersection, he swung the BMW left, going south and putting the pedal to the metal. "I'm going to try to outrun the train to the next street before crossing over."

"That's crazy," Sonny said. "We're *not* going to beat that train!"

Hannah and Sonny shot at the two cars following them, but the cars didn't back off, and returned fire.

Chris continued to gain velocity, running neck and neck with the train. "We're going to make it!"

"We're not going to make it," Sonny shouted.

"We're going to make it," Chris repeated, swerving around the car in front of him in order to push farther ahead. Now he was in front of the train, but there were no roads for him to cross, and if the road ahead filled up with cars, he wouldn't be able to maintain his headway. Then an intersection, *Sepolion*, came into view, which crossed the tracks over to the other side.

Sonny changed his tune. "We're going to make it."

Chris wanted more speed, but there was no more.

We're not *going to make it.*

Lord help us, please.

6

Chris ran off the road, and the car fishtailed as he turned right. The BMW straightened out on the road, and he barreled through a railroad-crossing barrier, breaking it off its joint. Then he crossed the tracks in front of the moving train, and he stomped the accelerator. The car wheels spun, losing traction. Hannah braced herself for a collision.

Chris let up on the gas enough for the wheels to bite into the ground, and the car passed over the tracks.

Michael, remaining low in the backseat, couldn't see anything. "What? What happened?"

"You don't want to know," Sonny said.

Michael poked his head up, but Sonny shoved it back down.

"You did it, Chris," Hannah exclaimed. "You shook them off our tail."

"You southern boys really know how to haul moonshine," Sonny said.

Chris zigzagged through the streets before heading south on *Voreiou Ipeirou*. He exhaled long and hard, relieved to finally be out of the Albanians' line of fire.

"Why don't the Europeans try to stop their dependency on Russia for natural gas?" Hannah asked Michael, picking their previous conversation right back up now that their six was clear.

"Russia uses the gas money to buy politically connected companies in Europe," Michael said, "and those companies donate to local politicians. Russia and Italy each invested five hundred million euros to fund projects in both countries."

"So it's no coincidence Italy has supported Russia in Ukraine and has been opposed to sanctions against Russia," she said.

Sonny turned and Chris saw him wrinkle his face in the rearview mirror. "That commie gas can pay for a lot of troops and ammo to kill Ukrainians."

"So if you and others succeed in building the Trans-Adriatic Pipeline," Chris said, "Azerbaijan could supply natural gas to Europe and decrease their dependency on Russia, weakening them."

"Exactly," Michael said. "With sanctions against Russia for its military intervention in Ukraine and low oil prices, Russia needs the gas money now more than ever."

Chris tightened his grip on the wheel, his knuckles turning white. "So Russia pulls the strings behind 21D to kidnap you in an effort to stop the Trans-Adriatic Pipeline."

"Bastards," Sonny muttered, watching out the back window again.

Hannah shook her head. "Not good."

Chris assumed Hannah was referring to Michael's kidnapping, but then a black Mercedes turned toward them, going the wrong way on a one-way street, set on a head-on collision course with the BMW.

"Maybe they're circling the area around the embassy, too," Sonny said. "Waiting for us."

Foremost in Chris's mind was surviving the impending head-on collision. He slammed the brakes and the ABS system engaged, the brake pedal pulsating under his foot as he steered away from the Mercedes. But there wasn't enough space on the road to avoid the oncoming vehicle completely.

"Brace for crash!" Chris called out, keeping his foot on the brakes to minimize the speed of impact. Within a second, the brake pumped more than ten times as the vehicle attempted to maintain control and keep the brakes from locking up. He made sure his hands were on the wheel and not obstructing the path of the air bag. He put his head back against the headrest and tried to relax before the heavyweight crunch.

The front corner of the Mercedes struck the front corner of the BMW with a loud crack, and pieces of vehicle splashed over the road. Inside the BMW, air bags blew out, and the vehicle spun. Chris's face, chest, and arms struck the hard pillow of air that hadn't been there an instant earlier. The impact of the bag was so violent that he wondered why his head was still attached, and his wrists burned from the speed at which the pillow had grazed his flesh. He pushed the air bag down with a hand, so he could see. The road ahead was clear, but it was jammed with traffic to the rear.

Sonny caught his breath as if the wind had been knocked out of him. "Armed male in the Mercedes that just hit us," he said.

If Sonny spotted the armed man, it was likely the armed man had recognized them, too. Driving around in a car with bullet holes in it wasn't helping them be covert. Smoke rose from under the BMW's hood, and the engine had shut off. Chris attempted to start it, but it wouldn't turn over. He tried again, but the engine didn't respond.

"Engine won't start," he told the others.

"Armed male exiting the Mercedes," Hannah said, pushing her air bag out of the way.

"We're in a shit state if we don't get out and hoof it," Sonny said. "Pronto."

"Let's go," Chris said.

Sonny helped Michael out of the backseat, but Chris's door wouldn't budge. He crawled over the center console and followed Hannah through her door. Once outside, Sonny helped Michael move off the street while Hannah took aim behind their car. Chris followed the direction of her pistol to the black Mercedes, where the armed male stood, raising a pistol in Sonny and Michael's direction. Hannah got off the first shot. She missed, but she was close enough that the enemy ducked out of sight before he could fire.

Three pistol-wielding blond-haired men—who looked more Slavic than Greek—used their Mercedes for cover. One of them held his pistol in one hand and pulled out his phone with the other. A second Mercedes, also heading the wrong way on the street, stopped in the middle of the road, and more Slavs pointed their weapons in Chris and Hannah's direction.

Chris glanced over his shoulder to check on Sonny and Michael, and he caught a glimpse of Sonny's foot disappearing between two buildings.

"Let's go, Hannah," he said.

"I'm right beside you."

They hurried away from the BMW and the street. The air around them erupted with bullets, and a brief stabbing sensation shot through his shoulder, a flash of pain running up his neck. It made the back of his head ache, but he was too busy to pay it much attention. He felt like a rabbit that had just been flushed out of its hole by a squad of hunters, and it was only a matter of time before he and Hannah ended up in a steaming bowl of rabbit stew.

They dashed between the two buildings where Sonny and Michael had disappeared, and the air around them stopped snapping and crackling. Chris and Hannah ran west along the sidewalk of a one-way street, Sonny and Michael ahead of them—but they needed to go south to reach Olympus. It was only five hundred meters away, but it might as well have been five hundred kilometers.

"Hannah, I need you to cover our asses while I run point," Chris said.

She nodded. "Got it."

Chris sprinted out in front of Sonny. "I'll take point."

"Make it quick," Sonny said, half carrying Michael.

Up ahead and across the street was a thick little forest of trees. Chris stopped there and took a peek around the corner of a building. A black Mercedes was driving toward him. He led his team north.

"You're going the wrong way," Sonny complained through clenched teeth.

"They're waiting for us between here and the embassy," Chris said. "Need to try to circle around and find another way in."

As Chris led them north between buildings, men's voices came from the south, speaking Russian. *"Gde oni?"* Where are they?

Chris patrolled north through the concrete jungle until the Russian voices became distant to the south. He found a good hiding place under a landing of a staircase outside an apartment building. It was a tight fit, but it kept them out of sight for the most part.

We need a vehicle.

He signaled for the others to stay hidden while he searched. It was slim pickings, but parked on the street was a dark-blue Nissan Qashqai, a combination of a compact car, station wagon, and SUV. Chris picked the lock, hopped inside, and hot-wired the engine before driving to the others.

Chris got out to let Hannah drive and helped Sonny and Michael into the rear before hurrying to the passenger seat and slamming the door behind him. She drove counter-clockwise in a wide circle around the roads surrounding the embassy.

Chris surveyed the streets for trouble but saw no sign of Xander, the Russians, or the Albanians. He looked back at Michael. "What do you know about Xander?"

"He's a Greek energy mogul with powerful Greek and American contacts, both liberal and conservative," Michael said.

"And he's been on the phone with your kidnappers," Chris told him.

Michael seemed to slump down in his own skin. "I talked to him at the embassy party. He seemed like such a gentleman."

"He does leave a good first impression," Chris agreed. "It's the second impression that's a killer."

Sonny grunted. "I didn't like his first impression, either."

They circled around to four blocks south of Olympus. At a stoplight, Hannah checked her phone. "I got a text message from the chief. He wants us to proceed to Olympus as planned."

"Easy for him to say," Chris said. Another black Mercedes came into view. "Black Mercedes to the north."

"I see him," Sonny confirmed.

Hannah drove calmly. "Did he see us?"

"Don't know," Sonny said.

"He's running the red light," Chris said, trying not to blow a gasket in his nerves. "They're all around Olympus, waiting to ambush us. Either we can try to break through, or we can change course and try to make it to Minotaur."

Their present vehicle had no GPS, so Chris used the one on his phone and touched the screen, setting a new destination. "We have a better chance making it to Minotaur." He gave directions.

Hannah drove onto a roundabout for a brief moment before exiting and turning left, taking them southwest.

Chris glanced at his phone. "The port leading to Minotaur is about seventeen klicks from here."

"The Mercedes is following us," Sonny said. "The passenger is talking into a cell phone."

At the intersection of *Epidavrou* and *Lenorman*, a white BMW ran a red light and swung out beside them. Before Hannah could avoid the vehicle, the distinct sound of 7.62 mm bullets banged. The noise of the shots echoed off buildings, pumping up the intensity of the sound. The projectiles struck the rear passenger door next to Michael with the fury of a jackhammer, making Chris's body shudder. The shots came so fast it almost sounded like full auto. He had been in gunfights with amateurs and professionals, and this sounded like the latter.

His heart rate jumped and his breathing became shallow and rapid. He had no time to slow it all down, only time to react. He turned his head over his right shoulder and spotted the shooter. "Xander!"

Michael was down on the floor, and Sonny returned fire, blasting through Michael's window at Xander, but Xander had already ducked to avoid the salvo.

From Chris's angle, he couldn't shoot Xander without possibly hitting a cluster of pedestrians, but he did have a clear shot at the driver. Chris pressed his pistol against the window, to prevent getting sprayed in the face with the glass, and squeezed the trigger. He thought he hit the driver with the first shot, but there was no immediate reaction as he continued to squeeze. His second shot clearly landed, spraying crimson on the shattered window. Chris fired again for good measure.

The driver's head flopped to the side, and Xander's BMW veered off the road until it struck a building, crumpling the front of the vehicle and stopping it.

Hannah sped forward, racing southwest. Chris checked the view to the rear. Xander's white BMW sat dead on the side of the road.

"Shit!" Sonny exclaimed.

"Are you hit?" Chris asked, turning toward him.

Sonny held one hand against Michael's head and another on the side of his neck, his fingers feeling for a pulse. When he pulled his hands away, they were bloody. "At least one of Xander's rounds penetrated the door. One of them hit Michael in the head," Sonny said, sadness filling his voice. "He's dead."

Chris's soul dropped out of his body, and a heavy cloud of discouragement descended on him. The cloud was so thick he thought he might choke on it. As a child, while his parents were diplomats in Damascus, Chris and a classmate were kidnapped in front of their elementary school. Chris was later rescued, but Nikkia died in captivity. A part of Chris died with her that day, and the part that survived wished it had died, too. He'd packed away the sorrow he felt then, but seeing Michael's dead body had opened up old wounds. Now he wanted to cry but didn't have the energy.

Hannah called the chief and reported. When she hung up, she said, "They want us to go to Minotaur."

The ride to the port of Pairaeus was a blur. Chris was too out of it to notice what had become of their shot-up vehicle. They were met by a small US Navy vessel, which shuttled them across the Mediterranean Sea, but while Chris went through the motions, it was as if the black cloud of despair had magically transported him from Athens to Crete.

7

Xander's servant led Animus through the house to the master bedroom, where the walls were as white as the exterior of the mansion. The swinging windowed doors to his veranda were locked, but the curtains were open, displaying the Aegean Sea as it reflected the sapphire sky.

"I'm checking my bug-out bag to make sure I have everything needed to sustain myself until we reach London and our mission cache there," Xander said. "The Americans will be looking for us here. The Hellenic Police will be looking for us, too." He took a look around. "I'm going to miss this house." He peered out the window. "And the view." His eyes returned to his bug-out bag. "But in this job, adapting is the key to survival, and adapt we must."

"Yes, sir." Animus was going to miss Athens, too. He was born here, and although he thought he'd die in Athens, it now occurred to him he might die in London. Even if he survived, he might very well be the lone survivor. But dying was something Xander never talked about, and Animus didn't dare to mention it for fear of crossing some unmarked line.

"Is Evelina packed?" Xander asked.

"Almost," Animus said. "That's what I came to talk to you about."

Xander stopped what he was doing. "My bag was all packed a minute ago, and I guess it will all still be there no matter how many times I check." He turned to Animus. "Is there a problem?"

"Evelina doesn't seem sure she wants to go with us on this mission."

"Does not seem sure?" Xander said with disbelief in his tone.

"She said she doesn't feel she has enough training or experience."

"What do you think?" Xander asked.

"I agree. But I didn't tell her that. I didn't tell her anything. I just listened."

"Do you think she should come with us?"

Animus looked him in the eye. "I think she's right."

"I agree," Xander said. "She *should* stay here."

"You do?"

"Yes, I think she is no match for the people we are dealing with…" Xander glanced at his watch.

"But…?"

"But she told me something different. She told me she still blames the West for December twenty-first when her mother was killed. It is why we still call ourselves 21D in the first place. Evelina wants revenge. More than ever. She told me she wants to go with us no matter what."

Animus was puzzled at the contradiction. "Why would she tell me she's not sure and tell you she's going no matter what?"

Xander shrugged. "She probably does not want you to know these demands she is placing on me and the mission."

"She's afraid I'll be angry," Animus said.

"While she is not prepared, I am afraid she will take off like a loose cannon if we leave her here. She will do her own thing and interfere with Phase Two. We will not be able to protect her. It will be better for her, and us, if we go to London together."

Animus nodded sadly. "I just don't want anything to happen to her."

"Nor do I."

"She's the love of my life," Animus said.

"Me, too. But if we let her go off on her own, she will be in more danger and more likely to disrupt our mission."

Animus swallowed. "Yes, sir."

"Did you reserve the hotel rooms?"

He cleared his throat. "There is a symposium in London and most of the hotels were booked. The closest to our target was the Sofitel St. James, but there weren't enough vacancies for our whole team so I also reserved rooms at the Grosvenor House."

"It is probably better that way. If one hotel is compromised, the whole team won't be compromised. And we'll be less suspicious if we're not all in the same building. Top-notch work."

Animus smiled.

"I will stay in the Sofitel with some of the men," Xander went on, "and you and Evelina can stay in the Grosvenor House with the rest of the team." He looked at his watch again. "It is time."

8

C hris, Hannah, and Sonny arrived at the Naval Support Activity in Crete and turned Michael's body over to the SEAL Team Six commander of Blue Squadron. The SEALs placed Michael in a body bag and zipped it shut. One moment, he was full of life, and now his body was an empty shell. The part of him that mattered most was gone, like a projectile fired through the barrel of a gun, and there was no bringing it back.

The Blue Squadron SEALs' faces and shoulders drooped as they loaded Michael onto the plane. They'd gotten all psyched up for a rescue, and they weren't even given a chance to try. Now there would be no back slaps, high fives, or stories of momentous heroism—only feelings of helplessness and defeat. On top of all that, Michael was dead.

The plane's hatches closed, and soon the big bird ascended into the clear blue sky. The higher it ascended into the expanse of the heavens, the smaller it became, and Chris felt himself become small with it. Then it was gone.

He wanted his senses to become numb. He wanted to take the emotions welling up inside and shove them in a box and store them with the others in the depths of his psyche, never to see the light of day again. But his emotions were loose. They started coming out of one eye, and soon a tear crept down his face. He was conscious of being in a public place, with Hannah and Sonny standing beside him on the tarmac, and he wiped it away.

Beneath his feet, the tarmac seemed to tilt and spin, like the teacup ride at Disneyland, and nausea overcame him. When Nikkia had died, little Chris had sat in a closet and wept, and now he longed for a closet to hide in.

Breathe, he tried to remind himself. He inhaled weakly, but he didn't get much oxygen. It was more like a convulsion, an inward sob.

He sensed Hannah's eyes on him. He turned to look at her but couldn't maintain eye contact.

"Chris?" It was her voice. "Your shoulder... It's all wet."

Chris peered down at it. Wetness spread across his dark polo shirt like a sweat stain, but when he touched it with his finger, the wetness was thick and sticky. He pulled his finger away and it was red. More than once he'd been on an operation where he and his Teammates were flying home and a guy would suddenly realize he'd been shot. With all the adrenaline and laser focus on the mission, guys sometimes didn't notice until later. He kept staring at the blood, still not feeling a thing.

Now Sonny was staring, too. "Dude, I thought that was water or some shit. You've been shot."

"We need to get you to a doctor," she said before flagging down a sailor for help.

"When did you get shot?" Sonny asked.

Chris pressed his hand on the wound, and the pain came, slicing through his flesh as he applied direct pressure. "I... I don't know. Maybe after we crashed the BMW... I thought I felt a sharp pain, but with my adrenaline banging and everything else going on, I guess I forgot about it."

With the sailor's help, Hannah and Sonny got him to the Branch Health Clinic on base. While a Navy flight surgeon took care of Chris, Hannah stepped out of the room to make some calls. The surgeon removed the bullet, cleaned the wound, patched him up, and gave him some meds. He told Chris to avoid strenuous activity, which Chris interpreted as, *Give your shoulder some rest when you can.*

When Hannah returned, he was already finished in the clinic, and they walked with Sonny to the parking lot to claim their new vehicle.

"The Agency took our shot-up car, and the Navy is loaning us this for use on base," Hannah said. "How's your shoulder?"

"Doc said to rest it when I can," Chris said, fudging the truth.

They sat in the car with Sonny in the driver's seat this time. He turned on the engine. "Where to?"

Hannah gestured toward the airfield. "We fly back to Langley for debrief."

Chris's brow furrowed. "Back to Langley? Why?"

"The mission is over," she said.

He shook his head. "Don't take me out of the box and wind me up just to stick me back in the box again. Please don't do that to me."

"What're you saying?" she asked.

"I'm saying I want to get Xander. Dead or alive."

"Hell, yeah," Sonny cheered. "This has just turned into a kill-or-capture mission."

Hannah gave Sonny a blank stare.

"Well it has, hasn't it?" Sonny asked. "We're not going to let that piece of shit get away with this, are we?"

"I can tell Langley we think Xander is trying to interfere with the construction of TAP, and I can request a mission to capture-or-kill him for the kidnapping and murder of Michael Winthrop. But I don't know what they'll approve."

Chris nodded as Hannah took out her phone and made the call.

"We should clean up a little so we don't stick out," Sonny said. "Then stop by Xander's house. He's probably not dumb enough to return home after what he did, but we might find clues to where he's hiding out."

Sonny drove to the Gulfstream jet, where they freshened up. While they were on the plane, Hannah received a phone call. After she ended it, she turned to Chris and Sonny. "That was Langley. They're going to send up our request."

Chris and Sonny smiled at the news.

"It's no guarantee," Hannah said, "but it's a start."

"We better get busy," Chris said.

"Better to ask forgiveness than permission," Sonny added. "Let's go."

Sonny drove them off base to a local restaurant in Crete for a meal, but Chris didn't have much of an appetite. The trio sat in a quiet corner of the restaurant, talking in hushed tones.

"We could drive within a couple blocks of Xander's house and do a quick vehicle recon," Chris said.

Sonny nodded. "If it looks safe, I say we move in on foot and take a closer peek." He took a bite of roasted lamb in a pita wrap filled with tomato, onion, and tzatziki.

"If Xander is there, and he's not heavily guarded, we can bag and drag him," Chris said.

"And if he's not there?" Hannah asked.

"We search for clues as to where he might be."

"And if we encounter Xander's assistant or others?"

Sonny swallowed a bite of his gyro. "We wrap 'em up."

Chris nodded, and Hannah pursed her lips. She was warier than they were about going against orders. Or not waiting for them.

They spent the rest of the meal eating in silence, Chris only picking at his food. When they returned to the base, the Navy gave them a ride to the Greek mainland where the Agency loaned them another vehicle. And soon they were parking their new car within a block of Xander's estate.

Hannah turned to Chris. "You know we'll blend in better as a couple than as individuals."

Chris took hold of her hand. It wasn't hard for him to act like he had romantic feelings for her. He opened the door to all his boxed-up emotions and stepped inside, and his feelings for her were in the crate closest to the door. He didn't need a crowbar to pry off the lid, either. She turned her face to him. Her eyes were smiling, and he sensed that her feelings for him were close to the door, too.

They strolled through the neighborhood of white stone mansions. The Aegean Sea came into view, and they stopped at a street corner and carefully observed Xander's place. It seemed dead in comparison to the last time they'd visited. They continued until they reached Xander's property, where they followed the cobblestone pathway to the front door. Hannah and Sonny readied their pistols, covering Chris while he picked the lock. Once it was disengaged, he opened the door and the three of them slipped inside. Chris drew his pistol then, too.

Beyond the entrance hall, they passed the grand piano and walked across the black marble floor. The spacious main room with the grand fireplace seemed empty without the crowd of people. They searched the house, but Xander's laptop was gone and there was nothing of significant interest left, not even his staff.

They spent the rest of the day and all night in the mansion, waiting for Xander or one of his staff to return. Chris didn't think he'd have to resort to pain killers while they waited, but the swelling around his bullet wound pressed against a nerve that ran between his shoulder and the base of his skull, causing him torment all along the nerve. He muttered some f-bombs before surrendering to a pill to relieve the hurt.

Swearing had always been a vice of his, but only once in his lifetime had he used the Lord's name in vain. It was in elementary school, and guilt had riddled him immediately after. He never did it again. Once he began studying to become a pastor, he'd stopped swearing cold turkey, and when he became an assistant pastor, he'd continued to abstain. However, when he resumed doing black ops part time for the Agency and came under fire, he couldn't stop the curses from falling out of his mouth. Old habits really did die hard.

Hannah and Sonny let him sleep while they took the first watch. Chris rested on his left side to give his shoulder some relief and fell into a deep sleep…

It was right after the Switchblade Whisper mission, and Chris flew from Dallas to Arlington to pick up Hannah in the dark of the morning. He drove from her house to the National Mall, and they sat down beneath Abe's feet, on the top step of the Lincoln Memorial. They drank hot cocoa as they watched the sun surge up the horizon, the sky becoming a swirl of orange and grape sherbet, split open by the Washington Monument. The trees cast shadows on the ground, creating a V-shaped border. The long mirror image shone in the reflecting pool, which was smooth until ducks floated by, releasing ripples across the water.

Moisture formed in the white edges of Hannah's chocolate-brown eyes.

"Is everything okay?" Chris asked.

She sipped her drink, the sun casting a warm radiance across her face. "I've been here before, and I've seen sunrises, but I've never been here at sunrise. It's too beautiful."

He'd seen sunrises around the world, and he'd seen Hannah, but he'd never seen Hannah at sunrise. She was too beautiful. He wanted to tell her so, but he worried that words would somehow get in the way. When she turned to look at him, he kissed her, and her lips tasted like the sweetest cocoa.

By morning, Xander still hadn't shown. On the upside, although still feeling discomfort in his shoulder, Chris was in less pain. The medicine and the sleep seemed to have helped.

They returned to their Athens hotel to change and discuss what to do next. When a call came from Young, Hannah put it on the speaker.

"NSA just picked up Xander's cell phone signal at Athens International Airport," he said.

"Showtime!" Sonny exclaimed.

They dashed out of their room and to the parking lot. Hannah remained on speakerphone with Young, who was communicating real time with NSA, updating Xander's location. Once in their car, Sonny drove them to the airport, arriving there in fifteen minutes.

"Can't tell if Xander is inside the main terminal or outside," Young said.

They parked and headed in that direction. "We're nearing a main entrance, now," Hannah said.

"Xander seems to be left of your position," Young said. "Possibly outside of the terminal."

Chris thought Xander would be going to the airport to catch a plane. *Why would he be outside of the terminal?*

The three shifted to Xander's direction, but he wasn't there. "The only person over there is a smaller guy, dark complexion," Hannah said.

"He may not be Xander," Young said, "but maybe he has Xander's phone."

"Okay, we'll check it out. Call you back soon," she said and then hung up, tucking the phone in her pocket.

The three approached the man.

"Excuse me," Hannah said when they got close enough for him to hear. But the man waved her off and walked past, heading in the direction of the parking lot.

The SOG three turned around, and Sonny called to the man, "Hey, asshole!"

The man picked up his pace to a trot, and the trio trotted after him. Then he full-out ran. Chris, Hannah, and Sonny ran, too.

The man looked over his shoulder, huffing and puffing. "Why you chase me?" he asked.

"Because you're running," Sonny called.

"Stop chasing me!"

"Stop running!"

The man kept running until Sonny tackled him, both of them landing on the concrete.

"I not do anything," the man said.

Sonny patted him down for a weapon and discovered a cell phone. Then another. And more. "Why do you have six cell phones?"

"I salesman."

Hannah quickly dialed Young back and asked him to call Xander's phone.

One of the man's cell phones rang. Sonny took it and checked the caller ID before answering and turning the phone off. He glared at the man. "Where'd you get this?"

"I don't know."

"You better start giving some answers," Sonny threatened, "or I'm calling the police."

"A big guy," the man said.

"Where was he?" Sonny asked.

"Near security." The man tried to sit up, but Sonny pushed him back to the ground. "Which security?"

He pointed to a spot in the terminal.

"Was he heading into security or walking by?"

"Going into security."

Sonny pocketed Xander's phone. "When?"

"Thirty minutes ago."

"We better hurry," Hannah said.

The three of them hurried into the airport, abandoning their informant, and stopped near a line of people funneling through security. Xander was nowhere in sight. Chris did notice a nearby TV monitor, though, tuned in to CNN International.

"In Athens, a terrorist group known as 21D kidnapped a British civil engineer, Michael Winthrop, son-in-law to America's White House Chief of Staff. When a fire broke out next door to where Winthrop was being held hostage, he used the diversion to escape, and as Hellenic police moved in to rescue him, a shootout occurred. 21D killed Winthrop, and police killed a number of the terrorists..."

Chris and his team knew the real story. It was them, not the Hellenic police, who shot it out with the kidnappers and lost Michael. He was used to his work going uncredited, but he wasn't used to losing a hostage. Xander would pay for it, too. Chris tightened his jaw and focused.

The trio pressed closer to the security line to search for Xander, but still nothing. Chris examined the surrounding area when he spotted a familiar figure. "That's Animus," he said, "heading for the ticket counter. He might be meeting up with Xander. Let's follow him."

They kept their distance and spread out. Chris tried to keep at least two people between him and Animus, and he searched for a place to duck out of sight in case Animus doubled back. The man kept going, though, and joined a line of customers at the Air France ticket counter. When he seemed near the end of his transaction, and before he turned around, Chris snuck into a restroom and waited, his heart pounding. He estimated how long he thought it would take Animus to leave the area and near security. While waiting, he heard footsteps approach the restroom door.

That could be him.

Chris hid in one of the stalls as sounds from the airport lobby entered the restroom. Footsteps echoed, closer and closer. Within the small confines of the stall, Chris felt ambushed. If the other person in the restroom was Animus and he started shooting through the door to Chris's stall, he'd be trapped. Whoever had entered used the urinal, but Chris couldn't see who it was. He could peek over the door, but he'd risk being seen. His heart pounded even harder and he pulled out his pistol, preparing to defend himself if the shooting began.

But the man left, and Chris gave him time to depart the restroom before stepping out of the stall. He left the men's room and scanned the terminal. Sonny briskly walked toward him, but Chris couldn't see Animus. Hannah was missing, too.

"If you shake it more than once, you're playing with it," Sonny quipped.

"Where's Hannah?" Chris asked, ignoring the joke.

"She's going to find out which gate Animus went to so we know his destination. She already bought a ticket and gave me her pistol to pass security."

Chris's eyes widened, concern churning in his gut. "What if she gets into trouble and needs backup?"

"She said she'll call before the trouble gets troubling."

"We should've given her backup."

"And do what with our guns to get past security?" Sonny asked.

"We have diplomatic passports. Maybe we can pass through the crew line without being screened."

"You're assuming Athens airport security gives a shit about our diplomatic passports."

"We could stash our pieces in a locker."

"Just chill," Sonny said. "We'll do her more harm than good. Animus is more likely to spot three of us than Hannah alone. He's also never met Hannah. You, he'd recognize."

"I don't like this," Chris said.

"If you weren't banging her, maybe your tactical judgment would be clearer."

Chris took a deep breath. "I'm not banging her."

Sonny shrugged. "Whatever you call it."

Chris pulled out his cell phone and tried to keep his anger from bubbling over. "If Hannah rings for help, we're keeping our guns and we're busting through that security checkpoint. You got it?"

"Damn straight."

Chris and Sonny walked to the security gate and took seats close by. Chris kept an eye on the clock, but it only made the time go slower, so he tried not to think about it.

When more than half an hour passed, he couldn't bear it anymore. "One of us should—"

"Shh," Sonny said, cutting him off.

Chris wanted to call her, but he knew the sound of her cell might alert Animus or Xander. Then Chris's phone rang. The caller ID read *Hannah*.

"I'm okay," she said immediately. "The line at security was long, but I got through and found Xander, Animus, and Evelina in the same lobby for the flight to Paris, but Xander is sitting separately, like he doesn't know them. Obviously, they're up to something, so I called Langley and requested some of our guys in Paris put surveillance on the three when they arrive."

Knowing she was safe, Chris heaved a sigh of relief.

"What?" she asked.

Chris didn't say anything.

"You were worried about me," she said.

He swallowed. "Yes."

"See you in a minute," she said, and he could almost hear the smile in her voice.

Chris wasn't completely worry-free until she finally reunited with them in the arrivals area.

"Can we have the Gulfstream meet us here and take us to Paris?" Sonny asked.

"The Agency is going to fly us," Hannah said. "The Gulfstream will have to catch up with us later."

9

our hours later, they were in an Agency plane flying
over France. "What do we do if our mission to kill-or-
capture Xander is denied?" Hannah asked.

"He kidnapped and murdered a US citizen," Chris said,
anger heating his face. "Michael was our responsibility, and a
US citizen's murder can't go unpunished. If we receive a message denying the op, we can just pretend we didn't receive the
message. Ask for forgiveness later, like Sonny said."

Sonny was silent.

"Are you still okay with that?" Hannah asked him.
"Pretending we didn't receive the message?"

"Yeah, I'm okay with that," Sonny said. "Xander took out
our hostage, and he's got to pay for it."

"How about you, Hannah?" Chris asked.

"I'm fine with continuing the op now. But if we get explicit
instructions to back off... I don't know. Disobeying direct orders from on high bit me in the butt once, and I'm not too
roused about getting bit again."

Sonny raised an eyebrow, intrigued. "What orders did you disobey?"

"I'm going to check radio traffic," she said, leaving the question unanswered, and headed to the cockpit.

Chris had almost dozed off in his seat when Hannah returned. "We received a digitally formatted Flash Precedence message," she said. "I decrypted it, authenticating Langley's digital signature. The message was short and direct: *Kill or capture Xander Metaxas.*"

"Now we won't have to ask for forgiveness," Chris said, relieved their op was now sanctioned. Now he was following orders.

"It's time to bring the hate," Sonny said.

Their jet descended below the clouds over Paris, and the quilt of farms surrounding the Charles de Gaulle airport became visible. After they landed, French customs and immigration officers boarded and checked their diplomatic passports.

"What is the purpose of your visit?" one of the officers asked.

Sonny's words echoed in Chris's brain. *It's time to bring the hate.*

"To visit the US embassy," Hannah answered for them.

"Business?" the officer asked.

Hannah nodded. "Yes." Her phone rang, but she paid it no attention.

The officers honored the diplomatic passports, not searching the diplomats or their plane. They seemed to have more pressing matters to attend to. After they left, Hannah checked her phone and returned the call. When her conversation ended, she said, "The Paris surveillance team picked up Xander. He was driving northward on the *Autoroute du Nord.*"

Chris peered out the plane window and spotted a driver sitting in a silver Renault with the engine running. "Who's he?"

"Silver Renault, guy in a brown suit?" she asked before looking out the window.

"Yeah," Chris said.

"Our driver from the Agency," she said. "His name is Don. If it isn't, we're in trouble."

They exited the plane, and their driver met them on the tarmac. He introduced himself as Don.

Hannah offered her hand. "Hannah."

He shook it. "Welcome to Paris."

"Happy to be here."

It seemed like a casual exchange, but it was an exchange of predetermined bona fides, including their appearances, so each knew that the other was whom he or she was supposed to be. She nodded at Chris and Sonny, signaling that Don was legit.

Don helped them load into the Renault before speeding off the airport property and hitting the *Autoroute du Nord*. They hadn't gotten far when the traffic crawled past an accident.

Traffic resumed speed as they passed an amusement park to the right. They sped by the patchwork of farmland they'd seen during their descent into Paris, but now Chris could see a herd of Holstein Friesan cows grazing in one of the fields. He'd once heard a French diplomat explain how eco-friendly their farms were. Farmers ran water through a pipe beside the milk to cool it down, significantly reducing their energy costs, and the same water exited the pipe and entered a trough for the cows to drink. But from the outside, the farms didn't look so different from American farms.

They crossed over a gentle bend in the *River Somme*. It was the sight of one of the bloodiest battles of World War I, with over a million killed or wounded, but now the river was tranquil. Chris had seen his share of the horrors of war, and rather than dwell on it, he focused on the serenity of the bubbling water.

Traffic became sluggish again, this time for construction. Chris breathed deeply, channeling the calm waters, even though his mind was screaming at him to hurry.

Hannah's phone rang. She listened for a moment, then hung up. "Xander's heading northwest on *Autoroute des Anglais* now," she said, the instructions clear.

Don nodded and turned off onto the highway leading to England.

"Maybe England is where Xander's next target is," Hannah said.

"Michael worked for United Kingdom Petroleum," Chris said. He used his smartphone to search the internet for United Kingdom Petroleum's headquarters. "I've got their address in London."

"At the rate we're going," Sonny said, "Xander could swim the English Channel and walk to London before we get there."

Chris chuckled at the truth of the statement. "Now, if Xander is heading to UKP, he could get there a number of ways, right, Don?"

"Yes, sir," Don said. "From Calais, he could take a ferry, drive, or ride the train through the Chunnel."

Chris nodded. "Okay, so we'll just have to figure out which way he went."

"That won't be difficult at all," Sonny said, sarcasm dripping from his words.

"Well, it's all we've got."

🐚

Nearly three hours after leaving Charles de Gaulle Airport, the trio arrived in the city of Calais, France's gateway to England. Hannah received a call from the surveillance team, and she put it on speakerphone. "Xander parked his car at a restaurant here in Calais and went inside. When we checked to see if he was eating, he wasn't there. He must've already slipped through the kitchen and out the back. His car is still sitting in the parking lot."

"You lost him," Hannah said. She heaved a deep sigh.

There was no reply.

"Do you think he made that move in the restaurant out of caution, or did he make it because he knew you were following him?" she asked.

"Hard to say."

"You check the ferry, and we'll check the Eurostar," Hannah said.

"If he abandoned his car," Chris said, "he might plan to take the train across."

"Or he could've had another car waiting for him," Sonny said.

"True," Chris agreed. "Xander isn't a freshman at losing a tail, I'm sure."

Don drove them to the Eurostar Station at *Calais-Fréthun*, where he dropped them off. They spread out on foot, making themselves less conspicuous and a more challenging target. They blended into the crowd and entered the station, giving the appearance of normal passengers, but they were observing everyone and everything, looking for any clue as to where Xander was. They examined the area, including the restrooms.

After searching the station, Chris and Sonny stopped in front of a fast-food stall.

"This is like trying to find a preacher in a whorehouse," Sonny said.

Chris frowned. "Instead of trying to follow Xander, we could try to anticipate where he'll be next."

Hannah joined them. "I just received a call from Young. He said when he hacked Xander's laptop, his team download-ed some web-browsing history Xander had tried to delete. Young's team discovered a lot of internet activity regarding UKP headquarters and its neighborhood in London."

"London," Sonny said.

"The train leaves in twenty minutes," Hannah said. "And we still have to buy tickets and make our way through security."

Because they were carrying pistols, they wouldn't be able to pass through the X-ray machines, so after getting their tick-ets, Hannah led them through the lane for crew and VIPs. A train conductor passed through the lane ahead of them, and when the trio reached the security guard, Hannah showed her diplomatic passport. As the guard examined it, a puzzled look came over his face.

The security guard scratched his head, and a crew mem-ber came up behind them. The guard looked at Hannah, then back at her passport, again and again. He asked to see Chris's and Sonny's passports, as well.

Meanwhile, the crew member behind them tapped his foot impatiently. When he tried to pass them, Sonny stopped him with a stiff arm. "Hey buddy, we were in line first. You wait like the rest of us."

The crew member became angry and shouted in French. *"Fils de salope!"* Son of a bitch! Then he complained about being late for his shift. Chris could communicate in French, in addition to being fluent in Arabic and Russian.

Sonny didn't know French, but the crew member's body language was clear, and Sonny smiled, eating it up, which only made the crew member raise his voice louder and spit out more obscenities.

The security guard told Hannah to wait for his superior. After arriving at the crew/VIP gate, the man gave the passports a cursory inspection.

Chris knew his passport was created by the Agency's finest, and his confidence in the document was the critical link between the passport and the official's approval. Such confidence could mask a minor error in a document. Likewise, the lack of confidence could raise suspicion, even if the document was perfect. Chris's faith in his passport was solid, and the head security officer waved them through without a fuss.

As the trio walked to the Eurostar platform, Chris observed the other passengers. None of them were Xander or Animus. Minutes later, the bullet-shaped train pulled up in front of them and stopped. Its doors opened with a hydraulic hiss, and Chris's team boarded. They located their seats and sat down.

"Who's going to search the train?" Chris asked quietly.

"It won't take all three of us, and we don't want to stick out like turds in a glass of milk," Sonny said.

"I'll be the least conspicuous," Hannah said.

Personally, she was the last person he'd send. He didn't know what he'd do if something happened to her. Professionally, she was the obvious choice. He wanted to go along as a tail, but that came from his personal feelings, not his professionalism.

Hannah looked to Chris, as if waiting for a response. He kept his mouth shut and forced his head to nod approvingly.

Hannah smiled, stood up, and walked away. She passed through the doors into the next compartment and was out of sight. She was a pro at recruiting and running agents, and she was an accomplished MMA middleweight, but her shooting, although better than most CIA officers, wasn't at the level of Chris's or Sonny's. And it might not be at the level of Xander's, either. Hopefully they wouldn't have to find out.

Speaking English with a slight French accent, the conductor announced the time in France over the loudspeaker and that the Eurostar would arrive in London in one hour. As the train pulled forward, the conductor repeated the announcement in French. Outside, sunlit poles and barricades disappeared, replaced by the blackness of the Chunnel, the Channel Tunnel. Inside, artificial lights flicked on, pushing out the darkness.

Across the aisle, a couple kissed, seemingly oblivious to the world around them. Chris remembered the first time he'd kissed Hannah. It'd been in an FBI safe house near Washington, DC, and he wished he could put the world on pause and go back there again. But the world didn't pause, and his thoughts returned to the mission. He had to stay alert.

Sonny fidgeted in his chair, glancing over at the couple, too. Finally, he stared hard at them, as if his eyes could make them stop, but they didn't. "He's sucking the ugliness out of her," he said with dismay.

Chris couldn't help but smile, but the kissing couple remained insulated in their own world.

"Why can't I have a girl?" Sonny said. "He's kissing her. I don't know what's going on between you and Hannah, but it's more than I got. I got bubkes."

"Every Tier One operator I've ever known could get a girl to go out with him," Chris said. "Why would you be any different?"

"Yeah, I can get a date, but the girls who are decent and nice are afraid to death to talk to me. They think I'm going to be mean to them or something. I need a girl who understands me."

"You'll find her."

"What about you?" Sonny asked. "What exactly is going on between you and Hannah if you're not banging?"

"We dated after the Switchblade Whisper op. The distance wasn't ideal, but we made it work. I'd fly out to see her in Virginia, she'd come see me in Texas."

"How'd that work out?"

"We enjoyed the time together," Chris said. "But we ultimately decided just to be friends."

"Oh." Sonny actually sounded disappointed and stopped his line of questioning.

Nearly half an hour later, with no more conversation and no sign of Hannah, the Eurostar exited the tunnel. The artificial lights cut off, and rays of sunshine poured in from the outside as they passed the base of the White Cliffs of Dover.

Where is she?

Chris checked his watch, then turned his head to peer out the window at the green English countryside. The bullet train continued gliding hundreds of kilometers per hour, passing hop gardens and orchards. He was trying to distract himself but it wasn't working. He checked his watch again, realizing he was still on French time. He adjusted it an hour back, so he was on London time. Then he inspected his cell phone, making sure it had automatically made the switch. He contemplated calling her, but he put his cell phone back in his pocket, putting the phone call out of his mind, as well. He glanced over at Sonny, who was updating his watch and examining his cell phone, too.

Chris said a silent prayer for Hannah's safe return and tried to take in the countryside, but he couldn't. The next time he checked his watch, only another minute had passed. He had no more patience. "I can't wait anymore."

He stood, and Sonny didn't argue this time. Chris walked down the aisle and opened the doors with more strength than he needed, causing them to bang against the frame as loudly as his anxious heartbeat. *Breathe,* he told himself. He used to breathe deep and slow, visualizing something calm to lower his heart and breathing rates, but now he could skip the visualization and cut straight to the calm. *Breathe.*

He'd only walked partway into the adjoining car when Hannah entered the doors at the opposite end. She seemed okay, so Chris turned around and returned to his seat beside Sonny.

Soon, Hannah joined them.

"Well?" Sonny asked.

"Nothing," she said. "I can't find a trace of him. There were some private compartments I couldn't search, and I didn't examine every inch of the train, of course, so it's possible he's here, and I missed him. I don't know."

Soon, the English countryside gave way to small towns then big cities, bigger and bigger until they started blending together, and it became difficult to tell where one city ended and the next began.

"We need to find a nice hotel close to UKP headquarters," Hannah said. "Not only for us, but Xander wouldn't stay in anything less than five-star himself. We need some idea of where he could be hiding out."

Chris nodded and called around for reservations.

"There's an international financial symposium in town, and most of the hotels are already booked," he reported afterward, "but the Grosvenor House still has vacancies. I reserved two rooms. The hotel also happens to be within a five-minute walk of the US embassy."

"We can use a taxi," Hannah said. "But rather than go directly to our destination, I think we need to plan an SDR. Maybe take the cab to a different hotel, go inside to shake off any surveillance, and take another taxi to our actual destination. After checking in, we'll do another SDR, leaving the hotel and pay a visit to the London CIA Chief at the embassy to solicit support."

"You're the SDR expert," Chris said, referring to Hannah's Agency expertise in Surveillance Detection Routes.

"Works for me," Sonny said.

The bilingual conductor announced they were arriving in London then, and the train came to a stop at Saint Pancras International Station. Because Chris still had no idea where Xander was, he was hyper-alert. After stepping off the

Eurostar, they found a black cab with an illuminated yellow sign on the hood that read *TAXI*.

Chris didn't see anyone following them, but something deep down in his bones told him something bad was about to happen.

10

Still unable to shake his unease, Chris discreetly inspected his surroundings. Because their actual destination was southwest, he had the driver take them in the opposite direction, northeast to Nags Head Towne Centre. Chris paid the driver, and then he and his teammates hopped out and melted into the crowd, exited the other side of the shopping center, found another taxi, and told him the route they wanted to take to their hotel. An added benefit of using a second taxi was that the first driver didn't know their final destination, and the second driver wouldn't know where they started.

The driver took them past the London Zoo, Regent's Park, and the Sherlock Holmes Museum before riding along Park Lane, where they entered through black wrought iron gates and stopped in front of the Grosvenor House, which stood seven stories tall, one of the sky-kissing hotels in London.

They went through the revolving doors and entered the lobby. "See anyone?" Chris asked.

Hannah shook her head. "We're still clean."

"Saw some dudes in need of serious dental work," Sonny said.

They checked in at the front desk and went up to their rooms—Chris and Sonny in one and Hannah next door, both their windows overlooking Hyde Park. Chris drew his pistol and press-checked it, finding a cartridge ready in the chamber. He looked in the closet and behind the shower curtain, but no one was there waiting for him. The room was clear.

He ejected the magazine from his pistol and pressed on the top round. It hardly moved, indicating that the cartridges were packed in tight and the magazine was full. After reinserting the magazine into his pistol, he examined the extra magazines on his belt, and they were maxed out, too. Unable to figure out the source of his paranoia, he dismissed it.

An hour later, they entered the US embassy. Sonny stayed in the reception area while Chris and Hannah entered the Agency chief of station's office. It was a spacious room for a London office, and the station chief sat in a high-backed leather chair behind a grand wooden desk.

"Leave the talking to me," Hannah whispered to Chris. "I just need you with me for moral support."

"Do you know the chief?" Chris asked.

"Afraid so," she said with a slight tremble in her voice.

The station chief looked up from his desk. "What do *you* want?" he snapped.

Chris and Hannah approached his desk. "We tracked a Russian spy," Hannah said, "Xander Metaxas, code-named Lullaby, here to London, and we could use some support in finding him, sir. Help from both the Agency and the local British authorities."

He didn't offer them a seat. "If you tracked a Russian spy here, then you should already know where he is. You do not need my help finding him."

"We lost him as we were entering the country. We think he might be targeting the headquarters of United Kingdom Petroleum," she said.

"You have a lot of nerve setting foot back here in London. After all that happened last time." He lowered his head and examined the paperwork on his desk.

Hannah stared at him.

The chief raised his head from his paperwork. "Why are you still here?"

"We've spent days working this case, and I'd appreciate it if you could take a moment to discuss supporting us," Hannah blurted in frustration.

"Yes. I have taken a moment to discuss this with you." He lowered his gaze back to his paperwork.

Chris didn't like the way he was treating Hannah, but he held his tongue to give her space to do her job. If suffering this bureaucratic fool led to support for the mission, Chris was willing to forego expressing his displeasure.

"We have to get Lullaby," she said.

The chief looked up from his desk again, and his brow furrowed. "The last time you were in London, were you not told to cease and desist? More than once?"

"Yes, sir. But I'm here because this man killed the son-in-law of the White House Chief of Staff. I'm here to stop him before he does more damage."

"How do you know the man who killed the White House Chief of Staff's son-in-law is Lullaby?"

"We have a voice-recognition match between the killer and Lullaby," Hannah said.

"And what is the reliability of your voice recognition match?" he asked.

"About seventy-five percent. You and I both know nothing is ever one hundred percent."

"Last time you were here, you pissed off Scotland Yard, MI6, and a whole host of other alphabet soup agencies. Now you are persona non grata. I do not need drama around here. Not your kind of drama. You can make out a report for the police."

Hannah's jaw dropped slightly, but then it tightened. "Are you serious?"

"The receptionist can give you directions to the police station." His eyes returned to the papers on his desk.

"Your job is to gather intelligence," Hannah said.

The chief's eyes rose before his head did, and his tone became heavier. "Be careful, Officer Andrade. Do not say something you will regret."

Chris had had enough of this guy and his attitude. "How can you gather intelligence while you're sitting on your ass?"

The chief turned his gaze to Chris and picked up a stack of papers on his desk. "This is intelligence, officially provided to me by my MI6 liaison at Vauxhall Cross, and I will not have either of you disrupt the relationships I have cultivated here."

"These relationships were cultivated years before you took your post," Hannah said, raising her voice. "That intelligence in your hand is carefully filtered horse piss."

"We have an official agreement in place not to conduct espionage in the UK, and the UK does not conduct espionage in the US," the chief said.

"When it's convenient for the British," she said. "We may have similar interests, but we are not identical. They spy on our country just like we spy on theirs."

"Are you going to leave here on your own, or do I need to call the RSO to escort you out?" the chief asked.

"You're nearing retirement, right?" Hannah asked, narrowing her eyes. "I know you spent most of your time in Langley, but you get paid more for working overseas, and your retirement pay is based off your last three years of service. So you thought you'd come over here to London to coast through those last three years."

"So?" the chief asked.

Chris took a step forward. "I think what she's trying to say is that for most of your career you've been hiding in Langley where it's safe, riding on the coattails of officers like Hannah, who have been out in the field risking their lives doing the real work. Now that you're nearing the end of your career, you come out to one of the safer stations like London to boost your final retirement pay. The shitty irony of it all is that when a real officer like Hannah asks a desk jockey like you to do your job for once in your lifetime, you can't be bothered to help her!"

The chief sat open-mouthed for a moment before he closed his lips. "Are either of you carrying weapons? Because you're not authorized to be carrying weapons here. And Andrade, I have already told you that your London privileges expired. A long time ago. You have twenty-four hours to leave London."

Hannah pulled out a piece of paper and thrust it in front of the chief. "This is a Flash Precedence message from Langley, directing my team to kill or capture Xander Metaxas. Either you are in support of this mission or you are against it."

The chief's expression went blank, as if he'd been on the receiving end of a stun grenade. He held out his hand. "Let me look at that."

Hannah gave him the paper, and the chief carefully read it. "This better not be a forgery."

"It isn't a forgery," Hannah snapped.

The chief stared at the paper before he let out a long sigh. "The British authorities are not going to allow you to operate here, not even in an advisory capacity. The best I can do is to report to MI6 that I have received reliable information that this Xander Metaxas, code-named Lullaby, is preparing an attack on UKP. I will look the other way while you conduct your operation here in London, but I cannot provide you support. If you are caught, I will deny any knowledge of this conversation and I will tell the British authorities you are a rogue officer."

"You do that," Hannah said. She turned to Chris. "Come on. This is going nowhere. He's more useless than the chair he clings to." She marched out of the chief's office with Chris at her side.

11

hris, Hannah, and Sonny returned to Chris and
Sonny's room in the Grosvenor Hotel. "What happened the last time you were in London that pissed
everyone off so much?" Chris asked.

"I don't want to talk about it," she grumbled.

They sat down with Sonny at the small table in the room,
and he tapped his fingers on the surface. "What do we do if
Xander or one of his goons tosses a grenade in here? Is one
of us going to jump on it and save the others? We really need
an SOP for this."

It was a legitimate question, one Chris had answered with
his former Teammates. Every SEAL was different, but each
member of the Team needed to know how they would react to
such a threat.

"I'll jump on it," Sonny said nonchalantly.

"You don't have to do that," Chris said.

"I've got no wife and kids," Sonny said. "Nobody depends
on me."

"I've got no dependents, either," Chris said, "but I'm not jumping on a live grenade. I'll throw it back to where it came from. Or in a safe direction."

"And what if it blows up in your hand before you throw it?" Sonny asked. "Then we all die. Total waste. Better to lose one of us than the whole team. I'll jump on it."

Chris looked at Hannah.

"I'm the same as Chris on this one," she said. "I'll try to get rid of it, but I won't do a suicide leap."

"So if either of you get to the explosive first," he summarized, "you'll chuck it. If I get to it first, I'm going to jump on it. That's our SOP."

Chris was impressed with Sonny—there wasn't even a hint of bitterness or sarcasm in his voice—and he was a little embarrassed, too, but at least he was honest. When Chris was in his early twenties, he made his first deployment to Iraq. He was part of an overwatch when a terrorist lobbed a grenade into their sniper hide. One of his Teammates jumped on the grenade just before it exploded, saving the guys but killing himself. *Greater love hath no man than this, that a man lay down his life for his friends.*

Sonny was that man.

Chris and Hannah nodded in agreement. He cleared his throat, the dryness of it uncomfortable. "Man, I could go for some cold water."

Sonny turned to Chris. "Me, too. Get us some ice, bitch."

Chris stayed seated. "I was going to, but since you put it that way, I'm thinking warm water would taste better."

"So sensitive." Sonny forced a smile. "Okay. Do you think you could get us some ice? *Please?*"

Chris chuckled. "Yeah. I think I could do that." He stood, picked up the ice bucket, and headed out.

He walked down the hall looking for an ice machine but found none, so he headed downstairs to try the floor below. He spotted it, filled the bucket, and then exited the floor.

As he headed back upstairs, he saw the young woman with the easy-going smile and light-brown hair: Xander's daughter, Evelina. He wanted to slip out of the hallway to remain covert, but he was between floors. There was no immediate exit, and she'd already spotted him.

Shit!

She smiled. "What a surprise!" Evelina seemed to jump up and down without leaving the stairs.

Although he wished he could disappear, he acted as if he was happy to see her. "Yes, quite!"

She stepped down the stairs, moving closer. "We were lucky to find a hotel. I told Animus there were nice ones farther out, but he insisted on this area. This was the only one that still had vacancies."

Chris had already assumed she was with Animus, but now she'd confirmed it. He was happy to have found Animus, but she would soon tell him about this encounter, and he would alert Xander they were closing in on him.

"Are you here for the international symposium?" she asked. "They said that's why most of the hotels were booked."

"Work," he said.

She took a step down, closer to him. "Are you alone?" she whispered, her voice smoldering.

He didn't want to give away the presence of Hannah and Sonny. "Right now I am," he said, leaving wiggle room to change his story later. But now he had to figure a way to keep her from alerting Animus.

"Can we go to your room?" she asked softly, almost nervously, as if she were at the top of a high dive preparing to take her first plunge.

He knew she was playing him. She probably played Michael Winthrop, too. Chris's head spun faster and faster, spinning out of control. Feeling off-balance, he shook his head. "I'm sorry."

Evelina hesitated. "I know we hardly know each other." She dropped her bucket, and it bounced to Chris's step before rolling behind him. Her hand caressed the front of her skirt, her fingers moving down below her waist. As her hand stroked her thigh, her wrist pulled up the lower hem of her skirt.

Right here? In the stairway?

This was getting out of control. He could knock her unconscious here, but then he'd have to drag her back to his room and someone might see them. It would be better to invite her to his room and wrap her up there. "On second thought, going to my room sounds like a great idea," he said.

When he saw she had something in her hand, he couldn't mentally process what was happening. He felt like he was outside of his body watching himself as she drew a Walther PPK .380 from a thigh holster.

Without thinking, his shooting hand had already clawed his shirt up his right hip, and the web of his hand closed high on the pistol grip. His adrenaline jacked through his arteries, accelerating his thoughts so fast the rest of the world seemed to decelerate.

As she brought her weapon up, she kept it close to her body so he couldn't bat it away.

Although he knew this might be his last gunfight, he focused on popping his pistol out of the holster. When the muzzle broke free, he rotated it until his hand, wrist, and arm came into alignment. Close enough to feel her breath, there was no need to aim—no time. *Just squeeze.*

Her eyes widened and her mouth twisted, as if surprised at how quickly and brutally the first shot had struck her gut. And she had no time to react to the second shot. As she stood frozen on the step above him, Chris brought his muzzle up and squeezed again, sending a final round up through her lower jaw, through the roof of her mouth, and into her brain. She fell forward, almost as if she were still alive and expecting him to catch her, but he sidestepped, letting her drop. He turned and saw her body strike the steps with a thump before sliding to a stop, making a part of Chris cringe.

The surprise, speed, and violence of the moment astonished his thought processes, almost paralyzing him, and his hearing had become fuzzy. It might've been the effects of the adrenaline, but adrenaline usually had the opposite effect on him, making his hearing keen. The more likely source of his hearing loss was the mind-joggling noise of shooting in the narrow confines of the stairwell. At least the deafness was temporary.

The stairs below were covered with sparkling ice cubes, and two gray buckets lay at the landing. The adrenaline dump had helped him focus on survival, but the same adrenaline seemed to have shut out most everything else. Gradually, the pinhole of his senses expanded. There was a mess to clean up, and he'd made a lot of noise. His fingerprints were on the ice bucket, which was now missing from his room, and there was a dead body on the stairs. He had to get out of the immediate vicinity before someone identified him, or worse, the police arrived. But first he needed to search her for intel. Doing so, he discovered a cell phone in her jacket and pocketed it.

Then Chris climbed the steps, and just before he reached the exit to his floor, he heard hurried footsteps above him getting louder and louder.

Animus stood at the top of the next flight of stairs with his pistol drawn. "Evelina!"

Chris had already aimed at Animus, but the adrenaline made his hand jitter. Animus stepped to the side, and Chris followed him with his sights. He jerked the shot, causing the projectile to strike wide and miss. *Damn!*

Suddenly, the intimate puff of wind on the side of his face created a sensation he'd experienced in combat before. The velocity of the incoming round created shock waves behind it, which crashed into each other. *Pop!*

In the chaotic swirl of combat, Chris hadn't heard the report of the handgun, but the *pop* of the mini sonic boom was unmistakable. Animus was still moving his pistol to bear on Chris, so the shot had to have come from someone else. Although he guessed the unknown shooter's location was somewhere above Animus, Chris didn't know exactly where. And if Chris stayed to fight Animus, the other shooter might succeed in making his next shot count.

The passageway leading to Chris's floor was the closest, but he didn't want to lead Animus to Hannah and Sonny, so he spun around and headed downstairs. In the same moment, a flurry of lead blasted the hallway. If he hadn't turned around and headed the other way when he did, Animus and the other shooter would've nailed him.

Chris bounded over Evelina's body, and when he hit the landing, his feet slid on the scattered ice. He caught the floor with his ass, desperately hanging on to his pistol as a hailstorm of bullets passed through where he'd been standing. If there was pain, he didn't have time to feel it. That was twice he'd cheated death in the stairway, and he wasn't counting on a hat trick. He turned and fired a burst in Animus's direction before racing downstairs again. He skipped three steps at a time as he descended the next flight of steps.

Now that he was on the floor below the ice machine, he breezed through the exit and rushed out of the killing zone. The stairwell he'd just left had become a deathtrap. He glanced at the elevator, but that could turn into a more confined place to be ambushed, so he ran away and turned down the hall. A cheerful man stepped out of his room, but when he noticed Chris, his cheer faded, and he backed into his room and closed the door. Chris glanced down at himself, red splatter on his shirt and pistol in hand. He looked like a gangster. Even so, he was determined to survive, and he didn't give a damn about appearances.

At the end of the hall, he burst through the doors to the north stairway and leaped up two stairs at a time, ascending two flights, until he reached his floor. He burst into the hallway. Hannah and Sonny must have already heard the gunshots, and at any moment they would rush to see if he was in trouble. Gunshots rang out from the southern stairwell.

Oh no. Hannah and Sonny are already there!

Just before Chris reached the southern staircase, footsteps came running up the stairs from that direction. Unlike the terrorists, who could shoot first and ask questions later, Chris had to identify the danger first. He aimed but kept his finger off the trigger. Hannah and Sonny appeared.

"Let's get out of here," Hannah said, dashing past him.

"Trouble coming!" Sonny shouted as he blew by Chris and Hannah. "I've got the point."

"I'll bring up the rear," Chris said, following behind them.

They descended the north stairs unmolested. As they blew through the hotel lobby, some customers and hotel staff talked and pointed at the stairs, while others went about their business as if nothing was happening.

Chris, Hannah, and Sonny departed the building and had to wait for traffic before they could jaywalk across a one-way street and onto a tree-filled island, where they waited again for an opening in the traffic. Finally, they caught a break in the flow of cars and crossed into Hyde Park, where they took cover behind London plane trees.

"What the hell happened back there?" Sonny asked.

Chris explained quickly.

"Holy shit!" Sonny said. "Did you see Xander?"

Chris shook his head.

"You think he's in there?" Hannah asked.

"Everybody else seems to be," Chris said.

Through the trees surrounding the trio, Chris spotted Animus and an albino man stepping out of the hotel, both holding pistols down by their sides. The albino wore a pork-pie hat, his white hair extending over his ears, and he had sunglasses covering his eyes and a white soul patch fixed between his lower lip and chin. He wore a black leather jacket and black pointy shoes.

"Whiteface looks like he just stepped out of a jazz club in Hell," Chris said, nodding his head toward the men.

Sonny and Hannah turned to look. "Whiteface was one of the guys in the stairwell who was shooting at us," Sonny said.

Police sirens sounded then, and six beefy Caucasian men came out of the hotel. Animus shouted at his comrades before pointing across the street in their direction.

"I think they're coming our way," Chris said.

Hannah nodded. "Sonny, take us out."

Sonny resumed the point. There were no more trees immediately to the west, only an open grassy area, so going there would leave them exposed. If they went north, they'd run out of park—and trees—to hide in. Thankfully, Sonny had the tactical sense to take them south, staying in the tree line next to a wide walkway. Although Sonny set a fast pace, when Animus, Whiteface, and their comrades crossed the street, the trio couldn't move fast enough.

Sonny sped up after a glance over his shoulder and approached a fountain where statues of a couple seemed to frolic, almost dancing, above the water as children around them dived and played in the sparkling liquid. The cheerfulness of the statues contrasted the impending doom of Chris's situation. The area immediately surrounding the fountain wouldn't conceal them, and Sonny guided them through the swath of trees to the right until they reached more trees.

With Sonny still on point, Chris had to keep watch behind them. Animus, Whiteface, and their gang were becoming more animated and picking up momentum. Animus raised his pistol in Chris's direction.

"Contact rear!" Chris shouted.

Hannah and Sonny turned and faced Animus and his men, preparing to deliver the pain. Animus got off the first shot, and it nicked Chris's shirt and he took cover. From behind a tree, Chris exposed only enough of himself to see and shoot, but a jogger in her mid-twenties stopped running and stood petrified near Animus. The shot was too close to take without risking a hit to a friendly, so Chris aimed at the next available target, Whiteface, but he rushed the shot and missed.

A small, potbellied elderly man who was walking two poodles through the park jumped at the gunshot. He dropped to the ground and hung on to his leashes. The dogs barked and tried to run away, but the man held on tight and shouted to his pets.

More police sirens sounded, and through the trees, Chris spotted a man who appeared to be a police officer standing on the sidewalk, talking into a radio, but he was unarmed and didn't stand a chance of fighting Animus's crew with a baton as his only weapon.

Animus's team engaged Chris's, and as mini sonic booms crashed against each other, the air snapped, crackled, and popped. Chunks of tree bark flew, and splinters of wood sprayed.

Animus seemed to follow Chris's cue, taking cover behind a tree, but a hulking enemy was caught out in the open. Chris shot Hulk's arm, sending him into a short spin, exposing his back, which Chris also fired at. The shot struck low, near the kidneys, but Hulk was still standing. Chris squeezed the trigger again. This time, Hulk fell over.

The air near Chris heated up, and a projectile narrowly missed his left arm. Although relieved the bullet hadn't made impact, he still had to eliminate the threat of Animus and his goons. One of them, wearing a green shirt and green trousers must've been shot by Hannah or Sonny because he crumpled to the dirt.

Chris's team had plenty of tree cover on each side for shooting and shielding their movement, but Animus's squad had too many men and not enough wood. While Chris, Hannah, and Sonny fired and maneuvered freely, Animus and his comrades were trapped like fish in a barrel. Animus was no idiot; he wisely ordered his men to retreat.

Chris took a shot at a black-haired man who moved slow like molasses and nailed him in the back, but the shot propelled him forward rather than drop him. Chris breathed hot and fast, and his heart rate spiked without restraint. Molasses was about to find cover behind a tree. Chris aimed again, but his sights wobbled, hovering over nearly everything except his target. Chris hoped to take the shot when his sights aligned on Molasses's upper back, but the shot missed.

As soon as Animus and his men reached a patch of woods for cover, he ordered his men to return fire. Chris wanted to chase them, but moving forward would put him and his team out in the open. He looked to Sonny, who wasn't making a move, either. Hannah looked to Chris. She was a master at recruiting spies, but Chris and Sonny were the masters of killing. They needed to do something to gain a tactical advantage, but he didn't know what. Patience could be a virtue, allowing the situation to unfold until an opportunity presented itself.

In the lull between the shots, one of the Russians started speaking, but Chris couldn't hear what he was saying or notice anyone responding. Chris could only guess they were calling someone for reinforcements. Even if Chris's team survived the initial fight against superior numbers without the benefit of surprise, they'd soon run out of ammo.

Off to the right, two policemen wearing bullet resistant vests and armed with submachine guns stepped out of a white police vehicle marked with an orange stripe on the side.

"We can't stay here," Chris whispered.

"No shit, Sherlock," Sonny said.

Hannah nodded.

Because Chris was the strongest shooter of the three, it made the most sense to pair up Hannah and Sonny. Chris pointed to them. "You two leapfrog back."

They didn't have to be told twice. They hustled back ten meters to the nearest cover, while Chris watched their six. But Animus, Whiteface, and their men weren't making even the slightest movement. *What are they up to?*

When Hannah and Sonny opened fire on Animus and his clan, Chris took that as his signal to fall back. He passed a young mother and her child huddled on the ground, and he wished he could help them, but it was going to be all Chris could do to save himself. The best thing he could do for the mother and child was to leave the area quickly to remove the danger. His feet pounded against the ground as he passed Hannah and Sonny at a run and went ten more meters to the cover of a tree.

Animus's crew shot at the armed police officers, and the police officers fired back. The police took out two of Animus's men, but they retaliated with full force. A shot hit one of the officers in the neck, immediately dropping him. The other officer seemed to be wounded in both his arm and leg. He limped as he tried to drag his fallen buddy to safety.

While Animus and his men occupied themselves with the police, Chris and his crew were able to put nearly a hundred meters of distance between them and the bad guys.

"Time to haul ass," Sonny said. He led Hannah and Chris southeast through the woods.

Police sirens descended on the park now. Chris glanced back. Animus and his comrades were still following Chris's crew. And *fast.*

As Chris, Hannah, and Sonny ran, the ground appeared level, but a dip in one spot caused Chris to trip. He dodged trees. Their roots threatened to topple him, but he stayed on his feet. When one foot came down, a root made him lose his balance, twisting his ankle and wrenching his nerves. The agony caused his eyes to tear up, but he held his tongue.

He didn't know how far he'd have to run, and having to do it on a bum ankle was not good. The pain in his shoulder returned from the shot he'd taken back in Athens, and he regretted not having done more physical training on his own after he left the Teams.

He gritted through the fire consuming his ankle and the stabbing in his shoulder, maintaining his pace. Animus could cause him even more pain, and if Animus turned him over to Xander, the man would surely clang Chris's chimes for killing Evelina. He would much rather die than be captured—especially now.

The trio had run half a klick, reaching the southeast corner of Hyde Park, and the nerves in Chris's shoulder and ankle had become numb. Although the numbness provided relief, he prayed he wasn't causing permanent damage.

They passed a giant dark metal statue of Achilles armed with sword and shield. Chris considered how excruciating a shot to the heel would be, then banished the thought. Getting shot in the shoulder hurt enough as it was.

To the northeast of the nearest park exit was a bus stop where a red double-decker bus was parked. Trying to catch it would cause the trio to backtrack closer to the enemy. Before Chris could weigh the option anymore, the bus pulled out.

They slowed down to a walk and holstered their weapons to blend in better with the civilian population. Now there seemed to be people everywhere: entering the park, walking on the sidewalk, crossing the street, waiting for a bus, and driving. They were going about their everyday activities, clueless as to what danger was on its way.

Sonny crossed the northbound Park Lane. Hannah and Chris followed. Then Sonny traversed a grassy square where there were few trees. Traffic ran across multiple lanes of the southbound street, and Sonny, Hannah, and Chris came to a stop as they waited for an opening to cross.

"Damn!" Sonny cursed.

While they waited, the distress in Chris's shoulder and ankle returned, and Animus and his clan were closing the hundred-meter gap behind them. Chris walked out into the street holding his arm out and yelling at oncoming traffic. He was sure a car would hit him, but the vehicles slowed down, honking at him as they crossed. *I'd rather get killed by a car than give Animus the satisfaction of killing me.*

Hannah and Sonny followed, and a young white guy in a white Audi honked his horn. His vehicle pushed forward, his bumper nudging Sonny.

Sonny banged his fist on the hood and shouted, "I'm walking here, shit-for-brains!"

The driver waved his hand and shouted back in Jafaican—a mix of Cockney, Jamaican, and something else.

Sonny flipped him the bird. "Up yours, sweetheart."

When they reached the other side of the street, they faced a tall concrete wall that ran for some distance and seemed to have no entrance. Sonny jumped and grabbed the top of the wall, pulled himself up, climbed over and dropped out of sight. Hannah went next, and Chris followed. Intense burning in his shoulder gripped him, but he made it over. On the other side, they scaled another wall.

They landed in a lush casino garden. Under a porch canopy, supported by fluted white pillars, a TV monitor displayed *BBC News*. The green card tabletops matched the color of the ivy and other plants. At the roulette table, men and women wearing business attire stopped gaming, drinking, and cigar smoking to gawk at Chris and his friends. The looks on their faces ranged from curiosity to fear.

Sonny took the point, briskly and confidently walking across the patio past the red horse chestnut and bay trees.

Hannah smiled at the guests. "Maintenance."

At the time, it sounded like a weak cover, but in the heat of the moment, no other excuse came to mind, so Chris smiled, too.

Some of the guests returned to their activities, but the croupier kept staring, her brow creased and her roulette wheel stationary.

Sonny passed the bar on his way into the building. Inside, they found another roulette wheel and more card tables, but this time they didn't attract as many eyes.

A man in a tuxedo approached Sonny. "May I help you, sir?" he asked, his tone haughty.

"Yes, actually. Can you show me the way out?" Sonny asked. "We're in a bit of a hurry."

"Right this way, sir." The man in the tuxedo led them off the gaming floor and down an arched hallway where chandeliers lined the ceiling. At the end of the hall, Chris and his team exited the building, returning to the streets of London.

To their left, three of the Russians rounded the street corner, discreetly holding their pistols down to their sides but not concealing them. It appeared Animus had split his men up to look for Chris's crew.

"These guys won't quit," Chris muttered.

Sonny's face twisted in determination. "We have to make them quit."

"Or at least slow them down," Hannah said.

Animus and another Russian appeared. Now there were five of them.

Across the street, the doorman to the Four Seasons Hotel greeted Sonny, who ignored him and entered the lobby. Chris and Hannah followed close behind. The lobby was clear except for a handful of guests checking in at the front desk. Chris's first impulse was to form a hasty ambush on Animus, but that would endanger the guests. He didn't like choosing a path of escape through populated areas, but in the heart of London, there wasn't a plethora of unpopulated places where he and his friends could stay alive.

As they made haste through the lobby, Chris threw a quick glance over his shoulder. The Russians followed behind, but they weren't displaying their weapons anymore. Sonny picked up his pace to a jog. The Russians picked up their pace, too.

Chris and his crew exited the hotel and slipped through the front doors of the Playboy Club. It was a classy joint similar to the first club they'd passed through, with expensive furnishings, a casino, and well-dressed guests. The main difference was the female staff, who wore black pantyhose, corset teddies, cuffs, bow tie collars, rabbit ears, and fluffy white cottontails.

A bunny greeted them at the door, and Sonny swiftly brushed past her. The door bunny cocked her head as if to ask a question, but before she could say anything, the trio had passed her.

Entering the club, Sonny voiced his disappointment. "Where are the naked women?"

Chris shook his head. *Only he would think about that at a time like this.*

Then, out of the corner of his eye, Chris saw Animus and his posse arrive behind them.

Sonny hung a left in the casino and took them through a side exit. Outside, a finely attired elderly gentleman stepped into a black cab. Chris and his friends joined the elderly gentleman in his taxi. The gentleman rattled with surprise, and he seemed about to say something but didn't.

Chris and Hannah smiled at him politely, but Sonny ignored him.

There was no passenger seat in the front of the cab and probably no room for a trunk in back, but in the middle was a three-seat bench facing two foldout seats. Chris unfolded the foldout seat and sat.

"Where to, sir?" the driver asked.

"Out of here," Sonny said. "Just drive."

"I need to know where to," the driver said.

"Buckingham Palace," Chris blurted. It was the first place that popped into his mind.

The elderly gentleman shook his head and couldn't seem to stop trembling as he spoke. "I do not know who you people are, but I am not with you, and I am not going to Buckingham Palace."

"Where are you going?" Chris asked.

The gentleman took in Chris's torn and stained shirt and sat still. Inside the Playboy Club, Animus and his goons hurried for the exit nearest the taxi.

"Buckingham Palace now!" Chris pressed.

Animus and his men reached for their pistols.

"Drive!" Sonny shouted.

The trio ducked and pulled the older man down with them. Bullets shattered windows of the Playboy Club, creating a frightening racket.

The taxi spun out, flying northeast on the one-way Brick Street.

"I thought the pickpockets in Madrid were bad," Hannah said to the driver, "but Madrid is calm compared to London."

"Shooting is not an everyday occurrence," the driver said with a quiver in his voice.

"I hope not," Hannah said.

Sonny peered out the back window, searching for their enemy.

12

Chris checked the GPS map on his smartphone. Because of the one-way streets, the driver would have to circle around to Hyde Park and the Achilles statue before taking a more direct course to Buckingham Palace. The Queen's Gallery at the Palace was well within walking distance of Victoria Station, which seemed like a great point of egress. If someone later asked the driver where he took his passengers, he'd only be able to tell them Buckingham Palace, and it'd be difficult to figure out where Chris and his companions went after that. "You can drop us off at the Queen's Gallery," Chris told the driver.

Chris had been so focused on their immediate survival he'd ignored the old man, who'd closed his eyes and balled up in the corner of the cab, his mouth moving without opening. "We're not going to hurt you, sir," Chris said.

The man's mouth stopped moving.

"We just need a ride to the Queen's Gallery, and then we'll disappear."

The elderly man opened an eye, but when he saw Chris looking at him, he closed it again.

As they neared the Achilles statue, Chris felt his heart rate pick up before he scanned to see if any of the Russian thugs were lingering in the park. When no signs of the thugs appeared, he managed to take in deep breaths, calming his pulse.

Within minutes, the driver stopped near the Queen's Palace, and Hannah paid him before parting company and melting with Chris and Sonny into the surrounding crowd. They examined the grounds for anyone who might've followed them, but there were no signs of surveillance.

When their taxi vanished, Chris said, "I'll take point to Victoria Station."

They strolled southwest like other sightseers leaving the palace. "The hotel room was ours for a week, right, Chris?" Hannah asked. He nodded, and she continued. "So that should give us time to get someone in there to make sure we didn't leave anything behind and check out for us."

"Someone from the Agency?" Sonny asked.

"The London chief is too much of a chair-hugger to send a cleaner for us," Hannah said. "Avoids espionage like the plague, but he attends to all the brown-nosing opportunities."

Sonny huffed. "Then who can help us?"

"I know a guy who might be able to clean up the hotel mess," she said with a faraway gaze. She pulled out her cell phone and made a call.

As they walked by Grosvenor Park on the way to the station, images of Evelina bleeding in the stairway flooded

Chris's mind. She was untrustworthy and had tried to kill him, but guilt still gnawed at him. A number of the enemies he'd shot, he'd never spoken to, but in Evelina's case, he'd interacted with her on more than one occasion. Instead of becoming desensitized to killing her, he'd become sensitized. He wondered what exactly her role in all of this was and what she hoped to gain by shooting him. Hannah nudged him as she hung up her phone and put it away.

"You okay?" she asked.

He gave her a tight smile and nodded. None of these feelings or thoughts were conducive to accomplishing the mission, so he needed to pack them in a box, push them into the warehouse of his mind, and stack them with the others. But then he remembered something: he had Evelina's phone. Maybe thinking about her wasn't all for nothing.

He put his hand in his pocket, confirming it was still there.

They descended the steps to the Victoria subway station, and Hannah quickly bought tickets and handed them out. "I contacted an old acquaintance, William Teach. He used to work for the Circus," she said, using a nickname for MI6. "But now he works for himself. He said we can stay at his house, and I'm hoping he'll be able to help us, too."

While they rode the Tube, Chris pulled out Evelina's phone and searched for intel. In her web search history there was UKP's website and another link for a map of the area around UKP. Then he connected to Young's website, so he could gather more information from Evelina's phone and analyze it. Chris shared what he'd found with Hannah and Sonny, and they agreed her web search history supported the theory that Xander's next target was UKP headquarters.

After five minutes, the train stopped, and the SOG trio exited at South Kensington Station, where Hannah led them on a walk several blocks to a house on Queensberry Place. Parked in front was a red Ferrari. Behind the car stood a six-story white stucco Victorian. A small set of outdoor stairs led to what the British called the "ground" floor. Below was a basement, and above the ground floor were the first, second, third, and fourth floors. The building shared walls with the houses on either side and had no front yard, but in this upscale neighborhood of London, the house was probably worth over twenty million dollars.

Hannah spoke quietly as she led them to the front door. "This place is a far cry from where William's foot soldiers live, mostly in the slums of World's End. And it's doubtful his neighbors know how connected he is to the underworld, if it all."

She rang the doorbell, and a man dressed in suit and tie answered the door, introducing himself as William's assistant. After Hannah gave her name, the man showed them in to a reception room and offered them a seat while he left to inform William they'd arrived.

They sat, and Chris studied the reception room. Three of the walls were brown with a leaf pattern and one wall was black and white with a leopard design. The furniture was a dizzying mix of colors and styles—classic Victorian, hip sixties, and two twisted lamps that appeared to be descended from outer space. The whole room shouted nouveau riche and made Chris's head ache.

Footsteps sounded, and William appeared, wearing a neon suit jacket and white shirt with the collar opened wide. He had black hair, a tan complexion, thick moustache, and an unlit cigar in his mouth. His strong, husky build seemed soft around the edges, like a former dockworker who now enjoyed a few too many fine dinners.

"Welcome!" he said with a big smile and outstretched arms.

Seeing the outstretched arms, Chris remembered last year when a duplicitous Agency bastard named Jim Bob welcomed him with outstretched arms. Jim Bob had nearly killed Chris and Hannah. Chris didn't trust William. Not yet. The man would have to earn it.

Chris and Hannah stood at William's greeting, but Sonny remained seated.

Hannah smiled and gave the man a hug. A knot formed in Chris's gut, and heat rose up his neck. He didn't want to admit it, but he was jealous. No one else's hands should be on her, but he had to contain himself. He took a deep breath and unclenched the fist he hadn't realized he'd formed.

"It's been awhile," she said.

"I thought I'd never see you again—especially not here in London. How are things?" he asked.

Hannah got other people to reveal themselves, but she revealed little, and often what she revealed was just another cover story, like layers on an onion. "This is Chris. And Sonny," she said with a smile that appeared to disarm William.

"Welcome," he said.

Chris reached out and shook his hand. "Hi."

Sonny had a sour look on his face like he'd eaten a lemon. "You said *welcome* twice."

William's smile began to fade, but Hannah laughed just in time. "Don't pay Sonny too much attention. He's like that with everyone. Sometimes he likes to stir things up a bit."

"Have a seat," William said, gesturing, "please."

Chris and Hannah returned to their spots, William following suit. He lit his cigar and offered some to the others, but only Sonny accepted, his frowning face lifting.

"Sounds like you're still getting in trouble," William said as he settled his gaze on Hannah.

"Same old, same old," she said.

He took a puff on his cigar. "Have you seen Maximilian lately? What was his last name... Wolf-something?"

"Wolf is dead."

"Dead? That's terrible... How?"

"It happens," she said matter-of-factly, not elaborating. "Speaking of business, yours seems to be doing well."

He took another puff on his cigar. "Always the tight-lipped woman of mystery," he said with a grin. "There's a lot of contract work to be done: Europe, Middle East, Africa." He shrugged his shoulders. "I got tired of gardening. Well, I wasn't very good at it, either. All my tomatoes died."

Sonny took his cigar out of his mouth and tapped it on the edge of the ashtray. "So now you're a mercenary."

"Same things I did in the Circus, gathering intel, acting on it, except now my work isn't as difficult and I get paid more. People with experience like us can make up to ten times what our governments paid us."

"I wouldn't know what to do with that kind of money," Hannah said.

"You saw the Ferrari out front," William said.

She shrugged. "I like my car."

William looked at Chris and Sonny, but they didn't say anything.

"Now I get paid what I'm worth," he went on. "And I don't have to answer to a ringleader. Hannah, you and I would make a most smashing team."

"Are you trying to take Hannah away from us?" Chris asked, unable to push down the aggression rising in his voice. "Break up our act?"

William casually blew smoke in the air. "Not break up the act. Merely offer a better contract."

Hannah shook her head. "Always the charmer."

"I'm serious," William said.

She looked at Chris and Sonny. "I already have a team."

William smiled. "If you can vouch for them—which I'm sure you can, otherwise they wouldn't be with you—I could use them, too."

Sonny blew cigar smoke at William. "We're not for sale."

Hannah shot Sonny a glare, but he was unfazed.

William changed the subject. "So you need a place to stay? You're welcome to stay here as long as you like."

"Thank you," she said with an even smile.

William grinned back. "Anything you need."

Chris didn't like the hungry way he looked at her, like he was eyeing dessert.

"I need a cleaner, too," she said.

He tapped his cigar on the ashtray. "That won't be free."

"I didn't think it would be." She paused. "And I need to find someone."

William stopped smoking on his cigar. "I can arrange for the cleaning, but I can't find someone for you. I don't do that for governments anymore."

She raised an eyebrow and gave him a sly smile. "I thought you worked for anyone. Anywhere."

"Not for anyone. Not anymore."

"Why not?" she asked.

"Not enough money and too much risk."

"You can clean up, but you can't find out where a person is?"

"I can clean up what's already been done," William clarified, "but I won't be a part of what's about to be done. Not for governments."

"I'm not asking you for my government. I'm asking you as a personal favor," she said.

William smiled and shook his head. "You look amazing. It's so good to see you again."

Hannah flashed him a petawatt smile.

"Who are you looking for?" he asked.

"Xander Metaxas," she said.

William stroked his chin with a finger. "Doesn't ring a bell."

"Code-named Lullaby."

The mention of Lullaby caused William's whole being to darken.

"So you know him." Chris said.

"Know *of* him," William said.

"What do you know?" Hannah asked.

William shifted his gaze to the carpet. "More than I care to."

"He took a hostage in Athens, the White House Chief of Staff's son-in-law. When the hostage tried to escape, Lullaby killed him."

"Maybe the hostage is lucky to be dead," William said.

"I'll advance you the money for expenses," Hannah said, "and if your expenses run higher, you know I'll cover them."

William shook his head. "I already told you I can't."

"Can you tell me what you know about Lullaby?" she asked.

"Like what?"

"Like his aliases or his mode of operation."

William's mouth became taut. "His mode of operation is like Ebola. He destroys everything. And he stays low under the radar until he starts infecting people."

It seemed the man knew more than he was letting on, so Chris piped up again. "Why does the mention of his name trouble you?"

William let out a sigh, still looking down at the floor, as if he were scrolling through his memories. Then he leaned forward in his seat. "*Troubled* doesn't begin to describe how I feel about Lullaby. When I was in the Circus, we had a top agent in Greece. Lullaby found out the agent was spying on one of his people, so he had one of the agent's relatives castrated. Then Lullaby sent the severed organs to the agent. After the agent had some time to reflect on matters, Lullaby put a bullet in the same relative's skull. The agent continued spying for us, so Lullaby had another of the agent's relatives killed, sending body parts to the agent again. The agent finally hung himself. Then Lullaby sent a message to our embassy saying the same fate awaited any future spies." He shook his head. "You don't want to mess with Lullaby."

Chris leaned forward in his chair and pitched his voice low. "Oh, but I do want to mess with Lullaby."

"Dead or alive," Hannah said.

"Preferably dead," Sonny said.

William slumped in his seat as if suddenly shouldering a massive burden. "Be careful what you wish for."

13

It was late in the evening when Animus and four of his men walked into the Sofitel London St. James Hotel. While Evelina's father was the reason he'd started dating her in the first place, he truly had come to care for her, even if she regarded their relationship as more of a business deal than true love. And now that she was gone, he missed her.

He and his men filled the elevator, but the elevator felt empty. And as they rode up, he felt as if his soul were going down. Although Animus didn't want to face the news himself, he had to give the news to Xander.

Animus stepped out of the elevator. "What the hell am I going to tell him?" He said it more to himself than to his posse. "I failed…"

"It wasn't your fault," his albino buddy, Ivan, said as they walked slowly down the hall. Animus didn't know why Ivan was such a loyal friend to him; he just was.

"I was responsible for her well-being," Animus said. "I failed to protect her."

"It wasn't your fault," Ivan repeated.

"I should've stayed by her side."

"You have to be careful how you word it to him," Ivan said.

"There's no careful way to word it. She's gone. If Xander kills me for it, at least I won't have to think about it anymore."

"He won't kill you," Ivan said. "He cares too much about you."

"We can't let him leave," Animus said. "There are police everywhere, and if he tries to go to her body, they'll try to apprehend him."

Animus took a deep breath before he knocked on Xander's door. The peephole went dark for a moment, and then light shone through. Gravity seemed to pull him down as he waited for someone to answer the door, heaviness pooling in his belly. Soon the peephole went dark again. The door opened, and a Russian named Sergey with smooth skin and hard eyes invited them in.

Inside the room, Xander stood and seemed to read Animus's expression. Xander's eyes widened, his face somehow burning with anger and pale with fear at the same time. "Where is she?!" he yelled, as if he already knew the answer. He rushed to the door and Ivan tried to grab hold of him, but Xander's hands swept him off to the side. Animus and his men picked up where Ivan had failed and pushed Xander back into the room, where they held on to him.

Xander struggled, trying to break free. "You sons of bitches. Where is she? Where is she?"

They dragged him back into the room and to the carpet where they dog-piled him. Animus strained to hold Xander down.

"Stop fighting!" Ivan yelled.

"Keep still!" Animus's men shouted.

Xander caught a piece of Animus's shirt pocket and tore it. Then he attempted to move both horizontally and laterally from under the heap. Animus battled to keep Xander from escaping, but seeing his grief made Animus's strength crumble.

Sergey pulled men off the dog pile in an attempt to free Xander, but Animus's men piled on faster than Sergey could tear them off. At the bottom of the dog pile, Ivan threw a punch, and Animus feared it was directed at Xander.

"Don't hurt him," Animus warned his men.

"Where is she?" Xander demanded, his voice becoming high pitched and frantic, his body twisting and turning. "Where is she?" Animus's men held him. "Where is she? Animus!"

Animus slipped to the side of the pile, and Sergey tore him away. He didn't have the steel in his muscles to return to the mass of men, and he didn't know what to say to Xander.

Xander's body trembled, and his eyes caught Animus's. "Don't try to avoid this."

Animus stood there speechless, unable to deliver the tragic news.

"Take me to her!" Xander said.

Sergey stopped resisting Animus's crew, knelt down, and patted his boss on the shoulder.

"Take me to her, damn you all!" Xander cried, his voice quaking.

For Xander's sake, Animus wanted to believe she wasn't dead, but he'd seen her corpse himself, and he was grasping at nothing.

"Bring my Evelina!" Xander yelled. "Bring her to me!"

His body became unsteady, as did the will of the men holding him, but Xander's emotions were still raw. Tears ran down

STEPHEN TEMPLIN

his face as he now seemed to fight inward, trying to embrace his denial but unable to hold on. Animus's men continued to hold him, and Xander's voice became garbled as if he were drowning in anguish, drowning in reality.

Only one word was discernible. *"Niet!"* No!

The rest was the gibberish of a man whose spirit was dying.

Animus could no longer distinguish between Xander's agony and his own. He shrank in on himself, feeling smaller as the room stretched wider and a wave of wretchedness swept over him, drowning his cries.

14

William's men must've been working hard even after Chris, Hannah, and Sonny went to bed, because when the SOG team awoke, they found their luggage sitting in the living room. Chris put antiseptic on his shoulder and bandaged it carefully. The evening's rest seemed to have helped, because he could move it more freely. Even his strained ankle didn't torment him to stand on.

While Sonny showered, Hannah sat next to Chris on the sofa. "The last time I was in London," she said, "I chased a man I thought was a terrorist for the Taliban. I bagged him on British soil before I flew him to a black site run by the Agency in the Czech Republic. The interrogation got a little rough, and it was discovered that the prisoner didn't work for the Taliban," she said, dipping her head. "He was a British citizen. Later, when the British government found out... well, they were livid."

"You're lucky your career survived," Chris said.

"After the British got their citizen back, they figured out he was a key recruiter for al Qaeda. Officially I was forgiven, but unofficially, I wasn't."

"Sounds like you did the right thing."

"I was younger and less experienced," she confessed, "but my instincts were good. Instinct is something that can't be taught. I see it in you, too. I've never told anyone that story. The only other people who know are those who were directly involved or heard it from the rumor mill."

He met her eyes and smiled. "Thank you for sharing it with me."

She pressed her lips into a firm line and nodded.

Before they could say anything more, Sonny came out in his business attire. They'd be doing recon around United Kingdom Petroleum Headquarters this morning and needed to blend in with the other business people in the financial district.

"Let's get some grub," Sonny said, clapping his hands together and rubbing them.

They approached the dining room, and William's cook invited them to sit down for breakfast and excused William for being late. The cook served cold smoked herring, eggs, toast, grilled tomatoes, and sautéed mushrooms with orange juice and coffee. Because caffeine would adversely affect his shooting, Chris avoided the latter but helped himself to the rest of the meal.

"What'll our cover be today?" Hannah asked before she took a bite of her eggs.

"Strip club owners," Sonny said, his mouth full.

Hannah grimaced. "You have a one-track mind. But I've never been in one, and I wouldn't know how to own and operate it."

"We could do some research," Sonny said with a waggle of his eyebrows.

Chris swallowed a bite of tomato and mushroom. "How about something to do with the outdoors? We all know about that."

Hannah nodded. "Outdoor clothing."

"We could call it Outdoor Mountain Clothing," Chris suggested. "OMC."

Sonny rolled his eyes. He didn't outwardly support the idea, but he didn't oppose it, either.

Hannah took a sip of her coffee. "We'll say we're based in the US and are expanding operations abroad to the UK."

"If Xander plans to attack UKP Headquarters," Chris said, "he'll probably check the place out before he hits it. Maybe we can catch him or his men while they're scoping the place."

"And maybe one of his goons will lead us to him," Hannah hoped aloud.

Chris nodded. "We could try to find an office space to rent nearby, too, so we can put UKP under surveillance."

"Who's going to pay for that?" Sonny asked. "We don't have an account for Outdoor Mountain Clothing."

"The Agency has given me a nondescript account I can use for payment," Hannah said.

"It won't take all three of us to put UKP under surveillance" Sonny said. "At least one of us could inspect nearby hotels and other places to figure out where Xander might be staying."

The others agreed, all seemingly pleased with their plan, and then focused on their meals. Breakfast was nearly over when William finally arrived.

"We're going to try to rent out an office space near where we think Xander will try to conduct surveillance and then wait for Xander or one of his thugs to show up," Hannah told him as she stood up, setting her napkin back on the table. "Can you hold on to our luggage until we're ready for it?"

William nodded, his gaze shifting from Hannah to Chris to Sonny and back again as they prepared to leave. "Of course."

"Thanks," Hannah said. "We'll be back." She patted him on the shoulder as she headed for the exit, Sonny and Chris hot on her heels.

They walked to Kensington Station where they hopped the Tube to Piccadilly Circus. They got off and weaved around several blocks to Duke of York Street. There, the presence of CCTV cameras permeated the city. Duke of York Street fed into St. James Square, a road surrounding a lush park facing the Naval and Military Club, the Buchanan House, and UKP on the corner.

Across from the UKP building and next to the park stood a uniformed police officer, wearing a checkered sleeve and helmet band. Armed only with a radio and baton, his mission seemed more of a hopeful deterrent than defense. Standing at the corner, there was a man dressed in a suit and tie, like any other businessman except for the white cord that ran from his ear down into his shirt. The City of London Police would surely do a better job of going undercover, so Chris guessed he was security hired by UKP. Nearby, he noticed a white van with tinted windows—possibly police, and hopefully not Xander's crew. It seemed the London Agency chief of station had really informed the British authorities as he said he would, and they were taking the threat with some seriousness.

"If Xander plans a kidnapping, assault, or explosives, he'll need large-sized vehicles like an SUV or van," Chris said. "If they follow the one-way streets, they'll come down from Duke of York Street before traveling clockwise around St. James Square to hit UKP."

Sonny's eyes focused on the building adjacent to UKP. "What the hell is that building?"

Chris shifted his gaze to look. "I don't know, but if it's office space, maybe we can rent it out and post surveillance."

Hannah headed toward the entrance. "I'll find out," she said.

Soon, she returned and said two companies occupied the building, with no available space to rent.

Chris shrugged, and they resumed their clockwise recce around Saint James Square. Across the street from UKP was another office building with a sign reading, *Offices and Suites to Let.*

"Hot damn!" Sonny said. "That's convenient."

They went inside and spoke to a receptionist, who connected them with their letting agent. The agent appeared and gave them a tour of available office spaces, all fully furnished and complete with a kitchen, lobby, receptionist, cleaning, and maintenance services. "We also have shower rooms and dry cleaning," the agent said.

The trio smiled at one another. They chose an office on the second floor, right on the corner of St. James Center and Charles II Street, giving them a view of the side of UKP's building and its main entrance.

"You also have a view of the St. James Gardens," the agent told them happily.

Chris smiled at her. He didn't give a damn about the garden view.

"Could we have a moment to discuss it, please?" Hannah asked.

"Yes, of course." The agent stepped out of the office and closed the door behind her.

"The trees in the square are blocking our view of the road around the square," Chris said. "We won't see the tangos until they're almost to UKP, and then it will be too late."

"We could set up surveillance cameras," Sonny said.

"We could," Hannah said. "I can ask Langley to fly out the equipment and a tech to install it. That would give us a view of the entire stretch of road."

"Or maybe Young can hack into the CCTV camera feeds," Chris said. "That might be faster."

Sonny grinned. "I like that even better."

"I'll give him a call," Hannah said, as she walked out of the room.

"Don't you hate it when I'm right, Sonny?" Chris smirked.

Sonny shrugged, then winked. "It's bound to happen once or twice."

When Hannah returned, she brought the agent with her, and they finalized much of the rental agreement for the office space. Once that was settled, they rented a vehicle, which they used to pick up their luggage from William's place, as well as to go shopping for sleeping bags, computer equipment, extra monitors, and food so they could live in the office while keeping UKP Headquarters under surveillance.

They were on their way back to the office when Hannah received a phone call; their Gulfstream jet had landed at Luton Airport, north of London, and was standing by.

"One more stop," Chris said, swinging the car around to head for the base.

They were going to need their rifles.

They were nearly finished setting up when darkness settled on the city. Young gave them a call and said he was able to hack into some CCTV feeds. He explained how to hook up their computer to begin surveillance. An image appeared on their screen, but it wasn't an image Chris was expecting.

"Something's wrong with the feed," Hannah said into the speakerphone.

"What's wrong with it?" Young asked.

The monitor was showing the interior of a club where a topless dancer gyrated around a pole.

Sonny was glued to the monitor. "Nothing's wrong with the feed," he said.

Chris gave Sonny's shoulder a good smack.

"I think you know what's wrong with the feed," Hannah said.

Sonny's brow creased in deep folds as he pleaded his case. "There's nothing wrong with that feed. We just need more feeds."

"This feed is coming from Duke of York Street," Young said.

"We need a view of the street," Hannah said, "not the inside of a strip club."

"I was just messing with you all," Young said, clearly trying to bring a little levity to the situation. "That was the Gaslight Club."

The screen went blank and a view of Duke of York Street replaced the image of the stripper.

Sonny slammed his fist down on his desk. "What the hell is wrong with you, Young?"

Young just chuckled quietly from across the Atlantic.

15

The day after Evelina's death, Animus sat alone with Xander in the older man's hotel room.

"How are you holding up?" Xander asked.

"I don't understand how those Americans slipped out of our hands," Animus said. "How are *you* holding up, sir?"

Xander breathed deeply. "When I was with Evelina, nothing else seemed to matter."

Animus nodded.

"Now I am angry," Xander said. "I cannot shed another tear for her. I am all cried out. I wish I could cry more, but I cannot."

Animus understood that feeling all too well. "Is there anything I can do to help?"

Xander patted him on the leg and straightened his spine, determination steeling his features. "We will continue with our plans to bomb UKP headquarters. After the bomb goes off, we will sweep through St. James Square and shoot everyone on sight. Then we will make our escape and contact the media and tell them 21D will continue its attacks until UKP stops construction of TAP. The West must stop its meddling in Greek affairs. For Greece and everyone, it is time to de-Westernize the world."

"Yes, sir," Animus said.

"First we need to build the bomb. Do you have the cannon fuse, diesel fuel, mixing buckets, and the thirteen barrels I told you to acquire?"

Animus nodded. "And the duct tape, plastic pipe, screws, power drill, and scale you asked for, too. We spread out the purchases with different men at different locations—just like you explained."

"You called earlier and said Boris has the nitromethane?"

"Yes, sir," Animus said. "He used his fake ID to pose as an FIA drag racing crew chief and paid cash for it." Using the cover of a member of the Federation Internationale de l'Automobile was his idea, and he was quite proud of it.

Xander rubbed his chin in silence for a moment as if reviewing a mental checklist. "And you already acquired the blasting caps, shock tube, and Tovex."

The Tovex was a highly stable water-gel explosive, and it wasn't easy to get. But they'd managed.

"Ivan snuck into British Seismic Exploration and took it. They've been gathering the materials and storing them in the safe house for weeks before you and I arrived."

Xander nodded. "I know you already told me, but I had to hear it again. I am not in my normal state of mind. I just need reassurance that something in the world around me is stable when so much has gone wrong."

"Well, all we need is fertilizer to shape the charge and oxidize the nitromethane," Animus said.

The corners of Xander's lips rose, creating more of a sneer than a smile. "Yes, we need fertilizer, and the UK is the ammonium nitrate fertilizer capitol of the world. You know what to do."

Animus nodded. Then he stood, walked to the door, and opened it. Before he left, he stopped and turned to look at Xander. "I'm sorry about Evelina."

"Me, too."

"Her killer was Chris Johnson, the American legal attaché who came to your party."

The muscles in Xander's jaw worked. "Ivan told me."

"I'm sorry," Animus said again.

He waved a hand, dismissing Animus. "I want to be alone now."

Animus nodded and stepped into the hall, closing the door behind him. The sound of something heavy hitting the wall sounded inside Xander's room, like a chair that had been thrown. Xander had always seemed in control, but Animus had never seen or heard him like this.

Animus walked down the hall, stopped at Ivan's room, and picked him up. The two exited the hotel and found their van in the parking lot. Ivan pulled a magnetic sign out of the trunk that read, *Wellington Farms*. He affixed it to the side door of the van before driving them northeast out of London.

"Xander said you told him Evelina's murderer was Chris Johnson," Animus said.

"I hope you're not angry," Ivan said. "I know you wanted to tell him yourself but couldn't."

Animus bowed his head. "Thanks."

They rode a little over an hour and a half in silence until they arrived at the importer's warehouse in Essex. Ivan dropped Animus off out front.

He was anxious about the whole transaction, but he hid his nervousness as he strolled through the front door and approached the clerk. "I'm Edward Wellington, and I ordered some ammonium nitrate fertilizer." Animus handed the clerk his business card.

The clerk shook his hand and read the card. "Oh, yes, Wellington Farms." He sounded bored, just going through the motions of his job as he put the card in his shirt pocket. "Will this be credit card or cash?"

"Cash," Animus said.

"If you'll fill out your company information on this form, please..." The clerk handed him a pen and a clipboard. "Once we input you into our computer, you won't have to fill this out again—just sign for it."

Animus filled out the form and signed at the bottom before returning it to the clerk.

The clerk took it and briefly glanced at the paper. "Can I see some ID, Mr. Wellington?"

Animus presented his UK driving license and showed his face boldly to make it clear he wasn't hiding anything.

The clerk took a cursory look at the license then Animus's face before returning his gaze to the paperwork on his counter. "Okay." His tone became apologetic. "We have to do this to protect against terrorists making homemade explosives."

Animus grinned and paid the man. "I understand."

"Thank you." The clerk turned and called out to one of the warehouse workers. "Fertilizer pickup!" Then he turned

FROM RUSSIA WITHOUT LOVE

to Animus. "Just bring your vehicle around to the side and park next to the first pallet."

Animus walked out of the warehouse with a feeling of celebration, but it wasn't over until it was over, so he kept his emotions in check. He hopped into the van and directed Ivan to pull around to the side, where the warehouse worker began loading the bags of fertilizer. Animus remained seated in the passenger seat to avoid small talk with the worker.

But when the young worker finished loading the van, he tried anyway. "What you going to grow with all this fertilizer?"

"You'll have to excuse us," Animus said. "We're in a bit of a hurry."

"Yes, sir. Have a good day."

The worker walked away and headed back into the warehouse, and Animus and Ivan smiled as they drove off the lot.

16

Young had hacked into the CCTVs of various private companies, including UKP, giving Chris and his crew views of Duke of York Street, St. James Square, and Charles II Street. The video was then digitally recorded, so they could analyze it. They'd stocked up on microwavable dinners, and while working on his meal of chicken curried rice, Chris peered out the window. Outside, the uniformed bobby and plainclothes security officer were gone. New men had replaced them, and the same white van with tinted windows was still parked outside UKP.

"Those poor bastards in the van must be hating life about now," Sonny said with a chuckle. "Eating cold food and pissing in a bucket."

Chris shrugged and stabbed his food with his disposable fork. He looked over at Hannah and she yawned. "Let's make shifts for the evening surveillance, so all of us can get some sleep," he said. "One on and two off."

Hannah and Sonny both nodded, and soon one person was pulling surveillance watch while the other two slept.

The next morning, they microwaved their breakfasts and ate together. Chris took a drink of orange juice. "Today," he said, "one or two of us can go out and look for Xander while one or two stay here on surveillance in case he shows here near UKP."

"We don't need two people on surveillance here," Hannah said.

"Yeah, I don't want to sit around here on my ass all day," Sonny said.

"I can stay here, if you like," Chris offered.

Hannah tilted her head and met his eyes. "Are you sure?"

"Yeah," Chris said. "We don't all need to be here. If I were Xander, I'd wait 'til the police get bored and leave before hitting UKP. If they don't leave, he'll probably call in some false alarms to make them leave—send them to the other side of London. If I see the police move out of the target area, I'll let you know. Or if I spot Xander or big trouble, I'll give a call, too."

"We'll do the same," Hannah said.

Chris shifted his weight from one side of his chair to the other, feeling uncomfortable. He had something on his mind and while he didn't want to bring it up, he had to. "Without the assistance of the police and the local Agency officers, there's a strong possibility we'll find ourselves in over our heads on this mission. What's our E & E going to be?"

"We can make our way through the city to the nearest taxi or hot-wire a car, and after we're sure we've lost any tails, rendezvous in the Gulfstream at Luton Airport," Sonny said. "The plane is still there, right?"

Hannah nodded. "It's still there, waiting for us."

"If I'm with one or both of you," Chris said, "I'll be happy to E & E with you through the city, but if I end up alone for whatever reason, I'll be safest escaping through the water before trying to make it back to the plane."

"The water?" Sonny asked.

"The River Thames," Chris said.

Sonny shrugged and started to gather his things. "Whatever floats your boat."

When Hannah and Sonny were both properly geared up, they headed out into the city to search for clues as to Xander's whereabouts.

Chris settled into his surveillance routine. He used binoculars to take a closer look and kept a notebook to record anything unusual, mostly vehicles and people, and a video time stamp, including as much detail as possible. As he watched, he got a feel for the flow of the area. At 0845, people on foot, riding bicycles, and driving cars seemed in a hurry to get to work. All pretty standard, but he watched for anyone or anything that didn't seem to fit the flow of the financial district.

One businessman stood out from the others on Duke of York Street. Although he wore a dark, conservative business suit similar to those around him, his pace was slower than the other businessmen, and instead of a tired, bored look on his face, he took in his surroundings like a tourist. In Chris's notebook, he nicknamed the man *Business Tourist*. The man walked along St. James Square, passing UKP before turning left on Charles II Street.

Later, the flow of traffic slowed, and the number of people on the streets thinned out significantly. In the afternoon, they became busy again as people went out for lunch and then calmed down again. Tourists, dressed in casual clothes and snapping photos, came and went at a leisurely pace. Chris compared morning and afternoon video, noting which vehicles and people stayed and which didn't.

Near 1700 hours, pedestrians, bicycles, and cars clogged up the streets with their movement. Hannah and Sonny returned, and over dinner they each reported their findings for the day. Neither of them had seen any sign of Xander or his goons. Likewise, Chris briefed them on his day. The trio also watched BBC News together, so they knew what was going on in the world around them.

The next morning, Hannah and Sonny were out beating the streets again as Chris stayed behind on surveillance, and then Business Tourist appeared again. He had his hand in his pocket today, but it wasn't just resting there. It was moving. Business Tourist could be concealing a piece of paper and a golf pencil, so he could write notes in his pocket, a tactic Chris had learned in training but hadn't put to use. Or the movement in his pocket could be some kind of remote signaling device. Or it could be a nervous tic, fumbling with his keys. Once again, Business Tourist passed in front of UKP.

Chris's gut told him the man was up to no good. Was he working for Xander? He could call Hannah and Sonny to tail him, but by the time they arrived, Business Tourist would be gone. Chris had to find out more, but he couldn't do that sitting in the office. The surveillance video on his monitor was being recorded, and that would have to do until he returned.

Chris quickly put on a tie and grabbed a suit jacket. He bolted downstairs, struggling to put the jacket on. Each step caused his shoulder and ankle discomfort. When he reached the bottom, he proceeded out of the building at a businessman's pace, ignoring the pain.

Blend with your surroundings. I am a businessman.

As he walked, he took a deep breath to calm himself. *Breathe.* He took another. He wanted to call Hannah and tell her what he was doing, but he didn't want to risk drawing Business Tourist's attention.

Business Tourist wasn't in front of UKP anymore, and Chris had to restrain himself from cursing out loud. But then the man appeared, strolling northwest on Charles II Street. Chris followed, on the opposite side of the street, keeping at least two people between himself and his target. The bustling crowds that worked to Business Tourist's advantage for blending in and moving also worked to Chris's advantage. Even so, tailing a moving subject on the street would be more challenging than sitting in an office observing the area round UKP. Now, not only did Chris have to keep up with his target, he also had to avoid being detected by him.

At the corner, Business Tourist looked both ways before crossing. It was possible he was just an average citizen trying to be safe, but if he was trained in countersurveillance, he'd use the technique to discreetly check for a tail. The subject crossed the street—if Chris crossed the street at that moment, he would mark himself as possible surveillance. However, the man had traversed over to the same side of the street as Chris.

So far, so good.

Even though Chris's thought process was calm, his heart raced and his skin became warm.

After passing Regent Street, more people were dressed casually, mixing with those in business attire. Business Tourist stopped at a bus stop and stood in line for a red double-decker bus. Chris's pulse kicked into hyper drive. It would be too much of a coincidence for him to stand in the same line, and walking past would give his subject a close-up view of him. But crossing the street, away from the target, would be marked movement.

Chris chose the lesser of the tactical evils and walked past Business Tourist, managing to keep one person between them. Now Business Tourist was behind him. He would be able to see Chris, but Chris couldn't see him. Chris faced straight ahead, but his eyes frantically searched the environment for something that would allow him to avoid the appearance of loitering, but not so far away as to lose the opportunity to re-sume tailing the man.

The Royal Opera Arcade appeared to his right, and Chris turned and entered. Both sides of the walkway were lined with upscale shops, and he spotted people around a sandwich shop so he joined them. Feigning indecision about what to order, he let others pass in front of him, managing to keep one per-son between himself and Charles II Street at all times. Chris waited for the man or a red bus to pass.

Maybe the dude is just a regular guy, and I'm on a wild-goose chase, here.

What seemed like half an hour was only a few minutes. Business Tourist turned into the arcade.

He never got on the bus. He was just getting in line in order to detect surveillance.

Chris wanted to move deeper into the store and hide, but the sudden movement would attract more attention than if he stood still. With each closing step Business Tourist took, Chris's pulse pounded harder. There was a guy with a thick white moustache between Chris and Business Tourist. He hoped the cover of Mr. Moustache was enough. Then Business Tourist passed, and Chris was certain he was up to no good.

He exited the opposite end of the arcade, and Chris followed. Then the subject went southeast for a couple of blocks. Again, he looked both ways before crossing each street. Soon, he arrived at St. James Park, east of Buckingham Palace.

Chris's heart sank. At this early hour, there were few people in the park for Chris to blend in with and conceal himself behind. And the park paths branched out in multiple directions, allowing his target myriad escape routes. Chris could either follow close and stick out as surveillance or he could follow from a distance and risk losing his mark. There was the option of doing a snatch-and-grab in broad daylight, but transporting a prisoner the distance to Chris's office without the assistance of teammates or the use of a vehicle was impractical. There was also the possibility his subject didn't work for Xander at all. Maybe Business Tourist was simply a thief, casing the area.

Chris chose to follow from a distance and was able to monitor his subject until he turned into Green Park, where the paths were more numerous and the trees denser. He had to close the gap soon, or he was going to lose him.

Business Tourist shifted into a faster walk, and Chris picked up his pace just before his target disappeared behind some trees. *Aw, hell!*

When he reached the point where Business Tourist disappeared, all he could see were trees and paths. Chris chose one of the diverging paths and followed it, but his target was nowhere to be found. He abandoned it and chose another, but that path was dry, too. If the guy was watching, Chris's actions would definitely appear suspicious. He searched until he came to the edge of the city.

Maybe I'm being paranoid.

As he turned down a gloomy alley to find a shortcut back to his crew's rented office, two white men in their early twenties approached from the opposite direction, smiling and joking with each other. They looked like twins, except one had a fuller face and smoked a cigarette and the other wore glasses. Both wore suits with their necktie knots loosened. They talked loudly about having stayed up all night and teased as to whether they should get some sleep or stay up all day, too.

They seemed comfortable in the shadowed alley, and from what Chris could tell of their ages, they should be in college or working their first jobs. The twins stared at Chris like they were looking through him—a way evil men had stared through him before—and he contemplated turning around and leaving the alley. But if these two were indeed bad men, Chris didn't want to flee like a wounded fish flapping around in the presence of sharks. There were no CCTVs in the alley, and it would be inconspicuous enough to resolve any problems here.

Chris greeted them with a nod, and they nodded back, but when he tried to pass him, they blocked him.

"Could you help us, sir?" the one wearing glasses asked.

Chris raised his eyebrows at the kid. "What do you need help with?"

"We need some money," the one smoking a cigarette said. Glasses laughed.

Chris shoved past them and walked briskly forward.

"Hey!" one of them called out, and the sound of their footsteps rushed after him.

He didn't want this to spill out into the open, so he stopped and turned around. "I have some important business to take care of, so I'd appreciate it if you could get to the point."

Cigarette removed the tobacco from his mouth and mocked Chris's American accent. Then Glasses pulled out a switchblade and flicked the blade open. "This is the point. Give us all your money. Now!"

They both smiled.

"No, *this* is the point," Chris said, and he fast-drew his pistol and aimed it at the chest of Glasses.

Their smiles dropped. Glasses took a step back and said, "Hang on, now. I was just playing."

"How do we know that's a real gun?" Cigarette asked.

"I don't want to make noise, but if you insist..." Chris aimed his Glock at Cigarette's crotch.

The kid threw up his hands and backed away. "Hey, we don't want any trouble, man. We'll go our way and you go yours."

Glasses folded the blade back into the handle of his switchblade. "See? No trouble."

Chris put his pistol back into its holster, concealed once more by his suit jacket. This time, when he resumed his journey out of the alley, the twins didn't follow.

With no clues as to where Business Tourist had gone, Chris returned to his static surveillance post. There, he tried to ignore the nagging reminder he'd lost his target. He reviewed the surveillance video recorded while he was out, simultaneously watching the live feed.

Nothing.

That evening, when Hannah and Sonny returned, he told them what had transpired. As he was showing them the surveillance video, Hannah raised a finger. "Didn't we see that guy in the lobby of one of the hotels yesterday?"

"What guy?" Sonny asked.

She pointed to the image of Business Tourist. "That guy."

"We saw so many people and so many lobbies," Sonny said.

"I've seen him, too. That's who I was following this morning." Chris rubbed the back of his head, frustrated. "He could've been reporting to Xander. You could've found Xander's hotel."

Hannah inputted something into her cell phone. "I wish I could remember which hotel we were in."

As they watched the rest of the recorded video of Business Tourist on one monitor, movement in the live-feed monitor caught their eyes. A marked police car picked up the uniformed officer in front of UKP, and the van with the dark windows rolled away.

"The police are pulling out," Chris said.

Next, the plainclothes security officer disappeared inside UKP.

"Wow," Sonny said. "If that ain't an official invitation for Xander to strike, it'll do 'til the invitation arrives."

"Maybe all three of us should stick around here for a while," Hannah suggested.

Chris and Sonny agreed.

Later, when they watched the news, the local weather forecaster came on the screen with a special report.

"A low pressure system is blowing in from the North Sea, and there will be high tides along the coast and heavy rains inland. The Thames

Barrier is being closed to protect the city. We'll keep an eye on the storm and keep you updated..."

Chris shook his head. "When it rains, it pours."

17

That night, in a roomy two-car garage of a safe house outside of London, Xander showed Animus how to construct a homemade car bomb. They placed boards inside the back of the van that would carry the explosives, then drilled the boards to the floor in order to keep the thirteen barrels stable while transporting them to the target area.

"Now we need to fill each bucket with the right amount of explosive," Xander said. His face was blank, emotionless, as they worked.

"Can I ask a personal question?" Animus asked.

Xander poured Tovex into a plastic bucket and weighed it with the scale to make sure it was the correct amount. "Yes," he said after a moment.

Animus couldn't contain the anger in his heart, and it overpowered his voice, making it tremble. "This has all become so ugly. How do you keep from being consumed by it?"

After adjusting the amount of Tovex in the bucket, Xander emptied it into one of the fifty-five-gallon barrels. "I am not sure I understand."

Animus tried to mimic Xander's calm and even manner, and measured the next amount of Tovex before pouring it into a barrel. "I feel so much rage at these Americans, and it's driving me crazy."

"Rage is good," Xander said. "Rage fulfills destiny."

"You lost your wife and daughter, yet now you seem so calm. I don't understand how you do it."

"It is the calm before the storm," Xander said. "Success is my revenge."

"Success?"

"I am not half-Greek like you, but you are half-Russian like me, and as Russians, we know how to immerse ourselves in fighting the West and delusions of glasnost and perestroika. I know you can feel what I am saying is true. Together, you and I will crush the American and his allies. Our success will be our revenge."

Animus nodded.

They completed portioning the Tovex into each of the barrels. Then they distributed liquid nitromethane, diesel fuel, and ammonium nitrate fertilizer into each of the drums. "Now we need to shape the charge," Xander explained. "We will pack the rest of the fertilizer around the explosives, leaving one wall of the van empty. When the bomb explodes, it will blast through the area of least resistance, the empty wall. That will be the one facing UKP headquarters. Because the blast will be directed in one direction, we will be able to post our little army around the area, using trees in the park for cover, to make sure no one defuses it. Anyone who survives the blast and tries to escape the building, we will shoot."

"Will this destroy the whole building?" Animus asked.

"It will destroy much of the first floor," Xander said, "and I hope the unsupported weight of the building will make the rest of it collapse. After the explosion, we'll sweep through St. James Square and shoot everyone we see." He duct-taped two PVC pipes to the floor, running from the explosives to the driver's seat. He grimaced and pulled so hard on the tape it looked as if he was strangling it. Then he slashed the tape with his knife. "Five years ago, on the twenty-first of December, the West was responsible for the death of my wife."

"It is why we call ourselves 21D," Animus said, repeating what Xander had told him previously. "In her memory."

"It is time to remember her again. And Evelina." He smothered the pipes with paint to blend with the color of the van's floorboards. "It is time for the *pogrom*." It is time for the massacre.

Then he stabbed a fuse through one of the pipes. "Now you do the other."

Seeing Xander's acrimony bleed through to the surface made Animus's heart wrench for the man and increased his desire to triumph in their mission. He ran the second fuse through the other pipe.

"Excellent," Xander said. "We'll join one end of each fuse to the thirteen blasting caps, which will connect to tubes of Tovex that will detonate the explosives in each barrel. And we'll hook up a detonator to the driver's side of the fuse."

"Why two fuses, then?" Animus asked.

"Just in case one does not work properly. In Moscow we say, 'If you are going for a day trip, take a week's supply of bread.'"

"I'm with you to the death," Animus said.

"The death will be theirs. Then we can begin Phase Three.

18

At 0745, Business Tourist appeared. Chris, Sonny, and Hannah geared up, and the guys took positions in St. James Square, Chris on foot and Sonny in a vehicle, while Hannah provided surveillance from the office. When a three-van motorcade turned down Duke of York Street, Sonny cut them off and pretended to have car trouble, so he could take a peek at who was in the motorcade.

The men in the vans and Business Tourist began shooting, and Chris and Sonny defended themselves. The lead van sped forward and hit Sonny's "stalled" vehicle with a smack and pushed Sonny's car out of the way before turning onto St. James Square and proceeding toward UKP. The van behind it, riddled with bullets from Chris and Sonny, rolled forward into the intersection but didn't make the turn. A black taxi sped around the square and plowed into the van with a horrific metal *crack*, smashing the front of the taxi and knocking the van over on its side. The taxi driver appeared to be pinned between the steering wheel and his seat. He wasn't moving.

Behind the first two vans, the third van didn't go any-where, but Xander and nine of his men—armed with AK-47 assault rifles—poured out of the tail of the vehicle. Chris tried to take a shot, but Xander ducked back behind the van before he could squeeze the trigger.

Sonny was vulnerable standing in the open without any cover or concealment, and he must have seen how outnum-bered he was, because he sprinted toward Chris, who covered him by laying down suppressive fire into Xander's group.

The first van had stopped in front of UKP. Its back doors flew open, and Animus and an armed gang of close to a dozen appeared.

Xander and his men faced Chris and fired at him from near the third van.

Sonny jumped over a fence surrounding the park area, and just after he weaved into the trees, an explosion lifted the tipped-over van completely off the street. The earth quaked, Sonny stumbled, and a geyser sprouted up out of the ground, spewing chunks of asphalt with it.

"Chris!" a voice screamed from the chaos. *Xander.* "I know you are here. I will find you, and I will kill you!"

A number of pedestrians had cleared out of the area, but some stragglers remained.

"I got your back," Hannah said, but her voice came from both Chris's earpiece and behind him. He glanced over his shoulder to see her there, HK416 at the ready. He didn't have the luxury of concern for her safety and was happy to have another gun in the fight.

Through Old Faithful, Chris spotted one of Xander's men, armed with an AK, as he executed a civilian. Chris put his red dot on the man with the AK and squeezed, and Sonny fired at another enemy armed with an AK. Two down.

Somebody from Xander's group fired in Chris's direction, but his shots struck nowhere near Chris. "They're shooting at civilians!" he shouted.

While the loud noise of the AK gave away the shooter's position, the SOG trio were using sound suppressors. Any sounds from their shots dissipated quickly, disguising their true location. A businessman stood in front of UKP petrified with fear, and a businesswoman tried to crawl to safety, but Xander's group approached steadily, blasting through them. There were too many bad guys and not enough good guys.

To the right, Animus's team seemed confused. Maybe they didn't understand why the other two vehicles in their three-van convoy hadn't joined them. Hannah whacked one of Animus's men, causing Animus and the others to hunker down.

The two groups of enemy combatants were each fifty meters away. Although Xander was probably deadlier than Animus, the younger man had a few more men by his side. Chris helped Hannah fire on Animus's group. The airy *pop-pop* of Sonny's carbine let Chris know Sonny was taking care of business, too.

One of Animus's men poked his head out from behind the van, and Chris poked it back with a bullet to the skull. It was a damn good shot, and Chris felt proud. While he anticipated another target presenting itself, a flow of water swept over his shoes. The broken main and rainwater were flooding in his team's direction.

Animus and his men moved out from behind the van and toward Chris. He aimed for Animus, who passed in behind a tree, and Chris lost his shot.

The police sirens were so loud it sounded like the area was surrounded, but Chris hadn't spotted a single officer or vehicle.

In Chris's peripheral vision, Xander's men continued to advance. Defending two flanks against so many combatants seemed impossible, but Chris spotted a beefy guy with an AK and took a shot. His aim was to the right and struck the man in the shoulder, spinning him. It wasn't enough to kill him, but maybe it was enough to put him out of action, at least for now.

A violent torrent of gunfire rang out from both Animus's and Xander's directions, causing the air around Chris to buzz and crackle as the projectiles zipped by. One bullet slammed the tree so close to his face he felt the shock wave in his teeth.

"Infidel," he said, using Hannah's call sign, "we can't hold them off much longer. You and Sunshine stand by to fall back."

"Roger," Hannah said.

Sonny grunted.

A round clipped the wool in Chris's suit, grazing his flesh.

"Fall back," Chris said. He fired three rapid shots in Animus's direction and then three in Xander's, trying to keep their heads down until Hannah and Sonny could find protected positions to the rear. Then he swung back to Animus and delivered three more shots.

All the enemy bullets seemed focused on Chris now, and the air burst next to his skin. When he heard Hannah and Sonny's weapons open fire—that was his signal—he wasted no time turning and running.

The water seemed deeper now, slowly pushing him toward Hannah and Sonny. It was better than being pushed backward, but each time he lifted a leg to move, the water sapped his movement and energy, causing him to decelerate. With bullets blistering the space around him, his upper body frantically tried to move faster than his legs could carry him, and he fell. A shit storm of lead blasted above, barely missing him. He desperately longed for Mother Ocean to wrap her cloak around him for protection.

Hannah and Sonny raised the bang of their firepower, giving Chris a moment's break from the onslaught. He hopped to his feet and retreated to a spot behind their position. He used a tree for cover and blasted at Xander and his men. Hannah and Sonny took that as their cue to get up and hurry to the rear. The purpose of the leapfrog was to break contact with the enemy, but the bad guys were gaining on Chris's crew, regardless.

Both Xander's and Animus's men had converged in the park and seemed hell-bent on annihilating Chris, Hannah, Sonny, and anyone else still alive in the park.

"Give up now, Chris, and I'll let you live!" Xander called.

Thanks, but no thanks.

Hannah and Sonny fired at Xander, so Chris rose to his feet again and retreated in their direction. His lungs burned from the exertion, and he'd strained for oxygen so much he thought he'd puke. Sloshing through the water as he ran, his M4 was out of ammo, and he changed magazines. A tree stood in his path, and he veered around, the tree taking a bullet-pummeling from the enemy.

Once Chris was past Hannah and Sonny's position, the firing around the trio became too grave for him to remain standing, even with a tree for cover, so Chris dropped down on a knee in the water, peeked around the tree, and returned fire. Bullets struck the liquid surrounding him. He was only moments away from being overrun. The streets, sidewalks, and park were littered with bodies. A man with a broken ankle ran away, his ankle flopping, and he fell repeatedly trying to flee the area.

As Chris's teammates raced to the rear, and with no help in sight, he felt alone in what were surely his final moments.

Lord, where are You?

He busted caps in Xander's and Animus's directions.

If it's my time to go, I'll go, but please help the others.

A voice called out on a megaphone from Xander's direction, but it was a garbled mess, and Chris couldn't understand what was said. Gunshots rang out behind Xander's crew. Then Chris distinguished one word from the megaphone. "Police!"

Xander's gang broke off firing at Chris and his team and redirected at the police, who must've been behind Xander.

Chris took his cue to escape to a more secure location. He turned and quickly splashed through the water toward Hannah and Sonny. The water level continued to rise as he joined his friends in the southern end of the park. Farther south, outside the park, and across the street was a row of cheaply made twentieth-century buildings.

Chris caught his breath. "Let's give the police a hand."

"Done," Sonny said.

While Xander and his men duked it out with the police, Chris fired at the back of a man who looked like one of the Albanian thugs Chris encountered in Athens. Maybe he was Talos. Chris exhaled, and in the calm, quiet pause between emptying his lungs and filling them up again, he eased the slack out of his trigger. Then the satisfying recoil pushed against his shoulder. Talos arched his back, but he didn't go down. Chris took a second shot. This time, Talos fell with a splash.

The rain came down so thick and heavy that seeing with the naked eye became a challenge, and discriminating targets with his red dot was becoming impossible, so he hit the quick release on his scope, removed it, stuck it in his pocket, and flipped up his iron sights. As he did that, two more tangos went down. It wasn't clear whether Hannah and Sonny had nailed them or if the police had done them a favor, but bad guys down was a good thing.

Chris lined up his iron sights and snuffed another of Xander's men, and the momentum of the firefight began to shift in his team's favor. As the trio's weapons spit bullets, the empty metal casings of the spent cartridges flew out the ejection ports, making plopping sounds in the water around them. As a pastor, maybe he should have felt guilt at killing so many, but his life and the lives of those around him were in danger. And as an experienced frogman, he couldn't kill enough of Xander's clan. Not until every last one of them was dead.

The beefy guy Chris had shot in the shoulder earlier came into his field of vision. This time, Chris had more time to focus—*pop!*—and beefy guy went down and stayed there.

The precipitation continued as Chris and his teammates knocked out the enemy one by one. Three more tangos splashed down, reducing Xander and Animus's men to roughly a dozen combined. The success boosted Chris's concentration, and he squeezed the trigger with calm gusto. Hannah and Sonny seemed jacked up, too. The change in momentum had to have a demoralizing effect on Xander and Animus, but they didn't show it.

The gunshots from the police side subsided, and the enemies turned on Chris, Hannah, and Sonny. In spite of Chris's team whittling down their numbers, Xander, Animus, and their men still outnumbered Chris's crew. They held their ground, but the enemies used trees for cover as they advanced, steadily closing the gap between them.

"This doesn't look good," Hannah said.

She was right. Behind them was a blocky twentieth-century building, an obstacle to their retreat. They could try to slip through one of the doors, but once inside, their movements would be constricted, and if the indoor shops were crowded, a gunfight would cause more civilian casualties. "Infidel and Sunshine, fall back around the west side of the building behind us. I'll cover."

They both bounded over the low fence surrounding the park and disappeared to the rear. The flooding water knocked over some parked bicycles nearby, and Chris let them float right on past as he focused on the enemy.

Xander's gang seemed uninhibited by Chris's fire, continuing to shoot and advance on him, so he flicked his selector switch to *full auto* and sprayed at them, hoping to discourage them from shooting at Hannah and Sonny. Steam rose from the heated barrel of Chris's carbine, and his bullet spray caused Xander and his men to direct their fire away from Hannah and Sonny, and give Chris their undivided attention. An enemy round struck the metal fence behind him, and bullets splashed the water, one striking his pant leg.

Bullets seemed to fly everywhere: left, right, above, below, front, and behind. One struck his chest, but one of the magazines of ammo in his vest stopped the round from striking flesh. The cell phone in his pocket exploded. Both the impact of the shot to the chest and his cell phone knocked him to the ground. He thought he felt the little communication bud fall out of his ear as he half-crawled away from the shots. He rose awkwardly to his feet, then a whizzing bullet ripped past his neck.

"You killed Evelina!" shouted Animus. "Now it's your turn to die!" His voice was so full of anger Chris's body faltered, weakness seeping into his muscles.

Snap out of it, Chris! he commanded himself.

Then his weapon ran dry and he had to move. As he ran, he repositioned his trigger finger and ejected the empty magazine, while with his other hand, he removed a full magazine from his vest and reloaded. He finished just before he jumped the fence between him and his retreat. Then he dashed across the street and bumped into a parked car, which stopped him before he could slow down.

A woman crawled through the water in his direction, seeking cover from the butchers. One of her legs appeared to be wounded. She wore a rose-colored dress that reminded him of one of the young women in his congregation back in Dallas. He grabbed her arm and pulled her to safety, using the vehicle as a shield. Like a flock of angry woodpeckers, bullets jabbed holes in the car. The woman shuddered and cried, but the rain came down so heavily Chris couldn't distinguish between the flow of rain on her face and tears. He desperately wanted to help her, but if he stayed where he was, they'd both surely die.

Above the terrible racket of gunfire and rounds hitting the vehicle, he said close to her ear, "Close your eyes and play dead. You're going to survive." It was a promise he'd made as a SEAL...more times than he cared to remember. Sometimes the promise was fulfilled, and sometimes it wasn't. It was a promise he couldn't guarantee. But whether the woman lived or died, she deserved hope. Everyone did.

Xander and his men must've guessed Chris would try to follow Hannah and Sonny around the west side of the building because Xander's gang blasted a hail of bullets in that direction, preventing him from meeting up with his team. He wanted to talk to Hannah and Sonny, tell them where he was going, find out if they were okay, but his cell phone had been obliterated in the firefight and his earpiece was gone.

One of Xander's men struggled to climb a section of metal fence surrounding the park, but he couldn't get over it. The half dozen or so who made it over the fence, or found the gate opening, came in Chris's direction just before he turned the building's east corner.

Breathe.

He sprinted with every part of his muscles he could muster, splashing as he ran. The water level seemed higher now, and it sucked his energy, but he tried to ignore it as he focused on picking up his thighs and putting them down, his legs like pistons.

Hannah and Sonny were nowhere in sight, but enemy shots came at him from behind. He cut sideways until he reached Carlton Street, where the groundwater became shallow, and raced south as swiftly as he could.

He arrived in St. James Park, a different location from the flooded park in St. James Square where he'd come from. He still didn't see Hannah and Sonny, but Animus and his men—numbering half a dozen—sloshed through the water after him. With the team split up and on the receiving end of superior firepower, there was no sense in pausing to look for one another and getting the whole team killed. Being split up had the added advantage of splitting up Xander's forces, but now Chris was on his own and had to escape. He switched into E & E mode and would try to make it to the River Thames. Hannah and Sonny would switch into E & E mode, too, pressing through the city.

There were a lot of civilians in the immediate area, some stopping and looking around. Chris was sure they'd heard the commotion up north, but these people had yet to find out what the noise was all about. He took cover behind a tree, turned towards Animus's men, aimed, and fired at the nearest enemy combatant, a barrel-chested man, stitching up his barrel. A pedestrian squealed.

Animus's men hid behind streetlamps, parked cars, trees—whatever was available. Animus only had a lamppost between him and Chris, so Chris took a shot, but he hit the post in front of Animus with a loud *thwang*, missing him. Chris *hoped* the near miss would slow Animus, but he *expected* it wouldn't.

People in the area shouted and ran for safety. Chris met up with a man who stood immobile with shock. Chris gave him a push. "Get down!"

The man fell out of Animus's line of fire. Off to the side, an older woman with white hair crouched down next to a man of similar age who was likely her husband, who was lying down. Chris couldn't tell if he was wounded or just being safe. He neared St. James Park Lake, and a woman wearing a dark skirt and jacket was running away from the shooting. She fell and hit the wet grass with a *smack*, but he wasn't sure if she'd tripped or been shot. She was too far away for him to help her, either way, and if he neared her, he'd bring Animus's wrath with him.

He tried to visualize a map of the area in his mind. The River Thames was about half a klick east.

If I can make it to the water, I can swim my way to safety. The water is my haven.

He ran past the lake, and as he came to a war memorial, he could see a dirt parade ground across the street and a massive building behind it. *Trapped.* To the right was the Cabinet Office and 10 Downing Street, where the prime minister resided. Police cars blocked off the street, and the officers were armed with submachine guns. They called out to Chris to drop his weapon and surrender, but with Animus so close to the north, he couldn't just stand in the open with his hands up, waiting to be killed.

In the distance was the London Eye, the enormous Ferris wheel standing over a hundred meters tall on the other side of the River Thames. Knowing he was close to the river lifted his spirit.

There has to be an opening somewhere...

Chris zigzagged between the trees, away from the police to the east. They opened fire. One bullet tore through the tail corner of his jacket and another ripped the heel off his right shoe, causing him to lose his balance. He tumbled and almost fell over. Police sirens, megaphones and shooting sounded from another area, but Chris couldn't focus on it.

He hoped Hannah and Sonny were okay, and he pressed forward harder, determined to get to rendezvous with them in one piece. He rounded the corner of the Ministry of Defense, where a police car screeched to a halt, and he ran past as two armed officers jumped out. They didn't shoot, probably out of concern for hitting innocent bystanders in the area. The sound of thumping footsteps came behind him. The police were chasing him, yelling at him to stop, which caused him to run faster. His thighs felt like gelatin, as if he had no more power in them. He wished again he'd done more physical training, but it was too late now. He almost turned right but realized it led to a dead end and continued straight, instead.

Shooting sounded behind him, but instead of the smaller caliber reports of police submachine guns, the shots were more like those of the larger caliber AK-47s. Chris glanced over his shoulder and one of the policemen had fallen... shot.

19

As Chris maneuvered through the streets, the sky continued to dump rain, and he wasn't sure where he was until he spotted a statue of King Charles I on a horse.

The center of London. Northumberland Avenue leads straight to the river.

Like most frogmen in deep danger, he headed for the water. If he could get to the river, he still had a chance of escaping death.

He hurried along Northumberland Avenue but couldn't see the river ahead.

Did I remember wrong? Is there another Northumberland Avenue?

Trees on both sides of the road formed a canopy overhead, blocking most of the skyline out. He ran a hundred meters, and he still couldn't see the water.

Lord help me, please.

Not knowing what else to do, he continued down the same road. The upper pylon of a bridge came into view. The more he ran, the more pylons appeared. Some pedestrians climbed the stairs while others crossed the bridge.

This has to be the place.

To his right was the London Eye—closer now.

I'm almost there.

It wasn't until he reached the intersection that he saw the River Thames. He didn't wait for a pedestrian sign to flash green and raced across the street. One driver honked at him, but he didn't care. On the other side of the road, he bounded over a wall. More honking behind him. Probably Animus's men. A loud *thump* sounded, followed by a cry of pain.

Chris hopped over another wall, stripped off his jacket as he neared the water, and dropped it on the ground. He didn't need his rifle and bullets weighing him down, so he threw his M4 in the river, and after tearing off his customized ammo-bearing vest, he threw it in, too, and both sank. His pistol still hung on his hip with some spare magazines of ammo, but they weren't enough to sink him significantly, and he kept them.

He dove in. With Animus and company close behind, he expected the shooting to resume at any moment. If he could swim three feet below water, and Animus and his men fired from the shore at about thirty-degree angles, the bullets couldn't kill him. Not wanting to leave anything to chance, he dove farther down and away from the embankment until he felt pressure on his ears and head. Thinking he had enough depth, he swam for distance.

Pop-pop went the AKs. Chris's cocoon of water mellowed their bangs. *Ploop-ploop* went the bullets as they hit the surface above. The River Thames put the brakes on each bullet, causing an aquatic audible *vzzz*. They sounded like zippers. He swam until his lungs ached for air, and then he swam some more. The current pulled him to the left, taking him east, and he went with it, happy to put more distance between Animus and himself. The outer edges of his vision became gray, and his head felt fuzzy. He needed oxygen, so he ascended slowly, but the gray edges of his vision became darker, and his vision closed smaller, becoming a tunnel. Now his need for oxygen was urgent. He swam harder toward the sky. His head broke the water's surface. With lips forming a tight circle, he sucked in a bite of oxygen, making his chest expand. Gunshots banged the air again, louder than they'd sounded underwater, but Chris couldn't sense where the shots landed. *Zing!* The sound was lighter than a heavy AK round and seemed to move more slowly, a ricochet, probably deflected by the water, like a skipping stone. If he'd been facing it, a ricochet could have put an eye out, but it wasn't likely to kill him. Even so, he didn't want a souvenir in the back of his head.

He dove underwater and swam again, but this time he didn't push so close to blacking out. And this time, when he came up for air, the shooting was farther away. The next time he dove, he realized he was shivering. He must've been shivering earlier, too, but now he noticed. His fingertips and ears were numb—even though one of his ears was a prosthetic replacement from an injury in Iraq, now he felt it, like a ghost appendage. His heart strained against the cold. As he tried to comprehend what was happening to his body, his thought processes seemed to slow down.

When he came up for oxygen the third time, he'd traveled well over a hundred meters, half the width of the river. And the current had taken him under the bridge and beyond. He turned to see where Animus and his goons were. Police had swarmed the area, but the tangos appeared to have fled.

The rain continued to dump on London. Chris's cold body trembled, and his respiration was shallow and quick. He tried to take slow, deep breaths, but his body resisted.

It wasn't a cold day, but having been out in the rain and swum the River Thames had resulted in a lot of wet time, which drowned the warmth in him. On top of that, he'd come down from his adrenaline high, causing his temperature to drop further. He'd burned through a lot of calories, and he didn't have much fuel left in his tank, so he was losing heat faster than he could replace it, experiencing hypothermia. Many people couldn't understand how someone could suffer from hypothermia on a summer day, but frogmen knew the danger all too well. In spite of the hypothermia threat, he wanted to make sure Animus and the police didn't know where he was, so he swam farther downstream past the next bridge.

A boat came his way, so he dove underwater to avoid getting chopped up by the propeller. He went straight down. The churning sound of the water became louder, and as he dove deeper, the water pressure squeezed his head. The boat's engine passed above him, and the rumbling noise in the water dissipated. Slowly he ascended, and he could taste fuel in the boat's wake.

Now his heart and lungs slowed their pace and the strain on his heart seemed to have lifted. At first he thought he'd succeeded in gaining control over himself, but something didn't seem right. As he tried to figure out what wasn't right, he experienced a mental fog. His arms and legs became less coordinated in the water, and he realized he was shivering violently—the hypothermia was worsening, and he needed to dry off. Soon.

Up ahead was a third bridge, or maybe it was the fourth—he was losing his ability to reason—and it was past time to head to shore. Still trying to keep a low profile, he continued underwater, rising up when he needed oxygen, until he made it to the other side.

Before coming out of the water, he realized he wasn't wearing a suit jacket to conceal the pistol and magazines on his belt, so he made sure his shirt and T-shirt were untucked, so they could cover his weapon and ammo.

He dragged himself out of the water and stumbled into the city, south of the River Thames. *Or am I headed north?* It was still raining, and it didn't seem to make much difference whether he froze to death in the river or in the rain. As he walked through street puddles, he felt like he was teleporting. He was at one street corner one moment and a different street corner the next. After doing this several times, he realized he was passing out as he walked, only to regain consciousness and find himself in a new spot.

Abruptly he stopped shivering—a bad sign. His outer body was shutting down while his core tried to stay warm. He wanted to strip off all his clothing, as if he could strip off the cold, but he wasn't thinking rationally. He feared his lungs and heart would stop.

Now he had little idea of why he was walking in the rain or where he was walking to, but part of him wanted to dig a hole, crawl inside, and lie down. The other part of him had a vague notion he needed to get warm—his survival depended on it. When he spotted a café, he realized he could seek shelter from the rain there and find something warm to drink.

He didn't remember stepping into the café or choosing a chair. Suddenly, he was just sitting at a table next to an unlit fireplace. He was the only customer. The waitress near him was a middle-aged platinum blonde, who welcomed him with a Scottish lilt and a universal smile. Her nametag read, *Catriona.*

"Something warm to drink, no caffeine, please," he said.

Catriona replied, but he couldn't focus on the words— probably giving him a choice of drinks? Then he realized there was a menu in front of him and a puddle of water on the floor around him, and he wondered how long he'd actually been sitting there.

He jumped forward in time again. Catriona nudged his shoulder. On the table sat a cup of liquid, steam rising from it. He grasped the handle. It was warm, and he lifted it until the rim of the cup touched his lips, and he tilted it back and drank. It was an herbal tea with a fruity taste he couldn't place. The heat traveled down his throat to his chest, slowly spreading through his body.

Catriona stood to one side of him, steadying his hand, helping him drink. On the other side, the fireplace was lit. The heat felt good. His clothes smoldered as the fire burned off the wetness.

"Have I been here long?" Chris asked her.

"Be careful you don't catch on fire."

"Thank you."

"I was afraid if you stopped drinking—" She glanced at a nearly empty glass teapot on the table. "Anyway, I'm happy you almost emptied it."

He smiled courteously, but he worried about Hannah and Sonny. Their escape-and-evasion plan was to return to the plane, and he hoped to still find them there. Chris tried to act casual as he rested his hands on his hips, checking for the firmness of his Glock and its magazines under his shirt. He sighed.

I'm still armed. Good.

Still, he had the uneasy feeling something was missing. He remembered ditching some of his kit in the River Thames. Before that, he lost his radio in the shootout in St. James Square. Then he touched his ear...

My prosthetic is gone!

Wet and with torn clothes and the heel missing from his shoe, he looked like a homeless man.

She seemed to sense he was concerned about something and gave him a small smile. "You don't have to pay for it."

The fireplace made one side of his clothes so hot his skin burned, so he turned his chair and heated the other side of his body. When that side became too hot, he turned again. As he made small talk with Catriona, he continued turning himself like meat on a grill until his clothes dried out.

His body didn't want to go back out in the rain, but his brain knew what needed to be done. "I need to get back to work."

"It's awfully wet out there."

"I wish I could stay. But my coworkers are depending on me."

She didn't seem to believe him. Maybe she thought he didn't have a real job. "Next time you come, you can bring them, too," she said kindly.

He thanked Catriona again, paid her, added a generous tip, and was on his way.

20

He took a taxi to a hotel on the outskirts of London, and in order to conceal his final destination from the driver, he changed to another taxi that took him an hour north to Luton Airport. After the second driver dropped him off at an office building near the airport, Chris waited until the taxi was gone before walking a block to his actual destination, a private hangar where the Agency's jet rented space under a nondescript name.

He climbed aboard the plane thinking he might be the first person to make it back to the rally point. The pilot was already onboard, and Chris was pleasantly surprised to see Hannah sitting there, drying her hair with a towel. She looked up at him, and her countenance brightened.

"Enjoy your tour of London?" she teased.

"I'm happy you're okay, too." He scanned the interior of the plane. "Where's Sonny?"

She continued to dry her hair. "Number Three."

"Number Three?"

She shrugged. "That's what he said."

Aft of the plane, the toilet flushed, and Sonny stepped out. "Ahh, I feel five pounds lighter." Sonny stared wide-eyed at Chris. "Dude, where is your ear?"

Chris had thought Sonny knew he had a prosthetic, but he guessed not. "Lost it," Chris said nonchalantly.

He passed Sonny and went to his baggage where he dug in and pulled out a spare ear. He affixed it to his head via the internal magnet that grabbed hold of the metal plate in his skull. When he looked up, Sonny was still staring.

Sonny turned to Hannah while pointing at Chris. "Did you see that?"

Hannah already knew about Chris's prosthetic, and she gestured, *So what?*

Chris took a seat, joining them.

"What happened to your rifle?" Sonny asked.

Chris explained.

"Sounds like Animus and his goons have taken a liking to you," Sonny said. "You're going to need a new M4 and phone."

"I'll make the arrangements," Hannah said. "And see if William can do some more cleaning up after us."

"What about you all? How'd you escape Xander?" Chris asked.

"Xander got bogged down in a shootout with the police," Hannah said.

Sonny grinned. "And we used the opportunity to slip away and find a taxi. Changed taxis at a nearby shopping center and came here. I imagine Xander isn't too pleased about us breaking up his little party."

"I'll be happier when we kill or capture him," Chris said. "And I don't think he's going to let us capture him."

"You want to kill him, don't you?" Sonny asked.

"Xander has killed a lot of people: in Greece when William was working for MI6, Michael in Athens, and all those innocent civilians here in London. And there's bound to have been killing we don't know about, too. People like Xander deserve two to the chest and one to the head," Chris said. "If he's willing to surrender, I'm willing to capture him. But I won't hold my breath waiting for that to happen."

"I'll do whatever it takes to get him off the streets," Hannah said. "If you guys were Xander, what would your next move be?"

"I'm not sure," Chris said. "It'll be harder for him to obtain explosives locally now."

"And if he obtains them from a foreign source, they'll be more difficult to smuggle into London," Sonny said. "Not impossible, but harder."

Chris nodded. "Law enforcement and media will be all over the target area."

"Making it more of a challenge for him to run surveillance and get into position to hit UKP," Sonny said.

"If I were him, I'd get out of Dodge until Dodge cooled off." Chris gestured toward his body. "Speaking of... I'm pretty drenched here, so..."

Hannah handed Chris a towel.

"Thanks." He dried his face.

Hannah's phone rang, and she answered. "Hello?" There was a pause as she seemed to listen. "They're here with me. We're all okay."

Hannah put the speaker on, and Young's voice came through. "You three had me worried. That shootout in London was insane."

"It was," she said. "What's up?"

"We just received a report that 21D claimed responsibility for the attack in London and said the attacks would continue if UKP didn't stop construction of TAP in Greece. The police apprehended two men armed with AK47s. Both were severely wounded and are still in critical condition. Neither fit the description of Xander or Animus."

She shook her head. "That's not good."

"It gets worse," Young said. "You know Xander's laptop? The one you and Sonny accessed and connected me to?"

"Yes..."

"Before I lost the connection, I was able to salvage some of the deleted internet activity, and I discovered he was using a public real-time satellite tracking website, called MarineFinder.com. We hacked into his account there, but he'd become inactive on the website and he left no record of his activity."

"How does that help us now?" she asked.

"Well, now Xander's account is active again."

"That seems to confirm the police don't have him in custody," Hannah said.

"We're monitoring his activity on the account, and he seems to be researching ports and ships in the Caspian Sea around Baku... in Azerbaijan."

"Why would he be interested in Azerbaijan and the Caspian Sea?"

A clicking sound came from Young's end, as if he was using a mouse. "UKP has ships there. It's the source of natural gas for the Southern Gas Corridor that runs all the way to Turkey, up to where the newly constructed Trans Adriatic Pipeline would carry the gas across Greece."

"Sounds like Xander is planning to hit UKP again," Sonny said.

"This time in Azerbaijan," Chris said. "Near the source of the natural gas."

"If that's his plan, we should organize a proper welcoming party for him," Sonny said.

"I can't say with surety Azerbaijan is his next target," Young said. "I can only pass along the intel and analysis as it becomes available."

"I understand," Hannah said into the phone. "Do you have a more likely target he might hit? Or hints of another target he might be looking at?"

"No," Young said. "Not at this time."

Sonny shifted uncomfortably in his seat. "We can't just sit here with our thumbs up our asses waiting to react after Xander makes his next attack."

"Then Azerbaijan it is," Hannah said. "The station chief there is a good man, and the Azeris have been supportive in the past. I'll ask him if we can expect cooperation from the locals." After thanking Young and ending the call, she stood, walked to the cockpit, and talked with the pilot.

A screech sounded as the plane hit the ground, stirring Chris from a nap and pulling his body forward. He opened his eyes to find Hannah and Sonny had fallen asleep in their seats, too. It was dark outside the plane window, except for lights on the airfield, other planes, and the terminal. *This is small for an international airport*, Chris thought, then he recognized it as Azerbaijan's military airport. He'd flown into it before on his way to Iraq. Azerbaijan allowed the US to land its planes and use its airspace during the wars with Iraq and Afghanistan. The military ties between Azerbaijan and the US were strengthened and expanded under Secretary of the Navy Ray Mabus. In the Caspian basin, with Russia to the north and Iran to the south, Azerbaijan was America's only friend.

Chris checked his watch—he'd slept for over five hours. He nudged Hannah and Sonny. "We're here."

They both jolted to attention, and all three pulled themselves together for the mission ahead as the pilot taxied. Finally, the plane came to a stop and the ground crew rolled up an air ladder. A van pulled up, stopped near the stairs, and a man stepped out of the driver's side.

Chris and the others grabbed their luggage and exited the plane. The local wind was so strong Chris thought it might blow him off the ladder, but he reached the bottom safely, where the man greeted them.

Hannah introduced the man as Mikhail from the Azerbaijan Ministry of National Security, the MNS. He had piercing black eyes, a thick stump for a neck, and cauliflower ears, indicating he was experienced with violence, possibly from practicing a martial art like judo, boxing, or playing a sport like rugby. Taking a hit to the ear could cause fluids to clot, killing part of the ear and leaving it permanently deformed. The cauliflower shape was a source of pride to some, but Chris felt no pride or shame in his missing ear. He preferred to keep his wounds private and wear his prosthetic consistently.

After loading everyone and their bags into the van, Mikhail sped off. Once off the base, he drove even faster. "We've alerted the local authorities about Xander Metaxas,

Animus Zacharoff, and their clan, and we're helping cover possible infiltration points," he said. "So far, there've been no reports of Xander or his men trying to enter Azerbaijan."

"The authorities in London were on the lookout for him, too," Sonny said. "Fat lot of good that did."

"But your superiors are more cooperative than America's seat-hugger in London," Hannah said to Mikhail.

"Our chief is a good man," he said. "But I must warn you he is worried about a possible leak in the police department, so the police don't know you're here or what you're doing. Only those inside MNS with proper clearance are aware of our mission."

They each agreed. It wasn't an uncommon thing to keep operations like this on a need-to-know basis.

Half an hour later, they were downtown. Although the military base wasn't much to look at, Baku was. Its modern skyscrapers boasted a variety of shapes and lines illuminated in fluorescent oranges, glacier whites, sparkling emeralds, and blue-blues, their reflections floating on Baku Bay. The parks reminded him of those in London. They passed what looked like a grand hotel, but Mikhail explained it was the Government House, where many of Azerbaijan's central government ministries were housed. "This is the control center for public expression and assembly," he said with sarcasm in his voice. "Paid for by oil and gas and corruption."

He stopped in the parking lot of an upscale apartment complex. "Here we are." After they stepped out of the van, Mikhail, carrying a guitar case, led them to an apartment on the first floor, unlocked the door, and let them inside.

"Welcome to the safe house," Mikhail said. "Make yourselves at home." It was a newer four-bedroom apartment with vaulted ceilings and granite countertops, matching the upscale neighborhood outside. Mikhail handed Hannah the keys and said, "I'm here to support you in any way I can." Then he gave the guitar case to Chris.

He opened it, and inside was an M4 like the one he ditched in the River Thames. And an iPhone. "Thank you."

"Langley asked us to give these to you," Mikhail said. "It was a bit short notice, but I hope these meet your needs."

Chris held up the M4. "Looks like a showstopper." There were magazines filled with ammo, too.

Mikhail excused himself to use the restroom, and Chris closed the guitar case before pointing to Hannah's laptop. "Mind if I borrow that?"

"Knock yourself out." She sat on the stuffed sofa in the living room, set the laptop on the low table in front, and turned it on. Chris sat next to her, and while he waited for her to fire it up and enter her password, he used a secure line on his iPhone to call Young.

After several rings, Young answered. "Hey, brother. I tried to edit your team out of public CCTV files in London, but there were some cameras I couldn't access."

The computer was on and the desktop showing, and Hannah slid over so Chris could take her place in front of it. He opened the web browser while he spoke into the phone. "Thanks," he said. "We're in Baku now."

"Wow, you three didn't waste time."

"You know the Marine Traffic website Xander was studying?" Chris asked, pulling up the site on the laptop.

"Of course."

"Can you tell me what ships he was looking at?"

"I can compile a list, yeah. Can I call you back?" Young asked.

"Yes, I'd appreciate it." Chris ended the call, and using Marine Finder, he located Baku and examined it. "Okay... Here in Baku Bay, there are four Azeri passenger ships, seven Azeri oil tankers, a dozen other Azeri vessels, two Iranian cargo ships, and a Russian river cruise ship called the *M/S Pyotr Tchaikovsky*."

Hannah looked over his shoulder. "It's doubtful Xander would attack an Iranian ship and cause unnecessary conflict," she said. "And it's not clear what purpose could be achieved by attacking one of the dozen other ships."

Sonny joined them. "The best targets are the Azeri oil tankers or, except for the *M/S Pyotr Tchaikovsky*, the passenger ships."

"If Xander wants to attack UKP-related targets, the oil tankers would make the most sense," Chris said.

"Yeah, but if he wants hostages or a lot of collateral damage, he might go for one of the non-Russian passenger ships," Sonny said. "Take 'em out all at once..."

21

Chris's cell phone rang, waking him. He'd fallen asleep on the couch in the Azerbaijan safe house, and the morning sun shone through the curtains. Mikhail was wide-awake sitting on a wooden stool at the kitchen counter and looking at his cell phone. Sonny lay on the floor snoring. Young's name showed in the caller ID.

"Hello," Chris answered.

Young's voice was full of excitement. "In Xander's Marine Finder account, he saved the names of four ships. All Azeri oil tankers."

"What were the names of the ships?" Chris asked.

"*Babek, Shusha, Binagadi*, and *Zengezur*."

"Anything else?"

"That's all I got," Young said.

"That narrows it down for us. Can you maintain a monitor on the Marine Finder account and keep us updated of any new activity?"

"Will do."

"Thanks, brother."

"Later."

Young ended the call, and Chris dragged himself into the kitchen. "Were you awake all night?" Chris asked Mikhail as he entered.

"Figured you guys could use some sleep," he said, "so I stood the watch."

"Thank you," Chris said. "Want some breakfast? We could use a good meal."

Mikhail smiled and nodded.

Chris rummaged in the refrigerator looking for something to cook. After spotting eggs and cheese, he decided on omelets. There were plenty of tomatoes, bell peppers, and onions, so he grabbed those. Searching for ham, he found none and remembered Azerbaijan was a Muslim country and eating swine was *haram*, unlawful. So he snagged some ground beef instead.

"Do you want help?" Mikhail asked as he put away his phone. "I can set the table. I can also make toast, but you don't want me to cook anything else. Trust me."

"Sure," Chris said with a chuckle. "Thanks."

Soon, Hannah came into the kitchen, yawning and her hair a mess, but as beautiful as ever. "That smells good. We're going to have to change your call sign to the Galloping Gourmet," she said.

Breakfast was ready, so Chris walked into the living room and gave Sonny a playful kick. "Wake up, sweet pea."

"Hey," Sonny complained, rolling over to face away from Chris, but he must've smelled the food because he sat up and said, "Breakfast!"

They all sat around the table and began to talk about their next moves while they ate.

"If Xander succeeded in slipping into the country," Mikahil started, "he could try to board a ship here in the Baku Bay, or forty-five klicks south of here is Sangachal Terminal, where they process the natural gas and produce oil. It'll be a lot easier to board the ships in port than at sea."

"We could recon both, familiarize ourselves with the area, until we figure out exactly what his plans are," Chris said, washing his food down with some water.

"We should prep most of our gear in the SUV," Sonny said, "so at a moment's notice we'll be ready for a variety of contingencies."

They all agreed.

Chris shared their call signs with Mikahail. "Infidel, Sunshine, and Reverend."

"My call sign is Jirtdan, but English speakers call me Dirt Dan," Mikhail explained.

"Does Jirtdan have a special meaning?" Chris asked.

"In Azeri, it means *little*. There is a fairy tale about a small boy named Jirtdan who helps his friends escape a monster by crossing the river. When the monster asked Jirtdan how they crossed the river, Jirtdan pointed to a millstone with a hole in it and said, 'We held that over our heads as a life preserver to help us cross.' When the monster held the boulder over his head like a life preserver, he drowned, and Jirtdan became a hero."

"I like Jirtdan better than Dirt Dan," Hannah said, smiling.

After cleaning up, they prepared to go out low profile, armed only with pistols on their person and keeping their rifles tucked away in the back of the SUV. Soon they exited the condo, and Mikhail drove them in a gray Toyota Prado SUV. Many of the vehicles on the streets of Baku were SUVs.

The four of them did a recon of Baku Bay, and in the afternoon they ventured the forty-five klicks south, remaining on the Caspian seacoast, to Sangachal Terminal, where there was a complex of pumps, storage tanks, and support buildings. That evening, they checked out both locations again. Chris took notes as he tried to put himself in Xander's shoes, seeking patterns of weak security and targets of opportunity.

In the evening, as they drove out to Sangachal Terminal again, Young called Chris's phone.

"What's up?" Chris asked.

"I don't know if this is helpful or not, but we were trying to gather more intel about Lullaby and we came across two reports from different sources that claim Lullaby ordered a hit on Xander's wife," Young said. "At the time, it was thought Xander had done something to irritate Lullaby, but it wasn't clear what. It was reported that Xander mourned deeply for her, but at that time, no one knew Lullaby and Xander were the same person."

"So Xander had his wife killed," Chris said, tapping Hannah and Sonny on the arms in an effort to share the info. "Why would he do that?"

"Seems like she outlived her usefulness to him."

"Seems that way." Chris pinched his nose between the eyes. "Thanks, Young. Talk to you later."

He hung up as they parked at Sangachal Terminal.

"What's that?" Chris asked, pointing to a puff of smoke in an unlit corner of one of the terminal's parking lots.

The four of them squinted from a street, a hundred meters away. It was a black Kia Sportage SUV parked with its engine running.

"The car is facing the sea," Hannah noticed. "Whoever is inside might be watching the ships. Should we take a closer look?"

"Nothing ventured, nothing gained," Chris said.

"And tip off Xander that we're here?" Sonny said, playing devil's advocate.

"I could pose as an Azeri security guard and check the car out," Mikhail said. "Unless someone else here speaks Azeri?"

"That'll work," Hannah said. "I'll take the wheel and keep the car running in case we need to get out in a hurry."

"Sonny and I can stand by from a distance to cover Mikhail," Chris said.

"Since when do you decide what I'll do?" Sonny asked.

"Pretty please?" Chris fake-begged.

"Since you put it that way," Sonny said, flipping him the bird and staying put in his seat.

Mikhail opened the door of the Toyota, its interior light already switched off. He stepped out and softly closed the door behind him. Then he walked in the direction of the SUV. Chris opened his door and stepped out, too, but before he closed it, Sonny got out behind him.

Mikhail closed half the distance to the SUV—fifty meters—and was well within an enemy's rifle range and still within pistol range for Chris and Sonny. They drew their pistols and covertly kept them down at their sides. At twenty-five meters, Mikhail was in enemy pistol range. Mikhail closed in on the suspicious vehicle from the rear. Chris and Sonny moved forward. In the middle of the parking lot, they had absolutely nothing to hide behind or use as a shield to stop flying bullets. They aimed their pistols at one of the SUV's tinted windows. If any shots were fired at Mikhail, Chris and Sonny would return fire first and ask questions later. Sonny stepped away from Chris, giving them separation so an attacker couldn't easily hit them both with the same salvo.

Mikhail looked in the rear window. When he reached the driver's side, instead of presenting a smaller target, the side of his body, he presented a bigger target, the full front of his body. He didn't even have his weapon drawn.

Is Mikhail so tactically stupid? Or is he sure this isn't a threat?

Chris's heart thumped faster and his breath chased after it.

Mikhail tapped on the window. No answer. He tapped again. A woman's voice screamed from inside. Chris's pistol hand perspired, and his heart raced. There was a flurry of movement in the SUV in front of Mikhail before the engine revved and the vehicle sped away.

Mikhail calmly turned and walked toward Chris and Sonny. Mikhail smiled so hard that it seemed his jaw might crack.

Chris lowered his pistol.

"What the hell happened?" Sonny asked.

"Kids," Mikhail said with a chuckle. "Making the beast in the backseat."

Chris's heart rate slowed as he holstered his weapon. He wiped his damp palm against his trousers. He shook his head, and they returned to their vehicle without a single lead.

On the drive back to the safe house, Chris gnawed on one question. *Where are you Xander?*

Inside the safe house, Chris studied a map of Baku Bay and Sangachal Terminal, and then he opened his guitar case and broke out his M4.

Hannah sat down next him. "I'm sorry to keep dragging you into these messes," she said with a somber voice.

Chris cleared his M4 in order to do a function check. "I came because I wanted to. After Xander killed Michael, nobody had to twist my arm to make me stay. I wanted to get Xander. Still do."

"This work is how I breathe."

"I know."

"But you don't need this work to breathe," she said. "Not anymore. Your life as a preacher gives you oxygen."

Chris made sure his weapon was on *safe*, with the bolt forward, and squeezed the trigger. The hammer didn't fall. "I'm not sure where this conversation is going."

"Xander and his goons are brass knuckles tougher than I expected."

He moved the selector switch to *fire* and squeezed the trigger. The hammer fell. "The only easy day was yesterday."

Emotion trickled into her voice, but she held it in check. "If something happens to you, I don't know what I'll do with myself."

Chris pressed down on the top cartridge in his magazine, making sure he had a full thirty rounds inside. "Nothing's going to happen to me."

"You've done more than most Americans to fight the bad guys. You've sacrificed more than enough for your country," she said. "If you walk away from this now, I'll still care about you the same way. We can still see each other just as often. We can still be friends.

He loaded the magazine into his M4. "Not more than enough. Not yet."

22

T he next morning, Young called. "The *Binagadi*, one of the four ships Xander is tracking in his Marine Finder account, is docked in Baku Bay. Also, we found his IP address, but he's using a re-router to throw us off his actual physical location. Even so, we installed a keystroke logger in his computer and found he's searching the web about the Shah Deniz Alpha gas production platform."

"Why would he search that?" Chris asked.

"If he destroys the Shah Deniz, he'll kill a lot of crew members and interrupt the flow of gas through the South Caucasus Pipeline," Young answered.

The pieces of the puzzle were finally coming together. "If the South Caucasus Pipeline shuts down, Europe will have to buy more of their gas from Russia."

"Right. So Russia will have more money for its occupation of Ukraine and to send its military to expand Russian territory into other countries."

"We have to figure out Xander's plan of attack and stop him." Chris ended the call and informed the others.

They planned on the fly and piled into the SUV outside, hoping to check out the *Binagadi* in port. Again, they made sure they had enough gear, including assault rifles and ship-boarding gear, like a caving ladder and extension pole, so they were prepared for a variety of contingencies. Mikhail drove out of the parking lot. Shortly after hitting the main road, they saw a white police car marked with a blue stripe on its side. It was parked on the side of the street up ahead. The police appeared to have stopped someone, and an officer was talking with him.

Another officer stood behind the stopped vehicle and directed traffic. As the parked car pulled out, the signaling officer motioned for Mikhail to pull over.

He slowed down. "Police roadblock. Not good." The SUV came to a halt on the shoulder of the road. Because Mikhail and the SOG trio were carrying loaded pistols on their persons and loaded assault rifles under a blanket in the back of the SUV, Mikhail was right. This was definitely not good. And although the police were authorized to shoot Chris and his crew, they couldn't shoot the police. Chris hoped their diplomatic passports would be honored by the local law enforcement, helping them to avoid a search. Now was not a good time for an international incident.

"Mikhail, do you have a get-out-of-jail-free card?" Hannah asked.

"I'll take care of this," Mikhail said.

The older policeman approached the driver's side and said something in Azeri. Mikhail replied and pulled out his wallet, but instead of giving the officer a driver's license or other such documents, Mikhail handed him several manta banknotes, the Azeri currency.

The police officer became indignant, raising his voice and waving the money at him. Mikhail had tried to bribe his way out of a ticket.

Shit.

Mikhail pulled something out of his wallet. More manta!

Damn, Mikhail, don't make it worse.

The police officer discreetly put the money in his pocket before puffing out his chest and waving his finger.

Mikhail nodded without protest.

After the policeman finished speaking and stepped away, Mikhail shifted into *drive,* pulled out from the shoulder, and returned to the road. Chris looked back to see the police pull over another car.

"Sorry about that," Mikhail said. "This has happened before. They just want to shake down drivers for some cash."

"Thanks for getting us out of it," Chris said. "I can't—" Chris's cell phone rang, interrupting him. "Uh, it's Young. One sec." He held up a finger. "Hey," he answered.

"SIGINT reported an increased volume of unidentified communication out of Baku, but they were only able to decipher a time, 0830, and a name, *Binagadi,*" Young said, "Pier Three."

"That's in six minutes," Chris said, then thanked Young and hung up.

He told the others, and Mikhail sped up without having to be asked. The four arrived in the harbor parking lot, but the *Binagadi* wasn't at the pier.

Then Chris realized what had happened.

"You're in the wrong parking lot," he said. "This is for Pier Two. The *Binagadi* is at Pier Three." Anxiety washed through him at the idea that Xander was boarding the *Binagadi* and they were about to miss him.

Mikhail drove them to the next parking lot, where the *Binagadi* was in view as the crew prepared to get underway. It seemed like a newer ship, probably built within the last five years, and stretched the length of a football field and a half. Judging by its size, it probably weighed around ten thousand tons.

Mikhail drove onto Pier Three, near the ship, and the SOG team dismounted the SUV and moved in. On the pier, there was a gangway security cabin, which normally housed a guard to protect the entrance to the ship. But there was no guard inside. Either the cabin wasn't manned, or the guard was dead.

Chris scanned the ship's deck and spotted Animus amidships before he disappeared inside. Near where he'd stood was what looked like the body of a senior crew member lying on the deck. Chris took in the rest of the situation, seeing two seamen working frantically to disconnect the gangway, the only connection between the ship and shore. A crane was already hooked up to the center of the gangway, ready to lift it away, and on the dock, two workers waited to steady it.

Shit. We're too late.

Two levels above the main deck, near the bridge, Xander appeared, opening a hatch and then vanishing inside, while his thug with the smooth skin and hard eyes—and armed with an AK—remained outside, yelling in English at the two workers on the pier next to the gangplank.

"Untie the ship!" he shouted.

Sitting in the backseat of the SUV, Chris and Sonny grabbed assault rifles and other gear and distributed it. They put on their inflatable assault vests, comms, and other kit.

Then the four of them jumped out of the SUV and ran toward the ship.

"Must remove gangway first!" one of the workers called out in broken English.

Smooth Skin fired his AK in the worker's direction. "Untie the ship!"

The workers scattered away from the gangway and hurried to the lines.

Smooth Skin turned his head and faced the foursome running toward the ship. Because Chris led as point man, the front was Chris's area of responsibility, and it was his job to protect his team by taking out the threat. Chris stopped, planted his feet in a shooting stance, placed the butt of his rifle firmly in the hollow of his shoulder and aimed. Smooth Skin brought his rifle up, too. But Chris got off the first shot. The bullet ripped into Smooth Skin's upper body, disturbing his balance and slowing him. As Smooth Skin tried to bring his weapon up into firing position, Chris shot again, tearing a new hole near the first one and knocking Smooth Skin back a step. But he was still standing. Chris squeezed the trigger again. This time, Smooth Skin toppled over. Chris aimed at Smooth Skin's body on the deck and took another shot. The jerk of movement under Smooth Skin's shirt indicated another hit.

Chris turned to say something to Hannah, but he'd been so mentally focused on Smooth Skin he'd fallen into tunnel vision, losing sight of her and the others. As he mentally opened up his field of view, he spotted Hannah, Sonny, and Mikhail on the gangway, which had already risen a foot off the pier. The weight of their bodies caused the gangway to dip on their end, smacking the pier with a loud *whack*. To keep from falling backward, they released their grips on their rifles, letting their weapons dangle by their slings, and grabbed the railing on the side with both hands. The shift of their weight caused the gangway to tilt, and they struggled not to fall onto the pier below.

Another of Xander's armed thugs emerged from the superstructure near the bridge. As he brought his weapon to bear on Hannah and the others, Chris popped him until he dropped.

A tugboat pulled the *Binagadi* away from the dock as the crane lowered the gangway and Chris's clinging teammates to the pier. Sonny shouted and motioned wildly at the crane operator to set them down on the ship, not the pier, but it was too late. The tugboat pulled the *Binagadi* out of reach, leaving them behind.

"Sonny, if you and Mikhail can retrieve the ship-boarding gear from the SUV, Hannah and I will find a boat to borrow," Chris said.

Sonny and Mikhail ran back to the SUV while Chris searched the area. He spotted a small, narrow boat with a deep V-shaped hull—a go-fast, popular with smugglers and SEALs because of its stealth, speed, seaworthiness, and attitude. It was also known as a cigarette boat. It was tied to a nearby pier, and he pointed to it, showing Hannah. Chris waved to Sonny, and when he flagged him down, Chris gestured to where he'd discovered the boat. Then Chris and Hannah hurried over to the go-fast and boarded.

Chris took out his Swiss Army pocketknife and used the Phillips head screwdriver to remove the screws from the hard plastic panel covering the steering column. Then he located the battery wires, stripped an inch of insulation off each, and twisted them together. Finally, he connected the ignition wire to the battery wires, causing a spark, and the go-fast's engine growled to life.

Sonny and Mikhail joined them, bringing the caving ladder and extension pole. Sonny helped Hannah cast off the boat lines and push away from the pier before they took their seats. Chris stood as he drove. He eased the throttle forward, and the engine hummed as the vessel advanced. He turned the wheel, aiming them southeast in the direction of the *Binagadi*.

The wind pulled at Chris and grabbed at the water's surface, creating whitecaps. Occasionally, the wind grasped harder, upsetting his stance and turning those whitecaps into waves.

"Hang on!" he called above the noise of the rushing wind. He pushed the throttle further, and the go-fast accelerated.

The boat hit the whitecaps like a race car hitting speed bumps—the impact traveled from the metal deck up to his leg bones and rose through his spine until his jaws vibrated. He pressed the throttle to its max nonetheless, making the boat whine and shudder. After he hit the first sizeable wave, the go-fast caught air and they flew like riding the wings of an angel. When the boat came down, it felt like being stomped under the foot of the devil. Although he bent his knees to protect them, they still absorbed most of the shock. He glanced over his shoulder to make sure the others were still with him. They were. And holding on tightly.

The go-fast soared off another sizeable wave. The boat landed before Chris's feet did, and gravity pushed down on him from above. The unforgiving metal deck greeted him from below, the impact of both forces meeting at his knees, bone-bashing. He glanced back at his crew—shaken but still hanging on.

He closed in on the *Binagadi* and slowed almost to half speed so he wouldn't rocket past her. It still felt like they were riding over speed bumps but not as fast or intense as before.

"Mikhail, I need you to take over at the helm while I try to hook the *Binagadi*. Sonny, if any AKs poke out at us, waste 'em. And Hannah, I need you to help steady me while I hook the ship."

Here goes.

23

C hris pulled up to the port side of the fantail before slowing to match the ship's speed. Then he signaled Mikhail to take the wheel. Sonny trained his weapon on the ship, ready to wax the first boogeyman who appeared. Chris picked up the caving ladder and extension pole and carried them to the bow. Hannah was right behind. Both the *Binagadi* and the go-fast rose and fell with the sea as they sailed forward.

While Sonny trained his weapon on the ship and Hannah steadied Chris, he attached the caving ladder and its hook to the pole. In the Teams, it was usually another guy's responsibility to hook the ship, but Chris had done it before. Normally, he did the deed with four boatloads of SEALs, two boats on each side of the ship. If one boat failed to hook on, the boat behind would move in and complete the task. Even if three boats failed and one succeeded, all the SEALs could climb up the one ladder that hooked on. Chris double-checked to make sure the hook was securely attached to the ladder. If he attached the hook to the ship and the ladder fell away, they'd be in a shit state, or worse; if he climbed the ladder and it separated from the hook and he fell thirty feet and landed on the go-fast, the fall would likely kill him.

"Just hold on to my belt from behind and steady me," he said quietly to Hannah. Normally, two SEALs would do the job of steadying him, but one Hannah would have to do.

He extended the hook above the edge of the hull, and he tried to hook it on to metal, but with both boats moving with the waves, it was tough to keep his balance. Hannah did a good job of preventing him from landing on his ass, though. His first attempt to hook on to the ship failed. His second attempt lined up perfectly, but Mikhail veered too close to the ship and bumped it, causing both Chris and Hannah to lose their balance. He silently cursed the man, hoping the noise of hull against hull didn't alert Xander and his gang.

On the third attempt, Chris successfully hooked on to a rail. Then he pulled down on the pole, causing the caving ladder to unroll like toilet paper until it reached his feet with ladder to spare. He collapsed the telescopic pole.

"Wait 'til I signal that it's clear to climb," Chris said. "I'll go up first, followed by Hannah, and then Sonny. Mikhail, once we're on board, you can back off and follow from a distance. After we get the ship stopped, we'll radio you in."

They nodded.

Chris mounted the ladder and climbed. With the wind and the movement of the ship, each step he took felt like a blessing. While at sea, he'd seen more than one Teammate thrown from a caving ladder. He climbed with his legs and used his arms for balance, rather than climbing with his arms and burning his muscles out quickly. Because it was daytime, it was much easier to see the steps of the ladder, but because it was daytime, it would also be much easier to be seen by Xander and his men.

When Chris reached the deck of the ship, he scanned the area for trouble. He saw none, so he went to work on the ladder. Once it was securely fastened, he looked around again for enemy signs. No one was on the main deck, but a man stood up on the superstructure. He was looking down at something in his hands, but it wasn't immediately clear what. As he lifted the object to his shoulder, it became apparent. He had a rocket-propelled grenade.

"RPG," Chris whisper-shouted into his comm.

There was nothing to hide behind to avoid the inevitable blast. *My only chance is to take him out before he takes me out.*

Chris aimed his rifle and squeezed the trigger, cutting down the enemy—but not before he could fire his RPG.

Swoosh. After the rocket took flight, it hit the deck next to Chris with a loud crack and knocked off the caving ladder. The time it took for the resulting explosion was interminable.

The RPG didn't explode, and his human instinct was *Don't pick up an unexploded bomb,* but the longer he waited, the higher the likelihood it would blow up in his face. He picked it up and threw it over the stern, away from Hannah, Sonny, and Mikhail. It vanished from view without a sound.

Thank you, Lord.

He looked over the port side. Hannah, Sonny, and Mikhail were fine. Hannah and Mikhail fished the caving ladder out of the water, but one of the hooks had snapped off. Sonny held up the ladder with the missing piece and asked over the comm, "Now what?"

There was strength in numbers, and Chris didn't want to go the mission alone. "I'll figure something out."

Up on the ship's superstructure, the RPG man was laid out on the deck, but now he rose to his knees. Before he could cause more trouble, Chris shot him again, flattening him.

Chris checked the port side for a boatswain's locker with some rope in it to secure the broken caving ladder. He found a hatch, and as a matter of routine, he aimed his weapon at it before opening it. Expecting to find rope inside, it startled him to see a man with long sideburns armed with an AK.

This is a passageway, not a boatswain's locker.

Both men jumped with surprise at the same time. Sideburns pulled the trigger first, but he hadn't aimed yet. *Clank clank,* the bullet ricocheted in the narrow passageway, hitting Sideburns in his own thigh. Chris was slower to pull the trigger, but his weapon was already aimed. He pumped two rounds into the man.

Sideburns dropped his weapon and clutched his chest. Frothy crimson spilled between his fingertips his lung was punctured and he was having trouble breathing. Sideburns dropped to his knees, and a smile appeared on his face.

"What's so damn funny?" Chris asked.

"You can't stop Mr. Metaxas," Sideburns wheezed.

Chris aimed his weapon at Sideburns's head. "Stop him from what?"

"Eat shit." Sideburns's smile broadened, and he closed his eyes.

Chris ended the conversation with a bullet. "Boring conversation, anyway."

Then he frisked Sideburns for intel and confiscated a cell phone, keys, and a wallet. He used the cell phone to call the automated number that Young ran 24/7. After the call went through, Young or one of his assistants would hack the phone and download its data and Young would begin analysis.

Chris maneuvered around to the starboard side to look for rope. With the disappearance of two men, Xander might be sending out a search party, and Chris wanted his crew at his side before the party started.

While looking for a boatswain's locker, he located a Jacob's ladder, bound by a strap and a metal latch. Chris spoke via his throat mic and used Mikhail's call sign. "Jirtdan, bring the go-fast around to the starboard side. I'm going to drop a Jacob's ladder for Infidel and Sunshine to climb aboard."

"Roger, wilco," Mikhail answered.

After scanning for possible threats and spotting none, Chris took a knee on the deck and undid the latch. Then he unrolled the Jacob's ladder over the starboard side. "Infidel and Sunshine, the starboard ladder is ready for boarding. I'll cover you from here."

"Roger," Hannah said, "Starboard ladder ready for boarding. You're covering."

"About damn time," Sonny said.

From Chris's current position, he had to look three ways to cover all possible approaches from Xander and his men: forward, aft, and up. "I'm moving aft for a better tactical view."

After shifting locations, he had most of the ship in front of him without having to bend his neck back and forth, up and down and risk missing something.

"Infidel boarding," Hannah said.

Chris hoped Hannah made it on board before Xander and his men appeared. Suddenly, there was movement. Whiteface, carrying an AK, appeared on the port side of the bridge.

Chris covered him. It was the same guy who was with Animus in London.

Whiteface looked down at the port side of the ship and the sea and then returned back inside the bridge. Soon, Whiteface stepped outside on the starboard side. Chris placed the red dot of his scope on the profile of Whiteface's upper body while simultaneously placing his finger snugly on the trigger. As Whiteface walked toward the edge of the ship, Chris followed with his red dot, tracking the side of his upper body. Chris held his breath to stop his lungs from moving, reducing the wobble of the red dot. Whiteface bent over the rails and looked down at the water, near where Hannah and Sonny were.

Chris squeezed the trigger slowly. He tried not to anticipate the quiet pop from the sound-suppressed barrel or the recoil of the butt into his shoulder. He tried not to think about when the shot would fire. It was best to be surprised. *Pop.* The sound was no louder than a kid's BB gun. Whiteface jerked, and he twisted toward the bow as if to see who hit him, but he was facing the opposite direction of where the shot had come from, and he seemed confused. *Pop.* Chris shot him in the back.

Whiteface's back arched before he dropped to the deck, crying out in Russian for help. "*Po-masch!*" He dropped his weapon and crawled for the bridge, but Chris covered him with the red dot and fired again, this time hitting him on his uninjured side. He stopped crawling.

"Ivan!" Animus's voice called out.

Ivan is no more.

Chris had focused so tightly on the bridge that he had to open his field of view again to possible enemy combatants on the rest of the starboard side. Hannah's head rose above the Jacob's ladder, and he assumed Sonny was directly below her.

An armed man hopped out of the starboard hatch of the bridge, stoking Chris's pulse and breathing rates. "Armed man, bridge, starboard wing," Chris reported over his radio.

Chris aimed at him, but he ducked before Chris could pull the trigger or Hannah could acquire him. Chris's heart and breathing sped up. Then more appeared.

"More armed men, same location. No Xander yet," Chris said into his mic.

He tried to figure who was the most senior of the men present in order to take him out first and weaken the remaining members, but it wasn't clear who was senior. Adrenaline dumped into Chris's system as he decided to take out the greatest threat first. But they all seemed equally threatening. While his mind raced trying to pick out the best target, the armed men spotted Chris.

Hannah, who was on deck by now, took a shot and missed as Sonny crawled up onto the ship.

Chris's panic rose. He had wasted precious time choosing a target, and now he wanted to shoot any and all threats. The darkness of warfare covered more and more of his light as a pastor. Gunfire erupted from the starboard wing of the bridge, and the heat of the rounds clapped the air near him. With his mind hazy and his vision blurred, it became a Herculean effort to focus on target. He knew his life and the lives of his teammates were in danger, so he jerked the trigger, hoping to hit one of the enemy combatants, but he missed.

"Take cover," he warned the others. The SOG trio ran toward the bulkhead and took refuge from the shit storm that rained down.

"How many?" Sonny asked.

"Five or six," Chris answered.

"Xander is still the prize," Hannah reminded them. As if they could forget.

Chris took a slow breath. He had failed to take an effective shot so far, but he shook off the discouragement. It was history, and there was nothing he could accomplish now by dwelling on it. The only thing he had any control over was the here and now.

"Xander and his men have less room up there to maneuver than we do down here," Chris said, getting his focus back. "We can whittle them down from where we are before making an assault."

Sonny nodded. "Smoke 'em."

"Let's do it," Hannah said.

"If Hannah can stay here and keep an eye on this hatch and the main deck," Sonny said, "it'll free up you and me to home in on the bastards near the bridge."

Hannah grinned. "My pleasure

It was a wise move, and it could help Chris ensure he followed the advice of his veteran SEAL mentor, a shooting guru named Ron Hickok. *Don't show your face twice in the same spot unless you want to get it shot off.* Because Chris had already been spotted aft, he moved forward. Sonny moved forward, too. Chris covered port and Sonny took starboard.

Thick black pipes ran along the length of the deck, and Chris lay down beside them, using them to provide partial cover and concealment. He slithered into a better position while watching the bridge and its starboard and port wings. More than anything, he hoped to spot Xander and take him out.

A spiky-haired man with an AK neared the rail and looked around. He seemed to have spotted Sonny, but Sonny's rifle spit twice and Spike dropped.

Hannah's rifle sounded. "Good night," she said quietly, as if to herself, but her voice transmitted over the radio, and then a man yelped.

Chris settled into a stable position, an advantage of being prone, which would aid his accuracy. Several people were inside the pilothouse on the bridge, but the windows were tinted and it was difficult to see who was inside. Outside, on the starboard side, someone hung his AK out and sprayed below. None of the shots zipped anywhere close to Sonny—yet. Chris put his red dot on the man's shoulder and squeezed. The shooter's shirt quivered slightly, showing Chris where he'd struck his target. The shooter almost released his weapon as he pulled away, back into the bridge.

Sonny reached the port side and went aft.

An aggressive gunman came out the port side then, aiming his weapon toward the bow, looking for trouble but failing to notice Chris lying down between the pipes. Chris's red dot aligned over the man's chest, and his finger applied pressure to the trigger. The recoil of the rifle pushed his shoulder, signaling the deed was done. The aggressive shooter sank out of sight.

Sonny aimed at a target near the bridge. Chris couldn't see who Sonny was shooting at, but he heard the *pop*.

Someone on the port side backed into Chris's view. Chris plugged him between the shoulder blades, and the man dropped.

Then the shooting stopped. Everything became quiet—too quiet.

Chris slithered toward the superstructure, and a bullet punched through the glass of the pilothouse window. *Tang!* The projectile struck a metal pipe next to Chris, the surprise of the shot jolting him. He dispensed with the slithering, hopped to his feet, and sprinted out of the line of fire. His body tilted as he ran, and he realized the ship was turning. *Tang!* A second bullet just missed his foot.

Chris joined Sonny and Hannah next to the port hatch out of the line of fire. There was Sideburns in a puddle of blood. "He told me I was *too late*," Chris said.

The ship straightened its course, and the deck leveled off. They were less than two klicks away from the Shah Deniz Alpha oil rig now. Chris had read that the rig's legs had to stretch a hundred meters below the water to touch bottom, and on top of those legs, thirteen meters above water, rested the platform that carried the drilling and production facilities with housing for well over a hundred crewmembers.

"Xander is on a direct collision course with Shah Deniz Alpha," Chris said.

"That's how he plans to interrupt the flow of gas through the South Caucasus Pipeline," Hannah said. "And he'll kill all the crewmembers onboard the Shan Deniz Alpha in the process."

24

Moving in for the assault, Chris hurried to the nearest ladder, and Hannah and Sonny followed. When he aimed his weapon up at the port side of the bridge, there was no one there. Expecting the enemy to appear at any moment, he observed the hazard spots with his M4 as he climbed the ladder, but no one showed.

"Something's wrong," Chris whispered.

They ascended several levels until they reached the hatch leading to the bridge. Chris positioned himself next to the hatch with Hannah and Sonny forming the train behind him. He glanced back at Hannah, who had a flash-bang device at the ready so when Chris opened the hatch, she could toss it in and stun whoever was inside. He pulled on the handle, but it didn't move, so he pulled harder. Still no luck. Then he used both hands to crank on it, but nothing changed. Then he heard it. From inside the bridge came a hissing sound.

"Sounds like they're welding the hatches shut," he said. "Let's find another way in."

Resuming point, Chris returned to the same ladder they had just climbed and went back down to the deck below where he found a hatch and opened it. He leaned into the opening with his eyes and his weapon, leaving the rest of his body behind the cover of the metal bulkhead. Xander and Animus were in the passageway. Chris trained his red dot on Xander, but before Xander turned and noticed Chris's presence, Animus stepped in front of the man, as if to shield him from Chris's fire. Chris squeezed, and Animus returned fire. Chris's shot struck Animus's flesh, and Animus's shot harmlessly hit the metal bulkhead.

Chris followed up decisively with another round, striking Animus between the shoulders. He fell with a gasp, but Xander had disappeared.

Ron Hickok's voice sounded in Chris's memory. *Sometimes the enemy will play dead on you. Shoot him until he's dead. Then you never have to worry about him surprising you—or worse—surprising your buddies.*

Chris put a security round in Animus's head, then stepped over his body to the spot where Xander had disappeared. The SEAL in Chris wanted to cheer, and the pastor in Chris wanted to say a prayer, but it was the SEAL who reasoned that he still had to get Xander. It looked like this passageway ran from starboard to port. Rather than present himself in the same upper location of the passageway, Chris dropped to a knee and leaned over. No one was there.

The sound of footsteps scampered away. Chris's first impulse was to pursue, but maybe the footsteps were from one of Xander's thugs and Xander was waiting around the corner to ambush Chris and his team.

Chris took a deep breath to calm himself, but it seemed to have little effect as he proceeded into the passageway. He didn't hear Hannah and Sonny behind him, but somehow he sensed they were there.

The passageway provided little room to maneuver on either side, making Chris feel trapped. If a foe came at him, the only way to escape would be forward, through the foe. Adrenaline unloaded into his arteries and his vision became crisp as the red dot of his sight covered danger zones. He searched for trip wires in front or a pressure release mat on the deck that could trigger a booby trap, but there were none.

When he reached intersecting passageways at the centerline of the ship, he looked for Xander, but no luck. He looked through the passageway which led to a ladder that reached up to the rear hatch of the bridge. As much as he wanted to chase Xander, the ship had to be stopped. Chris swiftly closed the distance to the ladder and ascended.

On the bridge he discovered the bodies of men who appeared to be the captain and his crew. Nearby was Whiteface in a puddle of blood. If he was playing dead, he could surprise Chris, or worse, surprise Hannah and Sonny. Chris eliminated the possibility of surprises coming from Whiteface.

Then Chris peeled right, knowing Hannah would peel left and Sonny would take the center of the bridge. There was a bullet hole in the windshield where someone had fired at Chris minutes earlier. He searched for surviving enemies.

"Starboard hatch is welded shut." Although Chris and his crew wouldn't be able to exit through the starboard side, it also meant no one from the starboard side would be able to enter.

Hannah tried to open the port hatch. "This door is welded shut, too."

Sonny jerked at the ship's throttle, but it didn't move. Then he attempted to turn the wheel, but it didn't budge, either. "They welded the damn throttle and wheel, too. Now we can't stop or steer the ship!"

Chris took a try at the throttle and wheel, just to make sure—not even a wiggle. The ship ran at a speed of ten knots, aimed at the Shah Deniz Alpha oil rig, one and a half klicks away. "Maybe we can't stop the ship, but we can get Xander."

"Do you have a death wish or something?" Hannah asked. "We need to get off now... before the ship crashes."

"Can't let him get away," Chris said.

"Hannah is right," Sonny said. "If Xander wants to go down with the ship, let him. If he surfaces, we'll be waiting for him."

Hannah's chocolate-brown eyes had a soothing effect on him as she locked them on his. "What's the best way to get off the ship?" she asked.

Chris could be reckless with his own life, but he couldn't be reckless with theirs. Like Sonny had said, Xander would either go down with the ship, or they would catch him when he surfaced.

"We can jump off the fantail," Chris said. He radioed Mikhail and told him they were coming and to contact the oil rig to inform them the ship was about to crash into them. "We only have about five minutes before the ship hits."

Chris, Hannah, and Sonny moved tactically out of the bridge, down the ladder and then into the passageway they'd just come from. Chris was careful not to take Sonny and Hannah into an ambush, but he still had to hurry.

When they reached the fantail, Mikhail was still dutifully in the go-fast, following behind. Chris warned Mikhail they were about to jump before turning to Hannah. "Right before you leap, start inflating your vest so you don't sink like a rock with all your gear when you hit the water."

She nodded.

"Go," he said.

She popped the CO2 cartridge in her vest and jumped, followed by Sonny.

As Chris turned and observed the deck, there was still no sign of Xander.

Where are you?

He ground his teeth and pulled his own cord, puncturing the CO2 cartridge to fill his vest with air, and he jumped. His mind cleared of everything except what he was doing, and he felt like a lead weight had been lifted. It was liberating.

Splash! He sank underwater, but his submersion was only temporary and he floated toward the surface. The first thing he checked was whether Hannah was okay. She was. Sonny was afloat, too.

Mikhail brought the boat up alongside them and helped Sonny out of the water and onboard first. Then Sonny and Mikhail helped Hannah and Chris aboard.

The ship was less than five minutes away from hitting the oil rig.

Before Chris could ask Mikhail if he was able to contact someone on the rig to warn them, he noticed Mikhail's face was pale. "Are you okay?" Chris asked.

"While you had your shootout, I ran into a little shootout of my own," Mikhail said.

"What happened?" Hannah asked.

"A yacht started following the ship," Mikhail said. "Then it rammed me and tried to knock me off course. I figured they were working for Xander. When I didn't change course, a gunman started shooting. So I shot back and took out the gunman and the pilot, and now they're both dead in the water." Mikhail chuckled. "Ow, that rattles my stones to laugh."

He turned awkwardly, and Chris didn't understand what was going on until Mikhail collapsed on the deck. Chris dropped to his knees beside him and opened his assault vest. Hannah took the wheel while Sonny trained his weapon on the ship.

Between Mikhail's neck and shoulder was a bloody mess. The round must've entered between his neck and the opening of the collar on his inflatable bullet-resistant vest. The whole front of his shirt was soaked with blood.

Chris pulled out Mikhail's blowout kit, removed a QuickClot Combat Gauze packet, and unbuttoned Mikhail's shirt to see exactly where the bullet entry was. There was a dark hole covered with blood, and Chris pressed part of his hand against it to stop the bleeding while using his fingers to open the packet. Then he removed the gauze and used his finger to poke it into the wound, applying direct pressure with his hand between pokes. Chris had similarly patched up a fallen Teammate in Iraq, who'd howled out in pain, but Mikhail made no sound. His eyes were open, but he didn't speak.

Shit, I'm losing him.

"Mikhail, how you doing?" Chris asked.

After stuffing the hemostatic gauze as deep as it would go, packing the wound, he used his hand to apply direct pressure with the remaining gauze. He leaned over and put his cheek close to Mikhail's lips to feel his breath, but there was none.

"Mikhail, talk to me. Talk to me, buddy."

Clank, clank, clank! It sounded like metal baseball bats striking the hull of the go-fast, but the sonic snap that sounded over Chris's head confirmed they were bullets. Sonny leaned into his rifle, the barrel spitting hate up at one of Xander's men on the tanker, who shrieked like a bird as he fired his AK down at them. Sonny muted him.

Chris maintained direct pressure for a couple of minutes until the bleeding stopped. Mikhail had closed his eyes. He'd lost a lot of blood and was still unresponsive. Chris reached into the blowout kit and pulled out a gray package containing an Israeli-designed military trauma bandage. He tore it open and pulled out the bandage, careful not to touch the sterile pad. After applying the pad to the gauze-packed wound, he wrapped the tail of the bandage around Mikhail's torso and clipped the excess with the pressure applicator.

"Mikhail, wake up. Wake up and talk to me." Chris wrapped in the opposite direction, tightening the bandage. Completing the wrap, he used the clip on the closure bar to secure it.

He flicked a glance at his watch. The ship was only about a minute away from impacting the oil rig.

Chris felt Mikhail's neck for a pulse—nothing.

"Mikhail is dead," Chris said, deflating like a punctured tire.

Hannah pounded her fist on the dash.

Sonny kicked the bench hard, making a loud *crack* before he dropped an f-bomb.

Chris had lost Teammates and mourned them, but he'd packed those feelings away in the tidy crates in his mind. Now those feelings of loss came tumbling out—loneliness, darkness, and a need to withdraw from the world. The guilt of botching the hostage rescue in Athens returned. Ironically the hostage's name was Michael, too. Different spelling, same ending.

Why? Chris turned his face to the sky. *Have I fallen out of favor with Thee?*

It wasn't outside the realm of possibility, he thought for a moment. Of course, he was unable to attend worship services. He'd brought his pocket-sized Bible with him, but it had stayed on the plane, and since leaving Dallas, he hadn't cracked it open once. He didn't pray as often as he did when he first became a pastor, not since returning to the world of black ops. This mission had worn on him, and he was too tired to read scriptures or pray—too tired in his body, mind, and spirit. Now Chris's bag of tricks was empty, and he'd committed the frogman's sin: allowing discouragement to creep in.

Crunch! The *Binagadi* plowed into the oil rig, taking out a section of it. The rest of the platform groaned and twisted before fire and smoke bellowed out. Alarms went off on the rig, and someone spoke over a PA system. Chris didn't have to understand Azeri to understand the gist of the speaker's words. Soon a handful of the rig's crew appeared, still strapping on their lifejackets, and launched lifeboats. Others donned fire-fighting gear and oxygen masks, but they seemed confused as to whether they should fight the fire or evacuate the rig.

The burning platform leaned into the sea. Another voice came over the PA system, and the firefighters disappeared back into the structure where they'd come from. More men wearing lifejackets emerged and headed to the lifeboats.

Chris tore his gaze from the horror, shifting to the ship. It had erupted in flames, too. It wasn't clear if the fire had originated from the ship or if it had spread from the oil rig, but there was no sign of Xander.

"Drown, Xander, drown," Chris muttered.

"I hope he shows, just so I have the satisfaction of plugging him," Sonny said.

"Kill or capture," Hannah reminded him. She stopped the go-fast and let it idle.

A stream of crewmembers evacuated the sinking oil platform, and Chris said a silent prayer the crew would make it out alive. He still hoped Xander would die, but he didn't pray it.

Hannah eased the throttle forward and motored around the ship.

Chris spotted someone in the water. "Xander!"

"We have to get to him before he reaches one of the lifeboats," Sonny said.

Hannah moved the boat in closer, and Chris and Sonny both aimed their weapons at him.

"Xander, surrender now, or we shoot you!" Chris said.

Sonny fired, but it missed. Chris didn't know if the miss was intentional or not, but Xander stopped, treaded water with his legs, and raised his hands in the air. He lowered his hands to help him tread water, then raised them again. He appeared compliant.

Some crew members evacuating the rig in lifeboats stared, but Chris and his team carried on with their capture. Hannah pulled up next to Xander, and Chris heaved him out of the water. All the while, Sonny pointed his muzzle at him.

"I hope you do something stupid," Sonny said.

"Bag and drag him, boys," Hannah said.

25

After fishing him out of the water, Chris kicked Xander's feet out from under him and slammed him face-first into the deck. Sonny aimed at Xander's head while Chris secured Xander's hands behind his back with plasti-cuffs, cinching them tight. Then he bound Xander's feet, too.

"You better hope this boat doesn't sink," Chris said. He searched every inch of Xander's body for weapons or intel. "He's clean except for a pocketknife." Xander carried a Swiss Army knife like Chris did. Chris opened it, and unlike his knife, Xander had modified some of the blades to serve as lock picks. Chris put it in his pocket.

"He must've ditched his weapons, comms, and everything else," Sonny said.

Chris's and Xander's eyes met.

"*Bayushki bayu,*" Chris said.

Xander's eyes widened for a moment, but his body was still.

"I know you had your wife killed," he went on. "And you made a scene of mourning her. That was her house in Athens, wasn't it?"

The edges of Xander's lips rose to a half-smile.

Chris glared at him. "I guess you needed her for her Greek citizenship."

Xander's eyes seemed to study Chris. "It is a matter of public record. I inherited the house. Among other things."

"How could you do that? To the mother of your daughter."

"Neither of them meant that much to me," Xander said coolly. "My wife had become suspicious and threatened my cover."

"Evelina didn't mean that much to you?"

"Evelina did not fit my needs for a protégé, but she did attract a number of candidates. Animus was the golden one. But they began to have troubles and she outlived her usefulness to me." Xander became quiet for a moment before the corners of his mouth broadened into a full smile. "Then you took care of the Evelina problem for me, and at the same time, you instilled in Animus a stellar hatred for the West. I discovered the vodka, but you distilled it for me."

Anger flared in Chris, so hot he wanted to put a bullet in Xander's head and heave him over the side.

Hannah revved the go-fast's engine.

"We need to get out of here before the Azeri Coast Guard arrives," Sonny said.

Chris nodded, trying to keep calm.

Hannah pushed the throttle forward and the go-fast motored ahead.

"Do you know how you caught me?" Xander asked.

STEPHEN TEMPLIN

Chris thought for a moment. "How do you think we caught you?"

Xander sneered. "Because we are alike. A hunter has to think like his prey in order to catch his prey. You think you are better than me, but you are not. You and I are one and the same."

Suddenly, Mikhail sat up in the boat. "Where's Xander?" he slurred, thrashing around frantically.

The outburst jolted Chris. The man's vital signs must've been too low for Chris to recognize as still having life in them. Or maybe he'd somehow misread them.

He tried to calm Mikhail. "We got him. We got Xander. You can rest now."

"Holy shit! I nearly pissed myself!" exclaimed Sonny.

Mikhail closed his eyes and his upper body dropped, but Chris caught him and eased him the rest of the way to the deck.

"I thought he was dead," Hannah said.

"So did I," Chris said. "We need to get him medical attention ASAP."

Hannah pulled out her cell phone and made a call while pushing the go-fast harder. "I'm on it."

Behind them, a helicopter approached the oil rig as it sank lower into the sea, and a string of boats headed toward the shore, away from the burning platform.

"We're going to look awfully conspicuous showing up on shore armed to the teeth like this," Chris said.

Sonny shrugged. "We can ditch the long guns."

A swarm of boats appeared on the horizon. "We got visitors," Chris said.

"Who?" Sonny asked.

Chris squinted his eyes, trying to make out more detail on the boats. "We're about to find out."

Xander let out a laugh.

Sonny gagged him. "You laugh one more time or make one more sound, and I'll personally screw a bullet through your skull."

Gradually, three Stenka-class patrol boats and one Zhuk-class patrol craft—leftovers from the Soviet occupation—and two forty-eight-foot-long rigid-hulled inflatable boats (RHIBs) came into view. "Azeri Coast Guard," Chris said.

"Probably heading to the oil rig," Sonny said.

Hannah shook her head, putting away her phone. "They're heading in our direction. We better strip down to our primary gear and play it cool."

The trio took off their assault rifles, assault vests, comms, and overt gear and stashed them in every available compartment on the boat, pulling out life vests and other gear to make room. Now their only weapons were concealed pistols and some ammo. When they took off Mikhail's gear, he awoke for a moment and shouted, "Happy birthday!"

Sonny shook his head. "Damn, Dirt Dan."

Mikhail drifted out of consciousness again and became quiet.

"How do we explain the two bodies on the deck?" Sonny asked. "I vote we just put some holes in Xander now and dump him over the side."

"Hopefully the Azeri Coast Guard sails by fast enough not to notice," Hannah said.

As the Coast Guard boats came closer, Chris's anxiety grew. The Coast Guard faced the go-fast head-on, forcing Hannah to slow the boat.

"This isn't good," Sonny said. From one of the Coast Guard vessels, a man spoke Azeri through a megaphone. When the Coast Guardsmen aimed their rifles at Chris and his teammates, the message was clear.

Hannah stopped the go-fast.

"This really isn't good," Sonny said. Chris, Hannah, and Sonny raised their hands in the universal language of surrender.

One of the RHIBs pulled up alongside, and armed men shouted in Azeri at them.

"I'm sorry," Sonny said, "I don't speak pig latin."

"Let me handle this," Hannah snapped at him.

An older Azeri, probably senior in rank, said, "You speak English?"

"Yes," Hannah said.

"You big trouble," the senior Azeri said. "You steal Minister of Defense rum-runner boat." Senior held up an iPhone. "Minister have GPS on rum-runner, and we track you with iPhone."

"Uh-oh," Sonny said.

Hannah held out her diplomatic passport. "I am a legal attaché for the United States of America, and I can explain."

Chris wondered how she was going to talk her way out of this one.

Senior's eyes stopped at Xander and Mikhail lying on the deck, and then he looked at Hannah. "Yes, you will explain." He motioned to his men to board the go-fast and said something in Azeri.

Hannah pointed to Xander. "This man is a terrorist. He crashed a ship into the Shah Deniz Alpha oil rig." Then she pointed to Mikhail. "Mikhail works for MNS, and we were helping him find this terrorist, but Mikhail has been shot and needs medical attention immediately."

"I don't know anything about this," Senior said.

Some of the Coast Guard men pointed their guns at the trio while others handcuffed them. Chris breathed deeply. He didn't like being handcuffed. After being kidnapped as a child, he never wanted to feel imprisoned again. And because no SEAL had ever been held prisoner of war, he had a reputation to uphold. But the Azeris weren't the enemy, and he went through the motions of compliance.

The Coast Guard searched Chris and his team, clearing out Chris's pockets, too, leaving him with nothing but lint. He tried to make out the type of handcuffs they'd used—ironically, the cheaper ones were made of softer metal, more prone to bending than breaking; whereas, the more expensive handcuffs were made of a stronger metal that was more brittle and easier to break. But he couldn't discern which type of metal these handcuffs were made of.

After the Coast Guard handcuffed Xander, they removed his gag and plasticuffs. "She's lying," Xander said. "They are the terrorists, and they kidnapped me. Her passport is a fake."

The Coast Guard rifled through the boat and found the assault rifles, assault vests, comms, and overt gear stashed in the compartments on the boat. Now they gripped their weapons more tightly and moved more anxiously.

"This is going well," Sonny grumbled.

"I can give you a phone number to call at the US embassy," Hannah told Senior.

A gray-haired man appeared from the cabin of the Stenka-class patrol boat, and he shouted out to Senior. Gray Hair seemed to be the highest-ranking man in the group, but Chris couldn't make out what he was telling Senior. When they finished talking, Gray Hair barked orders at his men before he left with two Stenka-class patrol boats, the Zhuk-class patrol craft, and a RHIB. Senior was left with one Stenka-class patrol boat and his RHIB. Gray Hair and his men sped away, pointed at the burning oil rig.

Senior called out orders to his men. One Coast Guardsman took the helm of the go-fast and motored toward shore with two men standing guard over Chris's team and Xander. The other Coast Guard sailors followed in the patrol boat and RHIB.

Senior said to Hannah, "I call US embassy first."

"Thank you," she said. "I can give you the phone number."

Senior took out his cell phone. "I have number."

While the senior Azeri made his call, Chris covertly rubbed the chain of his handcuffs against the metal of the boat, roughing up the links. The links of a smooth chain would slip against themselves, but rough links would gain more traction against one another. After scraping the chain links, Chris turned one hand around the other with a slight in-and-out motion, while keeping the other hand still. The chain links weren't biting, so he worked on scratching them up some more.

Senior shook his head in disgust. "You Americans and your damn robot phone answering."

As they neared shore, Chris rotated one hand again, manipulating the links in his handcuffs, and they finally bit into each other. *Bingo!* For a moment, the links seized up, but then he lost it. He tried to freeze them up again.

The Coast Guard boats and go-fast pulled up to a dock where the Coast Guard tied the vessels. As the Coast Guard escorted Chris and the others onto land, he tried to tighten up the links in his handcuffs again but failed. While walking, he attempted to rotate his hand slowly, so as to not alert the Coast Guard as to what he was doing.

Ching. Handcuff links popped, but they weren't Chris's. They were Xander's. Both of Xander's hands pumped freely as he broke into a mad sprint. The Coast Guard yelled at him, and one sailor ran after.

Adrenaline surged into Chris's system, but the sudden burst of dynamism coursing through his veins threatened to disrupt his dexterity.

I've got to stop Xander before he escapes.

He turned one hand over the other, but too much movement caused the links to slip. He took a deep breath to regain composure and tried again. The chain links bit into each other and jammed up. *Good.* Carefully, he applied pressure at an angle, using more torque than strength, until the link at the swivel snapped.

With his arms liberated, Chris sprinted toward Xander. He passed the Coast Guard sailors, but Xander was still twenty-five meters ahead. A gunshot sounded from behind. Chris didn't know if the shot was a warning fired into the air or a direct attempt to hit him, but he wasn't about to slow down and find out, and he didn't bother to turn around.

26

Chris chased Xander away from the docks and into the city. As juiced as Chris was, he couldn't seem to close the twenty-five meters between them. Xander was cranked. Chris wasn't in top condition, but he didn't allow Xander to put any more distance between them. Xander turned the corner of a building. After twenty-five meters, Chris turned the corner, too, but Xander was gone. A passerby stared at Chris's handcuffs, and he pulled down his shirtsleeves and tucked in the dangling chain to conceal the cuffs.

He had lost Xander. He wasn't straight ahead, so he had to have made another turn to the right or left. Or maybe he was waiting just around a corner to jump Chris.

Chris searched the ground for clues and noticed part of the pavement was wet. Not enough to form a complete footprint, but enough of the heels for Chris's trained eye to spot. The dampness led into the building next to Chris, so he tracked them.

He entered an office building of some sort, but Xander was nowhere in sight. On a desktop was a cupful of pens, pencils, and a pair of scissors. Some of the pens had metal clips, and Chris knew he could use a clip to unlock his handcuffs. He calmly took a pen and continued forward. Ahead, he found dirty wet spots, dulling the shine on the linoleum under the fluorescent lights. As he tracked the footsteps, he bent the metal clip on the pen as far as it would go then bent it back to its original position. He kept bending the clip back and forth until it snapped, creating a shim. He'd only taken one pen and was relieved to see the clip broke cleanly.

He followed the partial footprints to the exit and opened it. Outside of the building, he slipped the smooth, broken end of the pen clip into the space between the strand of teeth in one handcuff and the ratchet holding it in place. It clicked, and he pulled the strand of teeth out, opening the cuff, which he let fall to the ground. Then he repeated the process for the other handcuff and pocketed his homemade shim.

He shook his hands out and scanned the city. Xander would use every trick he had to evade capture. Xander's soles left a distinct mark, like a vertical tree bough with twigs branching horizontally. The soles also had deep lugs for traction, useful for steep or slippery surfaces outdoors. Chris followed the footprints, but they went dry. Xander had used busy public places on purpose, so he could hide among the people. He had sound instincts on top of his experience and FSB training, causing Chris to wonder if he'd even be able to take Xander down alone.

Chris assessed the situation. Xander had completed his objective of attacking the Shah Deniz Alpha oil rig, and now his main goal would be to get out of town. He had run away from the sea and into town, only to circle around and head back to the sea. *Why?* It all seemed part of ditching any surveillance, but maybe Xander was meeting someone at the mall, or maybe he had a countersurveillance team standing by to snuff Chris.

Not knowing where else to go, Chris continued forward until he reached Park Bulvar. The mall was six stories tall and its architecture was Eastern, but when Chris stepped inside, its interior design was Western. He quickly surveyed a map of the mall's layout. There were movie theaters, a supermarket, and restaurants that served Turkish, Russian, and Azeri food, among fast-food places Chris recognized—McDonalds, KFC, and Sbarro. He recognized a Nike shop, too, but didn't know the other retailers.

He ventured deeper into the building. While the shopping mall was dying out in the US, it seemed to be alive and well in Azerbaijan. He continued through the mall, trying to spot Xander or pick up his tracks again, but he'd lost him.

Chris stepped out of the mall and scanned the area closest to him—nothing. As he searched farther out, he spotted Xander seventy-five meters away, walking through a park. Chris hurried into the park, but Xander didn't stay put, strolling off the grass and along a pier that jutted out into the Caspian Sea. Tied to the pier was the cruise ship Chris had seen when using Marine Finder to scope out the bay: the *M/S Pyotr Tchaikovsky*.

How did he plan to get aboard? Chris had personally searched Xander, and Xander hadn't had a boarding ticket. Chris neared the pier, where he could see through the windows of a security booth. Inside, passengers showed their passports and tickets to a security officer, who seemed to be checking them against a passenger manifest on a laptop. A line of passengers proceeded through an x-ray machine before continuing to the gangway where a crew member greeted them for boarding. *No Xander.*

Chris looked aft to see if he might have boarded posing as a dockworker or ship's crew member. Contrasting the orderliness of the passengers, a gaggle of dockworkers loaded the *Tchaikovsky* with luggage and palates of boxed food and beverages. A chef inspected a container of vegetables. Still, there was no Xander in sight. He must have boarded already.

Chris continued forward without a plan to get aboard himself, searching for a weakness to exploit. With each step, his gut twisted. The Azeri Coast Guard had confiscated his ID, so he'd need a passport from someone who looked like him, but most of the passengers were older. Even if Chris's doppelganger was present, Chris wasn't as skilled at pickpocketing as Hannah, and lifting both a passport and a ticket from the same person seemed impractical. He could try to gain access as a visitor, but he'd still need his passport.

The controlled access for the dockworkers and ship's crew was guarded by a darkly tanned security officer who was paying more attention to what was going on inside his area of responsibility than outside. Chris's best shot at boarding the ship still seemed to be to pose as one of the dockworkers or ship's crew, so he headed in their direction, ignoring his first obstacle, the tanned security officer. Without slowing his stride, Chris ducked under the yellow security tape meant to restrict access. He needed a cover—fast. His mind spun feverishly: supervisor, galley hand, forklift operator, dockworker... Posing as a supervisor might be a problem if he ran into the actual supervisor he was impersonating. If he attempted to act as a galley hand, the chef would probably recognize him as an imposter. As for the forklift, there was only one, and the operator was running it. A common dockworker seemed the ticket, but the guys loading the luggage wore matching blue overalls, and Chris had none. His gut continued to wind around itself, but he didn't let it show on his face. Confidence was key.

Without moving his head around like a lost passenger, he covertly searched the area for something he could use as part of his dockworker guise—uniform, hard hat, soft hat—anything. He thought posing as an electrician might be a good cover, but there was no utility belt around, either. *Damn!*

After he reached a stack of boxes of vegetables, he picked one up, carried it over to the chef, and placed it on top of the other boxes in front of him. The chef looked like he was about to ask a question, but Chris passed him, maintaining a busy pace. He worried the chef saw through him, but he didn't dwell on it. He just kept going.

He passed an abandoned suitcase with a clipboard balanced on it. Chris snatched up the clipboard and took it with him. Maintaining his forward momentum, he stepped into the ship's cargo hold, careful not to get run over by the forklift as it transferred a load of boxed provisions to the ship. His guts unwound a bit now that he was onboard, and he wanted to give a victory shout, but, again, he couldn't show his emotions.

A wiry worker gazed at Chris's clipboard, then him.

I hope this isn't your clipboard.

Wiry said something in Azeri, but Chris didn't understand. He could continue walking deeper into the ship and risk raising suspicion or stay and try to engage in a conversation that might raise suspicion. He paused and stared at the man.

"Your paper empty," Wiry said in broken English.

Chris looked down at his clipboard. Wiry was right; the page was blank. Chris answered in Russian with a smile, but Wiry didn't understand, so Chris said in English, "You're right, the paper is blank. And that's the least of my problems." *Confidence. Breathe.* He took a shot of oxygen straight to his lungs and walked past Wiry.

Now he had to switch identities from worker to passenger, and he needed to ditch the clipboard. He climbed one of the ship's ladders to the main deck and found himself in the reception area. A crowd was lined up at the counter to show their passports and tickets to the ship's purser, who checked each passenger's data on his computer before he handed out cabin keys.

"I don't know who he is," a large woman said loudly in Russian.

Surprise was etched on the purser's face.

"He's not with me," the large woman said.

"Sir, where is your passport and ticket?" the purser asked.

The woman chuckled. "I'm kidding." She nodded at the skinny man beside her. "This is my husband." Then she handed his passport and ticket to the purser.

The purser smiled uneasily. "I almost thought you were giving me more work to do. Part of my job is to catch stowaways."

The passengers laughed, but Chris showed no expression as he passed the mob of people, avoiding the purser. Traversing the central passageway, he found sick bay and noticed the numbers on the doors of guest cabins that lined the port and starboard sides. Sitting in the passageway was a maid's cart, and there was a clipboard on top. The maid was inside a cabin with her back to him, making a bed, so Chris slipped his clipboard underneath the maid's as he walked past. When he reached the end of the passageway, a couple descended the stairs, appearing lost.

The woman spoke in Azeri, gesturing erratically as she glanced between him and her companion.

Chris thought he'd been discovered, and his stomach jumped.

Then she turned to her left and pointed at the sauna, directing her companion's attention to it.

Chris was relieved not to have been busted, but a voice came over the PA system, causing his gut to tighten up again. Maybe they were announcing that a stowaway was onboard and that passengers should report him.

I've got to find where the restrooms are, so I can hide out.

The announcement was repeated in Russian and then English. "All visitors must depart the ship now."

This was the critical moment when he still had a chance to abort the mission, but he'd come too far to give up now, and he was taking Xander down, dead or alive.

He ascended the stairs to the middle deck, which was similar to the deck below, with numbered guest cabins port and starboard, with one exception at the stern of the ship, where the Tatiana Restaurant was. But it was closed.

The PA system came on again. "All visitors must depart the ship *now.*"

He spotted a restroom and made a mental note of its location so he could hide out there later. Other passengers milled about, and Chris blended in with them, climbing the stairs to the next deck.

Seeing the pool up there put a smile on his face, and he imagined going for a swim. He took a relaxed breath. Near the pool was a bar and another restroom—hideout number two. The cabins on the deck were junior suites, double the size of the other rooms, and toward the bow was a lounge.

Although Chris was getting thicker and thicker into this situation, he had no visual confirmation that Xander was actually aboard the ship. He'd seen Xander go in the ship's direction, but he didn't actually see him board, and he still hadn't spotted him on the ship, either. But Chris's instincts told him Xander was here. He heard Hannah's voice in his head, pushing him on: *You've got better instincts than any shooter I know.*

He climbed the steps to the sun deck, the top deck of the ship. It was deserted. It would be ideal to catch Xander here at night. Because Xander was so slippery, and the situation so dangerous, this kill-or-capture mission had become a kill-or-be-killed mission. Eliminating him here and tossing him overboard seemed the best option. But Chris had to find him first.

The *Tchaikovsky's* horn sounded, signaling that the ship was getting underway. It pulled farther and farther away from the Azeri pier. Chris looked around, realizing how conspicuous he must've appeared standing alone on the sun deck, and he headed below to mingle with other passengers, but most of them were gone. The ship's library, TV room, and souvenir shop were all vacant. Even the mob of passengers at the reception area had cleared out.

They must all be checking in to their cabins.

As Sonny would say, Chris stood out like a pork chop at a bar mitzvah. His stomach twisted at the thought of Sonny, and with him, Hannah. When Chris escaped the Azeri Coast Guard and went after Xander, he hadn't noticed whether or not they had escaped, too. Whatever happened to them, he hoped they were okay. But he had to keep his eye on the prize.

With the majority of passengers off in their rooms, it was time to hide out. He descended the steps to the deck below and pulled on the restroom door handle, but the door was locked. When he checked the other restrooms, they were locked, too. Apparently, he wasn't the first stowaway with the bright idea to hide out in the restroom. His plan on the fly had crashed and burned. He could try to duck out in some inconspicuous place, like somewhere in the engine room, but if he was spotted, he'd suddenly become suspicious. The best place to hide was probably in plain sight.

He made his way to the lounge, where the Azeri couple he'd seen earlier was now seated at the bar. He took one of the low-backed stools next to them, and they seemed to be in their own little world, oblivious to him, and he was fine with that. Chris was a teetotaler, and he thought about ordering vodka for appearance's sake but figured it would be odd to order a drink and not drink it, so he'd just get a water.

Now, if Chris was going to successfully hide out in plain sight, he was going to have to engage in conversation, but he needed to figure out his cover story before he did anything. As a frogman, he was used to planning on the fly—literally while riding in a plane or helicopter to the target area—and he was used to the fluidity of changing situations, but this stowaway fluidity was worse than diarrhea.

"What would you like to drink?" a bartender in a black-and-white crew uniform said in Russian with a smile. He had a laid-back way about him that helped Chris unclench.

Without thinking, Chris answered in Russian, "I'll just have a water, please."

"Drinks are free," he said. "Are you sure?"

"I'm sure," Chris said.

As the bartender turned to get his drink, Chris scoped out the area. The bar was unremarkable with shelves of bottles of various shapes and sizes filled with liquor, standing against a mirrored wall. A Coca-Cola refrigerator unit sat off to the side—a sign that capitalism hadn't totally died in Russia—and the stainless steel counter was clean and shiny. He swiveled in his seat to scope out the rest of the lounge. Quartets of plush burgundy chairs surrounded small drink tables scattered throughout. Except for the bartender and the couple at the bar, there were no customers in the lounge, making it appear large and open. The air smelled clean, and one side of the space was mostly windows. Sunlight provided most of the light in the lounge, and outside the Caspian Sea sparkled.

An unpardonably pretty young lady appeared in the doorway to the lounge. Her hair was carnelian in color, red as she passed through the sunlight and brown when she walked away from the sunlight and sat down on the shady seat next to Chris.

The bartender placed Chris's water on the counter, and Chris thanked him. When the bartender asked the woman what she wanted to drink, she looked at Chris's water and said in Russian, "I'll have a vodka, too. No, make that a Bubble Gum Vodka."

"Certainly," the bartender said.

The woman looked at Chris and said, "I love this river cruise."

"This is my first time," Chris said.

The bartender brought the lady her vodka, and she took a sip. "Oh, you'll love it, too, especially Saint Petersburg. It's lovely this time of year."

"Looking forward to it." Actually, Chris didn't look forward to it, and he hoped he finished his mission before the ship got that far. The deeper he traveled into Russia, the more difficult it would be to escape.

"I work at a bank here in Baku," she said.

Chris smiled. "That sounds like a good job."

"Do you live in Baku?" she asked.

Damn. He hadn't thought of a place of residence yet. "Canada." He'd used the cover before, and there was no time like the present to resurrect it.

"Your Russian is good for a Canadian," she said.

He'd hardly spoken enough for her to know whether his Russian was good or bad—she was just being friendly. "My parents were diplomats, and we lived in Moscow for a while," he said. It was true, but his parents worked for the US State Department, not Canada's.

"My name is Kisa." In Russian, her name translated to *pussycat*, and he had to force himself not to react.

He smiled politely. "Chris."

"I like that name," she said.

Chris's throat became warm and dry, and he took a drink. "*Kisa* is a pretty name."

The ship's purser entered the lounge then, and Chris's stomach sank. But despite feeling he was about to be busted, he acted as if everything was normal.

The purser came to the bar and spoke in Azeri. Not understanding what he said made Chris more nervous. Whatever the words were, it caused the Azeri couple to look surprised. The purser eyed Chris.

"I'm sorry?" Chris said in Russian.

The purser spoke Russian back to him. "One of the passengers reported seeing someone sneak onboard."

"How?" Chris asked.

The purser's face was serious. "The passenger said the stowaway came in where the dockworkers were loading supplies on the ship."

Me. Now I can make a run for it and dive off the ship, but will I be able to swim to shore before the Azeri Coast Guard picks me up again? Boy, will they be pissed.

"What does this stowaway look like?" Chris asked.

"Tall and fit," the purser said.

Chris forced a grin. "Sounds like me."

The purser stared at Chris for a moment. "No, this man was older and had a gray beard."

Xander. He is *here.*

The purser leaned forward. "He should hope he gets caught before we reach Russian waters. Russia doesn't tolerate stowaways."

"How soon before we reach Russia?" Chris inquired.

"Tonight we'll sail off the coast of Russia, and tomorrow evening we'll pull into our first Russian port. At Olya on the Volga River," the purser said. "One of the oldest fishing villages in that region."

The deeper they penetrated Russia, the bigger the chance Chris would be busted, and he wondered what life in a gulag would be like, if he survived to that point. "We'll let you know if we see him," Chris said.

"Bet you didn't know this cruise would be such an adventure," the purser said.

Chris gave the man a wink. "Not a dull moment yet."

"Sorry to have bothered you. Enjoy your cruise," the purser said before departing the lounge.

So Xander is here, but where? He obviously wasn't using the hiding-in-plain-sight tactic.

"So what kind of work do you do?" Kisa asked, interrupting his train of thought.

Chris couldn't think of a suitable answer other than the cover story his team had come up with when renting the office in London. "I work for Outdoor Mountain Clothing. We're looking at expanding operations into Eastern Europe."

She took another sip of her drink. "So you're here on business."

Chris nodded. He chatted with her for a little while longer before excusing himself to take a look around the ship.

While he searched the ship bow to stern for Xander, he kept an eye out for a place to spend the night. As he passed through the ship, he stopped by the reception desk and picked up a copy of the cruise itinerary and map. He figured either Xander was hiding in one of the restricted crew areas or he'd somehow acquired a room. As for a place for Chris to stay the night, the TV room seemed like a good option. Falling asleep watching the tube might appear natural, but if Xander found him before he found Xander, he wouldn't have much space to maneuver and defend himself in the small TV room. Xander could effectively trap him inside.

Another option for Chris would be to fake like he was drunk and pass out in the lounge, which seemed like his best option, but as a teetotaler, he wasn't confident he could pull off the drunk act.

At dinnertime, Chris journeyed to the dining room to search for Xander and get some food, but the seats were assigned to passengers by cabin, and Chris's belly was shit out of luck. He read the names on the cards at the tables with no-shows, particularly the men. Maybe Xander whacked some poor dude and took his cabin. Chris wished he had a golf pencil and some paper in his pocket, so he could covertly write the names down.

Kisa arrived and spotted him before he could slip out of the dining room. She waved him down.

"Where are you sitting?" she asked excitedly.

"I'm not really hungry," he said. "I'm going back to the lounge to have a drink."

She smiled. "Drinking without eating, you must be part Russian. But you should really eat."

"I'll be fine. Maybe I'll grab a snack later." He talked to her for a little bit more before excusing himself.

He returned to the lounge, and he was happily surprised to find others there, too. If he was going to do his passed-out-drunk act, he better get started, so he ordered a vodka and chose an area to sit with a view of the lounge and easy access to the exit. He sat down on a chair next to a table partly covered with empty glasses, hoping passengers would think the glasses were his. On the other side of the table was a tipsy man who spoke to Chris, and during the course of their conversation, Chris gave the man his vodka. The man asked where Chris's cabin was and he tried to avoid answering, but the man insisted, so he gave a random number and told him dinner was being served in the dining area. The man thanked him before standing and making a slightly unsteady walk through the exit, leaving Chris with all the empty drinking glasses next to him.

"Thank you," Chris said, but the man was already gone.

He'd been hanging out in the lounge for about an hour when Kisa arrived and sat down next to him. She had a new glow about her as if she'd freshened up. She was attractive, enjoyable to be with, and her companionship helped him blend in with the other passengers, but she might figure out he was a stowaway. It also occurred to Chris that she might work for Russia's FSB, hunting for a prospective spouse, so she could obtain citizenship in a country like Great Britain or the USA—or Canada.

She seemed to notice the mass of drinking glasses beside him, and her eyes grew wide.

Chris shrugged.

She glanced at the ship's itinerary in his hands. "Anything interesting?"

He needed to check the restricted areas for where Xander might be hiding. "I was just looking at the schedule and thinking that after dinner I'd like to go on the ship's tour."

"I was thinking about doing that, too," she said.

"Great."

"After that there's a movie playing later tonight in the conference room up on the sun deck," she said. *"Brat."*

Chris knew *Brat* was Russian for *brother*, but he hadn't seen the movie. "What's it about?"

"It takes place right after the dissolution of the Soviet Union, and a young soldier loses his job in the Army so he travels to Saint Petersburg and joins the mafia. The movie received an award nomination at the Cannes Film Festival."

Chris smiled. "I'd like to see that." He really did want to see it.

"Would you like to go to my room for a drink?" she asked.

Maybe she was just inviting him to her room for a drink, or maybe this was a booty call, but Chris was a pastor and single pastors didn't do booty calls. "I'm sorry," he said.

"Maybe later," she said.

Chris smiled kindly without committing, but he still didn't really have a place to sleep without sticking out as a stowaway. *Maybe I can sleep on the deck in Kisa's cabin.*

They hung out in the lounge some more before going for a walk around the ship. Still no Xander, but they came upon a small buffet with leftovers from dinner. Chris filled a plate with beef stroganoff and a *bublik*, a Russian bagel with a large hole in it. "Are you hungry?" he asked Kisa.

"I had enough at dinner, thanks." Instead, she took one of the teacups sitting next to an ornate silver-and-enamel Russian samovar shaped like an urn. From the top of the samovar, she lifted a teapot and poured a small amount of concentrated tea—*zavarka* being the most common—heated from the steaming water at the bottom of the samovar, into her cup. Then she used the spigot at the bottom of the samovar to pour in hot water, diluting the tea to her taste. She sat down with Chris at a small table.

Sautéed beef in a sauce of Smetana, a heavy sour cream, assaulted Chris's taste buds. He tried not to make a pig of himself as he filled his empty stomach, but afterward, his body felt tired and his mind slow. He needed to rest, if only for a moment. He wished Xander was already captured and he was on a cruise with Hannah, but wishing didn't make it so.

In spite of Chris's fatigue, he and Kisa met with the other passengers in the reception area and the tour began. Their guide showed them the bridge, engine room, and other parts of the ship, and Chris closely inspected each area for Xander, but there was no sign of him.

As the tour ended, Chris spotted him. He was walking out of the cabin nearest the sauna and going up the stairs. It jolted Chris to such an extent it felt like his heart had stopped.

The bright sunshine had retreated, and dark clouds rolled in, rumbling with thunder. "Looks like a storm is coming," Kisa said.

"Could I meet up with you later at the movie?" Chris asked.

"Huh?" she said.

Xander was getting away, and Chris tried to appear nonplussed as he walked in the direction of Xander's cabin. "Could I meet you later?"

"Is something wrong?"

Everything was wrong, and it was about to get worse. "Everything is fine." He tried to smile but couldn't.

"Your eyes, they look different, like something is wrong."

He wanted to break into a sprint, but there were others in the passageway and he didn't want to draw their attention.

Kisa looked at the deck as they walked. "Mama says I try too hard sometimes."

Oh hell. He felt sorry for her, but he didn't have time for confessionals, and if that's what Kisa was doing, he wished she'd hurry up.

She said, "If you don't want me around, I understand."

He stopped in front of Xander's cabin. If he could get inside, he could wait there to ambush him. "I'll catch up to you in a little bit."

She smiled awkwardly, as if she wanted to believe him but couldn't. "Okay. I'll see you at the movie."

Chris attempted to smile again, but he didn't believe in it, and he knew she could see through him. Even so, he said, "See you there."

There was less bounce in her gait as she left him, disappearing up the stairs.

He frowned, guilt creeping in at hurting her, but Xander could return at any moment. He glanced down the hall. No one was looking in his direction, so he tried the doorknob but it was locked. He reached in his pocket and pulled out the clip he'd broken off the pen he took in Azerbaijan. He inserted the shim into the lock and attempted to pick it, but his tool was too simple and the lock too complex. He cursed himself for wasting time on what he should've known was futile.

He checked the hall again. There was a group of people there, but they were focused on talking to one another. Chris kicked the door, hard, near the doorknob, popping the door wide open. The group in the hall turned to see what the noise was as Chris slipped inside, closed the door, and locked it. He gave a tug to make sure the door would stay locked, but it opened freely. Upon examining it, the lock strike in the frame was knocked crooked, as was the lock set in the door. He straightened them before closing the door and trying to lock it again. This time, the lock held.

He took a brief examination of the compartment, and in the bathtub he found a man's body, dried streams of blood exiting his nose and ears. Chris felt for a pulse. Dead.

Chris shook his head, and it struck him that the average person would feel horror at such a sight, but his eyes had been forced to see so much worse, each time tearing another piece from the fabric of his spirit. Such experiences were what helped motivate him to get out of the military in the first place, before his spirit was stripped completely. The adrenaline and the brotherhood could no longer bind him to the job—until Hannah had pulled him back in. Now his venom for evil men was full again. He had a mission to finish, and there was no turning back.

He figured he could wait in the bathroom until Xander entered the cabin. Once he was inside, Chris could knock him unconscious and tie him up, but there was no rope in the room. Chris opened a dresser drawer and found the dead man's T-shirts. Those would work. Expecting each room to have lifejackets for its passengers, Chris was able to locate two in the compartment. He could use them for both Xander and himself. At night, when they neared a port, he could jump ship with his prisoner and swim them to the nearest boat and sail back to Azerbaijan. But it was risky. The water would be cold, and they wouldn't be able to survive for too terribly long.

As he waited in the bathroom, he took another look at the dead man's body. Xander probably viewed it with the same cold detachment as Chris did. Maybe Xander was right, Chris's ability to think like him was what had allowed Chris to find him.

If I were him, what would be my next move?

Xander would need to debrief. Then he'd jock up to do the next mission. For Chris, the debrief would be in Langley; for Xander, the debrief would be in Moscow.

How would I get to Moscow?

Xander could simply take the ship to Moscow and turn himself over to the local authorities there and wait until his superiors bailed him out, but Xander had been under deep cover for so long and he seemed proud of his abilities as a NOC.

I wouldn't turn myself over to the local yokels. I am a professional.

The PA system came on, and a voice announced the ship was nearing a port, where the *Tchaikovsky* would stop and take on supplies. The supply-port officials would probably have less manpower, training, and equipment to hunt for an illegal immigrant than big-city Moscow officials. By the time the search intensified, Xander would have already hot-wired a car and been on his way north. Then he'd ditch his stolen car in the next town and make sure he was "clean" of surveillance before making the rest of the journey to Moscow.

That's it. He'll jump ship here!

Chris rushed out of the room and up the stairs. He knew there was no convenient place to jump from on the middle deck, so he ascended past it to the next deck. There, he left the stairs, ran aft of the lounge, and dodged the other passengers. An imposing shirtless guy walked in the middle of the passageway, oblivious to others around him. As Chris ran by, he clipped the guy's shoulder, causing him to shout angrily. Chris eventually reached the pool. It was deserted.

Blackness blanketed the moon and stars, and rain diffused the illumination of the artificial land lights, which stretched long reflected limbs across the water. The sound of the ship's diesel engines churning, the rain pouring down, and the sky rumbling made it impossible to hear whether someone was swimming or not. The Caspian Sea extended like Tyrian ink from a bottle, and twenty-five meters away from the ship, Chris could barely make out what appeared to be splashes characteristic of a swimmer. The identity of the person wasn't clear, but the swimmer stroked toward shore, unlike someone who might've fallen off the ship and wanted to be rescued. The swimmer only had a hundred more meters to swim before reaching the bank, not a difficult swim.

If it's Xander, he's getting away.

Chris climbed over the rail and prepared to jump.

If that isn't Xander, I'm screwed.

The noise of hitting the water seemed so incredibly loud. It was always like that when hunting bad guys: Chris's own noise was amplified in his mind, and adrenaline heightened his senses. Before becoming a frogman, he wasn't as comfortable in the water, but through training and experience, it became instinct, allowing him to focus on the mission and nothing else: *get Xander.*

The cold water attacked Chris's senses, but he knew if he swam fast, his body would warm up. While the swimmer stroked freestyle, splashing toward land, Chris swam a combat sidestroke, making no splashes. The petrol in the water fumed so deep and thick in the back of his nostrils he almost choked on it—but if he held his face above water, his hips would sink as if he were swimming uphill, so he stuck his face in it and maintained his horizontal balance. Chris stretched his body out to increase his length, make longer strokes, and swim faster, and he cranked his hips and utilized his core muscles to rotate his body in the water, boosting his engine. He was gaining on the swimmer.

A ship's horn sounded, startling him, and an announcement came over the PA. "Man overboard!" It came from the cruise ship. "Man overboard!"

Before Chris could close the distance between him and the swimmer, the swimmer reached shore and climbed out of the water, silhouetting himself against the smattering of blurred lights behind him. It was Xander. Chris imagined being the water and avoided thinking directly about Xander, so as to not trigger any sixth sense in him. Then the man disappeared over the seawall.

Chris reached the shore and slinked over the seawall, as well, and into the mud on the other side, but Xander was already gone. Lying in the muck, Chris observed his surroundings. No one moved on him, so he assumed he hadn't been spotted. He rose to a crouch and stalked through a parking lot looking for his target.

The sound of glass shattering cracked through the night air. Maybe someone was shooting at him through a window, but Chris wasn't hit and there was no sonic snap of a round passing near him. The noise came from the parking lot ahead, and Chris noticed a small fleet of white trucks. An engine started up, and Chris hurried in the direction of the engine's sound, but he was too late. The truck was driving away.

Chris rushed to the row of white vehicles, where *Caspian Shipping* was written on the sides and backs of the trucks. He took the shim out of his pocket and inserted it into the keyhole of the driver's door but he couldn't unlock it. So, taking a cue from Xander, he searched for something solid to break the window with. As he was searching, he noticed a compass on a dash inside another white truck and decided he wanted that truck instead, so when he found a massive rock on the ground, he used it to bust through the passenger's-side window. Then he unlocked the door, climbed in over the glass, and sat in the driver's seat. He tried the shim again, this time in the ignition, but he couldn't start the vehicle. He wielded the rock like a caveman and busted the ignition cover. After hot-wiring the vehicle, he sped off to find Xander.

As Chris gained ground, the rain flowed through the broken passenger window, and he turned on the windshield wipers. He wished he had a GPS to help him locate a main road leading to Moscow. Although he could read Russian, there were no signs indicating the direction of a major street. He followed what seemed to be a main road leading north, but it terminated in a dead end and he had to backtrack. He followed the street until it veered west, away from the Caspian Sea. Then he turned onto another road leading north. As the windshield wipers beat a monotonous rhythm, he felt contained in a maze of little roads as he tried to navigate his way through a small village.

When he came to a body of water, he had no idea where he was. His compass indicated he was traveling north, but with the moon and stars being obscured by the rainclouds as they were, he couldn't use celestial navigation to confirm its accuracy. All he knew was that he was getting deeper into Russia. If his luck didn't change soon, he might have to abort the mission. He prayed he'd know where to go, but he didn't feel like he received an answer. He felt like he was on his own.

Just because he felt disoriented in a strange land didn't automatically mean the compass was wrong, so he decided to trust it some more and started driving west. The body of water ended as Chris continued to follow the road, but he ran into another dead end, so he had to turn and resume his northerly trek. In spite of the confusing array of streets and waterways, he finally ran into Route E119, which he hoped would go all the way to Moscow.

Although it was possible Xander had stayed put, he'd stolen a vehicle, and it was more likely that he was headed to Moscow. Xander knew customs officials and local law enforcement would be looking for the "man overboard," so he was probably headed north for the first big town, where he could ditch his stolen vehicle and find his connecting transportation to Moscow. Chris was lagging and had lost more time navigating his way through the small village, so now he had to play catch up. He pressed harder on the gas pedal, pushing the truck faster.

27

A bolt of lightning struck less than a klick away, and Chris was driving directly into the storm. Carefully watching the road in front of his headlights, he drove as swiftly as he dared on the slick dark asphalt, somehow managing to keep himself between the ditches. He had to find Xander, and fast. As Chris rounded a curve, he nearly rear-ended a white truck with its lights turned off.

Jackpot.

The road became straight again, and Chris accelerated, moving alongside the other truck, and got visual confirmation it was indeed Xander inside. Chris backed off a bit and used his bumper to tap Xander's vehicle behind the back wheel. Then he pressed down on the gas pedal and turned the wheel hard into Xander's truck, causing it to lose traction. Chris steered clear as Xander lost control and skidded off the road into a ditch. Chris was still going fast, so he passed him and circled back. Xander was attempting to drive out of the ditch when he returned, but he'd only managed to entrench his vehicle more.

Lightning struck, closer this time, flooding the forest with light. Xander leaped from his truck and ran into the woods. Chris pulled over beside the road, disconnected the ignition, jumped out, and gave chase. He ran for all he was worth, and then he ran faster still. A blinding flash of lightning struck, followed by a *crack* that sounded like a tree splitting open, and something heavy hit the forest floor with a loud *thud*.

The lightning will probably kill me before Xander does.

Branches whipped Chris's face and the uneven ground made him stumble, but he didn't let the obstacles slow him down. He ran until his lungs burned and his thighs ached, but Xander picked up his pace, too.

Chris wanted to avoid tall trees that would serve as a lightning rod and rebound the lightning out of the trunk and hit him. He glanced up, but all the trees were tall, and it would be impossible to avoid them.

The woods became thicker and darker as he ran, and Xander disappeared until a brilliant white flash of lightning spotlighted him. The forest thinned out into a clearing where a dacha—a Russian country home—stood. Chris thought he saw Xander enter it, and he ran across the clearing and attempted to open the door, but it was locked. He kicked it open and rushed inside. As he searched the living room for Xander, he also looked for any weapons of opportunity. When he passed through the kitchen, lightning struck again, and he spotted an ax embedded in a tree stump outside.

There's a weapon of opportunity if I ever saw one.

A creaking noise came from one of the rooms down the hall. Chris checked the first room but only found a bed and a dresser—the closet was empty, too. He checked the rest of the dacha, only to find that no one was home.

Maybe the house is settling, he reasoned.

He exited the dacha through the back door. The sound of movement in the leaves came from around the house, and Chris followed the noise. A rat. When he turned the corner of the building again, he saw the tree stump, but the ax was gone. His stomach dropped.

A jagged streak of light descended from the sky, branching out toward the earth. Its white branches sprouted more branches, smiting a nearby tree and causing an explosion at the trunk. Chris had been under effective mortar attack before, but this lightning strike gave him pause to check if he'd pissed himself. Just then, he heard a noise behind him. He spun around to see Xander standing there wielding the ax.

"I did not realize you were alone," Xander said.

Chris said nothing.

"You do not know when to give up, do you?"

Chris remained quiet. He hoped to grab Xander's arm before he could swing the ax, but he swung before Chris could move in to grapple. Chris stepped back instead, the blade just missing him. Xander was too quick.

Chris positioned himself next to a tree, and when Xander swung again, Chris stepped outside of the swing. Xander missed, and the ax imbedded itself in the trunk. Before Xander could pull the ax loose, Chris kicked him in the crotch. Xander lifted to his toes with a grunt. Then Chris swung at his enemy's solar plexus, but Xander released his grip on the ax, leaving it in the tree, and stepped back. Chris's punch missed. He had put so much oomph into it, though, that he overextended himself. Xander blew at Chris like a squall, exploiting his awkward positioning, and iron-fisted him in the side of the gut. Chris's air caught, breath ceasing to come as the wind was knocked out of him.

"Prepare to join Michael Winthrop," Xander said.

He punched at Chris's head, and Chris ducked, averting the blow. But Xander's other fist was too speedy, and the follow-up smashed Chris in the face, throwing him to the ground. It hit him with such devastating impact that he struggled to lift his body from the dirt. It rained so heavily that he didn't know if the stream running down his face was water or blood.

Xander retrieved the ax, his dripping hands clenched tightly around the handle. "You Americans are no match for Mother Russia. That is why you could not save Michael. You cannot even save yourself."

"I agree with one thing you said," Chris said.

Xander moved in closer with the ax. "What is that?"

"I don't know when to give up." Chris scrambled to his feet, but he staggered from the cast-iron aftereffect of Xander's punch. His body reacted slower than he intended. He didn't know whether he was about to throw up or pass out.

Xander's shoulders and arms moved back, body coiled as he lifted the ax and prepared to deal the final blow. Lightning flashed. Rain poured down Xander's face, and his eyes filled with insane rage.

Chris needed to move out of the way, but something was wrong, as if there was a disconnect between his brain and body. And there wasn't enough time for the effect to wear off.

This is the end.

Crack! Lightning struck the tree next to Xander. Then his countenance changed as if an artillery shell had struck him. In the next instant, something struck Chris, too. His skin clenched his bones. The noise was so deafening he thought his head had exploded. His body felt like it had been hit by flaming shrapnel, knocking him off his feet, and his vision whited out.

The outline of trees appeared on a blank white canvas and the morning aquamarine of the sky seeped through. The lightning and rain had stopped. In fact, all sound was gone. Chris had lost his hearing, but he was thankful he could still see. He smacked his lips at the strange metal taste in his mouth.

Nearby, a gray squirrel sat up on the ground, watching him with big black eyes. Then there was a faint sound of birds chirping. At first, he thought he'd imagined the sound, but it became louder, and he thanked God his hearing was returning. The air smelled fresh, and the forest was peaceful.

Chris fought to sit up. He noticed one shoe had a hole in the sole, probably where the lightning had entered from the ground. His other shoe was missing, and there was a charred hole in the bottom of his sock. He looked around and spotted his missing shoe, crawled over to it, and noticed it had a hole in the bottom, too. The lightning had entered one foot, traveled through his body, and exited his other foot, taking his shoe off with it.

Groggily, and without thinking, he put his shoe on. His legs were unsteady as he stood. He wobbled a little and put a hand out, leaning against the tree nearest him. Its bark seemed to be intact, confirming that the lightning current had traveled from the bottom of the tree trunk over the surface of the ground, rather than exiting the tree's side. Then he saw the ax in the dirt and picked it up. At first, the ax felt heavy, but as his strength came back, it became lighter.

Off to the side, Xander sat stock-still with his eyes open, as if paralyzed. His hair looked wiry, and his clothes were charred. One of his shoes and a sock were missing, and the bottom of his naked foot was fried.

"I need an ambulance," Xander said with a moan, battling to breathe and slurring his words. "Get me an ambulance!" He drooled out of one corner of his mouth.

Chris's hate for Xander bubbled inside him. Reverend Luther said hate could destroy a pastor quicker than most anything. He tried to heed the reverend's warning and took even sips of air into his lungs. With Xander already incapacitated by the lightning strike, he wasn't an immediate threat, he reminded himself. Killing him would be akin to cold-blooded murder, especially for a pastor. Even so, Chris was madder than hell.

Xander seemed to read his eyes. "You cannot kill me here," he said quietly, "not in my own country."

Chris had let the anger boil up until he was so full of it that all he could do now was explode. He moved into position and raised the ax high in the air.

"You cannot do this to me," Xander objected, "not in my own—"

Before Xander finished, Chris brought down the ax with a mighty swing, stopping Xander midsentence. The ax split a fallen tree trunk.

Chris's dark side chided him for not killing Xander right then and there, but he loved God more than he hated Xander. It was a small price to pay for giving his soul to a greater good.

28

Chris searched Xander's pockets and cleaned out the Azeri cash and a cheap pocketknife—probably taken from the poor passenger he killed on the cruise ship. Chris used the knife to cut some vines to use as rope, then hog-tied Xander.

"You make one wrong move or sound, I'll kill you," Chris promised. And it was a promise he intended to keep. He took off Xander's other shoe and sock, so if Xander miraculously recovered enough to make a run for it, he'd have to run in his burned bare feet. He stuffed the sock in Xander's mouth as a gag and used the vine to tie it in place. Then Chris dragged him through the woods for several minutes, having to stop for a moment to rest, before he found his vehicle.

Still not functioning at one-hundred-percent strength, Chris strained to hoist Xander into the vehicle. Then he crawled into the driver's side and started the engine. There would be trouble waiting for him to the south, near the Russian supply port where he and Xander had jumped ship and stolen the vehicles, so he drove to the nearest port and absconded with a boat, tarp, and two containers of fuel. He covered Xander with the tarp and cast off.

After motoring south on the Caspian Sea for a while, he was alone on the water with his prisoner. He uncovered Xander, who remained quiet and motionless. Xander had his eyes open, squinting at the sunlight, but he was still alive. The vines remained tied tightly. Chris undid the gag and let Xander breathe freely.

Chris observed him. "Did you think it would end like this?"

"I was fulfilling destiny," Xander said, slurring his words, spittle dripping from the corner of his mouth.

"So was I."

"I am KGB."

"FSB," Chris said.

"Whether I am called KGB or FSB, I am still alive and thriving," Xander said.

"It's true that you're alive, but I wouldn't call your present situation *thriving*."

"Everything I did, I did for my country. You should understand that."

"Maybe that was true for you at one time. It was true for me at one time. Immediately after 9-11, everything I did, I did for my country. But after a while, everything I did, I did for my Teammates. My guess is that now everything you do, you do for yourself."

Xander said nothing.

"Did you ever try to be anything different?" Chris asked.

Xander groaned. "I have. More than once. This is all I know how to do. This is all I want to do."

Chris shook his head. "It doesn't sound like you tried very hard, then. And now your days as a spook are over. Your body is so paralyzed you can hardly speak without slurring your words and spitting on yourself. You *are* something different. A prisoner."

The skin around Xander's eyes drooped as if under a tremendous burden.

"And now you have no protégé to carry on your legacy," Chris said.

Xander's voice shook as he spoke. "You have no idea how hard I searched for him. And you cannot comprehend the investment of time, the laser focus, and Herculean efforts I made to polish him."

"You speak of Animus as if he was a tool."

"He was. A very valuable tool... You and I are not so very different. We both devote our lives to creating valuable tools."

"Don't confuse your life with mine."

"As long as I live, I will remember you, and one day I will make you pay."

Chris thought for a moment. "You'll have to take a number and stand in line."

Xander gave an odd stare as if he didn't understand.

Chris spotted a vessel up ahead in the distance. He turned to Xander. *"Babushki bayu."* He gagged Xander with his sock again and covered him with the tarp.

Chris kept composed and didn't try to hide. On the boat was a net and a man who wore what looked like a wetsuit overall. He neared Chris's vessel, so Chris waved at him and cruised past.

He sailed until the gas tank ran dry, and he used one of the cans to refuel. Then he continued until the sun surrendered to the evening, and he arrived in Baku. There, he broke into a car, locked Xander in the trunk, hot-wired the ignition, and drove to the Agency jet at Heydar Aliyev International Airport. Chris was so exhausted and weakened he feared he might lose consciousness at any moment. He parked the car and stepped out. Hannah and Sonny must have seen him approach the tarmac because they met him on the stairs.

Hannah was the first to join him, and they greeted each other with a hug. Her eyes filled with concern. "Are you okay?" she asked.

"I'm alive," he said. "Xander is in the trunk."

Her face lit up like she'd been given a brightly wrapped birthday present.

"You're shitting me," Sonny said.

Chris barely had the energy to shrug. "See for yourself."

Sonny pushed past Chris and Hannah, skipping steps as he raced to the bottom. He reached the vehicle, opened the driver's side, popped opened the trunk, and hurried to the rear to peek inside. "Hot damn!"

When Hannah took her turn to look inside the trunk, she let out a *whoop* and high-fived Sonny. They wasted no time in dragging Xander out and dumping him on the tarmac. There, they searched him. When they picked him up to his feet, he fell.

"What did you do to him?" Sonny asked. "Looks like you stuck him in a bathtub full of electric eels. Holy shit. Dude can't even stand up."

Chris couldn't see Xander's face from his perspective, but he imagined Xander with slobber on his chin and a scared look in his eyes. He wanted to help them carry Xander onboard the jet, but he barely had enough strength to carry himself, so he boarded the plane and took a seat.

After Hannah and Sonny brought Xander aboard, Hannah told the pilot to go wheels up and take them to Langley.

While the pilot made preparations for flight, Hannah and Sonny checked out the homemade vine ties Chris had used on Xander and the dirty sock in his mouth. "You totally went primitive," Sonny said with glee. "I love it."

But they cuffed Xander to the plane, anyway, and put sensory deprivation headphones, blinders, and a black hood on him. Sonny volunteered to take the first watch over their prisoner.

Hannah returned to Chris and sat beside him. "You look like you've been shot out of a cannon."

"I feel like it," he admitted.

"Do you need medical attention?"

"Just some rest. Feels good to sit in a cushioned chair." He paused a moment. "How is Mikhail?"

"He's out of critical condition, but he's undergoing surgery again," Hannah said. "He's got some tough bark on him, though, so we think he'll be okay."

Sonny had a bag of nuts and munched on them like a damn squirrel at a movie theater while he watched Xander. Chris let out a soft chuckle, then met Hannah's eyes, his expression serious. "Did the Azeri Coast Guard mistreat you?"

"We had a cell to ourselves, and they were professional about it," she said. "The Agency bailed us out pretty quickly. It was no big deal. But don't worry about that now. We'll do the full debrief when we return to Langley."

He smiled. Being with her lifted his spirits. "I'm glad you're okay."

"I want to hear all about how you captured him, but you look like you could use some rest."

Chris smiled weakly. "Thanks."

"I have to make a couple calls," she said before giving his shoulder a gentle squeeze and leaving him.

Chris savored the catlike grace in her stride as she made her way to the cockpit. He closed his eyes, keeping her in his thoughts. At Harvard, he'd read the writer-philosopher Elbert Hubbard who said, *A friend is someone who knows all about you and still loves you.* Hannah knew more about Chris than he knew about her, but he hoped in time the scales would balance.

The plane's hull rumbled beneath him and an unseen weight pressed his body back into the seat. He opened his eyes and continued to feel the heaviness against the front of his chest as the jet accelerated and lifted off the runway. Baku's city lights became smaller and smaller and were eventually extinguished by the clouds. Soon, the weight melted off his body, and the plane reached cruising altitude.

Hannah returned from the cockpit, and Chris fluttered his eyelids open. She reclined his seat back before she sat next to him and reclined hers, and the cabin lights dimmed. He closed his eyes again, and just before he fell asleep he felt the softness of her hand on his.

And in the realm between reality and dreams, he thought he heard Sonny's voice. "Bubkes."

Chris, Hannah, & Sonny will return

To connect with Stephen Templin and for updates about new releases, as well as exclusive promotions, visit his website and subscribe to his VIP New Releases newsletter at http://www.stephentemplin.com.

GLOSSARY

Agency: Central Intelligence Agency.

AK: Abbreviated form of AK-47 and its variants.

AK-47: Contraction of Russian, *Automat Kalashnikova abraztsa 1947 goda* (Kalishnikov's 1947 automatic rifle). Holds thirty rounds of .308 (7.62 x 39 mm) ammunition.

Azeri: Shortened word for Azerbaijani people or the Azerbaijani language.

Blowout kit: Slang for first aid kit.

BUD/S training: Basic Underwater Demolition/SEAL training. Where all prospective SEALs must begin training, located in Coronado, California.

Bug-out bag: A three-day survival kit kept handy in the event of having to suddenly evacuate, or *bug out.*

Bubkes: Yiddish word meaning *nothing*, having no value.

Circus: Slang for MI6.

Comms: Communications devices.

Delta Force: US Army's Special Forces Operational Detachment—Delta. Has used cover name of Combat Applications Group (CAG) and Army Compartmented Elements (ACE), but its men simply refer to it as "the Unit." Recruits mostly from top-performing Army Rangers and Green Berets. Similar to SEAL Team Six, Delta Force is the Army's Tier One unit that conducts counterinsurgency and counterterrorism operations. For the most sensitive operations, they also work under the CIA's umbrella of Special Operations Group (SOG).

DEVGRU: Development Group, one of the cover names for SEAL Team Six.

E&E: Escape and Evasion. For each mission, SEALs make an E&E plan for what to do when they can't make it to the extraction. They also carry a small kit to help them escape and evade the enemy.

Federal Security Service: The *Federal'naya Sluzhba Bezopasnosti* (FSB), Russia's version of the CIA. Formerly part of the KGB. FSB headquarters is in the Lubyanka building, northeast of Red Square, in Moscow.

FSB: See Federal Security Service.

Gulag: Originally a Russian acronym for **G**lavnoye **U**pravleniye **Lag**ery, literally translated as the "Main Camp Administration," the government agency in charge of Stalin's forced labor camps. Although they imprisoned criminals, they also functioned to suppress opposition to Stalin.

KGB: Russian acronym for **K**omitet **G**osudarstvennoy **B**ezopasnosti, directly translated as Committee for State Security. From 1954 to the dissolution of the Soviet Union in 1991, the KGB served as part of the Soviet Union's military, acting as secret police within the country and spies abroad. Following the end of the Soviet Union, the KGB was divided into the Federal Security Service and Foreign Intelligence Service.

Kit: Gear.

Klick: Kilometer.

MI6: The United Kingdom's equivalent of the Central Intelligence Agency.

MNS: Ministry of National Security, Azerbaijan's intelligence agency, similar to America's CIA.

NOC: Stands for Non-Official Cover. An illegal resident spy. Rather than work as an official spy with diplomatic cover in an embassy, a NOC works away from embassies and trade missions. If captured, a NOC doesn't have diplomatic immunity, but he does have more independence and can mingle more easily in the target country in deep cover. Even if the embassy or trade mission in the target country is dissolved, the NOC can remain to continue conducting intelligence operations.

PC: Precious Cargo, such as a hostage being rescued.

Resident spy: An intelligence officer who operates in a foreign country for an extended period of time.

RHIB: Rigid Hull Inflatable Boat. A boat with a solid, V-shaped hull and large inflatable collar at the gunwale, often used by SEALs and other military personnel.

RSO: Regional Security Officer, who works for the State Department overseas and is in charge of law enforcement at US embassies.

SDR: Surveillance Detection Route. A tactical route taken to notice surveillance, which can also be used to lose surveillance, making oneself *clean.*

SEAL: US Navy commandos who operate in the environments of SEa, Air, and Land. The odd-numbered SEAL Teams (One, Three, Five, and Seven) are based in Coronado, California, and the even-numbered Teams (Two, Four, Six, Eight, and Ten) are based at Little Creek, Virginia. (If the Teams expanded, Team Nine would probably be created next.)

SEAL Team Six: Team Six selects from the best SEALs to serve in its Tier One unit, also known as DEVGRU. Team Six SEALs conduct counterinsurgency and counterterrorism operations. For the most sensitive operations, they work under the CIA's umbrella of Special Operations Group (SOG).

Selection: The course for weeding out who would become a Delta operator and who wouldn't.

SIGINT: Signal Intelligence. SIGINT collects electronic signals and can break encryptions and analyze who is sending/receiving signals and the quantities of signaling.

Sluzhba Vneshney Razvedki: Abbreviated as SVR. Russia's foreign intelligence service, successor of the KGB after the dissolution of the USSR.

SOG: Special Operations Group conducts high-threat military and intelligence operations that the US government may deny knowledge of, such as SEAL Team Six's raid of bin Laden's headquarters—each Team Six SEAL signed a contract temporarily placing him under SOG's command. SOG also utilizes Army Delta Force operators and others.

SOP: Standard Operating Procedure.

Southern Gas Corridor: A plan by the European Commission for Caspian and Middle Eastern countries (Azerbaijan, Turkey, Georgia, Turkmenistan, Kazakhstan, Iraq, Egypt, Lebanon, Palestine, Jordan, and Syria, and possibly Uzbekistan and Iran) to supply Europe with natural gas. The plan includes a network of pipelines, part of which consists of SCP, TANAP, and TAP.

SCP: South Caucasus Pipeline. The pipeline that carries natural gas from the Caspian Sea, through Azerbaijan, and to Turkey.

Spook: Slang for CIA officer.

TANAP: Trans-Anatolian gas pipeline, which would cross Turkey. Construction was estimated to be completed by 2018.

TAP: Trans-Adriatic Pipeline. A pipeline to carry natural gas from the Turkish border, through Greece, Albania, and the Adriatic Sea, to Italy. The route (with originating pipelines in parentheses) would be from the Shah Deniz gas field in Caspian Sea (SCP) à Azerbaijan à Georgia à Turkey (TANAP)à Greece (TAP) à Albania à Italy.

TECHINT: Technical Intelligence. The use of technology and gizmos to gather intelligence, as opposed to HUMINT, human intelligence.

UKP: United Kingdom Petroleum.

The Unit: See Delta Force.

ACKNOWLEDGMENTS

I'd like to thank SEAL sniper veteran Kyle Defoor for training me in assault rifle and pistol to help me prepare for this novel. In Afghanistan, Kyle was part of Operation Anaconda, where he fought in the Battle of Takur Ghar and was awarded a Bronze Star for valor. The operation succeeded in killing hundreds of Al-Qaeda and Taliban terrorists, taking away their control of the Shahi-Kot Valley.

I greatly appreciate Carol Scarr and Danielle Poiesz for their editorial advice on early drafts of this book.

Most of all, I am thankful for the support of my wife, Reiko, and children, Kent and Maria.

Since elementary school, **STEPHEN TEMPLIN** felt a need to write, dreaming of becoming a novelist. Now he is a *New York Times* and international bestselling author with the movie rights to one of his movies purchased by Vin Diesel. Steve's books have been translated into thirteen languages. He is a "hybrid" author who maintains active book contracts with top publishers such as Simon and Schuster and St. Martin's Press while also publishing independently.

After high school, he completed Hell Week, qualified as a pistol and rifle expert, blew up things, and practiced small unit tactics during Basic Underwater Demolition/SEAL training. Later, Steve left the Navy and became a missionary. Then, for fourteen years, he lectured as a tenured professor at Meio University in Japan, where he also practiced the martial art aikido. Currently, he lives in the Dallas-Fort Worth area.

To connect with Steve and for updates about new releases, as well as exclusive promotions, visit his website and sign up for his VIP New Releases newsletter at http://www.stephen-templin.com.

CPSIA information can be obtained
at www.ICGtesting.com
Printed in the USA
LVOW10s1938141116
512910LV00001B/55/P